THE KISS CHRO

DREAM A LITTLE DREAM

G.A. ANDERSON

Black Rose Writing | Texas

©2025 by G.A. Anderson
All rights reserved. No part of this book may be reproduced, stored in a retrieval system or transmitted in any form or by any means without the prior written permission of the publishers, except by a reviewer who may quote brief passages in a review to be printed in a newspaper, magazine or journal.

The author grants the final approval for this literary material.

First printing

This is a work of fiction. Names, characters, businesses, places, events, and incidents are either the products of the author's imagination or used in a fictitious manner. Any resemblance to actual persons, living or dead, or actual events is purely coincidental.

ISBN: 978-1-68513-613-0
LIBRARY OF CONGRESS CONTROL NUMBER: 2025930162
PUBLISHED BY BLACK ROSE WRITING
www.blackrosewriting.com

Printed in the United States of America
Suggested Retail Price (SRP) $23.95

Dream a Little Dream is printed in Sabon LT Std

*As a planet-friendly publisher, Black Rose Writing does its best to eliminate unnecessary waste to reduce paper usage and energy costs, while never compromising the reading experience. As a result, the final word count vs. page count may not meet common expectations.

This book is dedicated to the
Reich & Lukacs Families

DREAM A LITTLE DREAM

ABOUT THE HUNGARIAN WORDS

There are many Hungarian words and phrases in *Dream a Little Dream*. I've done my best to make their meanings clear. If you would like to hear those words spoken in Hungarian, please visit my website (www.anderson-author.com) and listen to the podcasts I have posted. Each podcast is short and amusing because Hungarian is a strange and wonderful language.

The word you will see most often is *Igen*. EE-GEN. Hard g. It means *yes*.

One more: *fuj*. FOO-Y. This is what we heard as children when caught doing something messy, and possibly gross—like the earthworm colony we made in the yard.

CHAPTER 1
MONDAY, MARCH 14TH
OREOS WITHOUT MILK

It takes exactly nine seconds to walk into my shrink's waiting room and find a seat. I know it's nine seconds because I hold my breath and count. I hold my breath and count because I'm anxious. Quietly, internally. Forevermore. I blame the bad day. The one when I lost my dad.

I've been working on accepting the changes, on embracing moments of optimism. And I am getting better. Not as perfect as a bowl of ice cream with chocolate-covered almonds or ribbons of marshmallow, but adequate, like an Oreo without milk. At least until the fight with my mom a few weeks ago at my uncle's apartment in Paris. A knockdown, way down, with tears, and screaming, and pent-up rage, promptly followed by the crowning touch—a monster panic attack. What I remember most vividly is wondering how much strain my eyeballs could take before they'd pop out of my head. After that, I hyperventilated and passed out on the gently mopped, bespoke parquet floor.

It's one of the reasons I'm back in Dr. Jonas' office, waiting my turn, counting steps, and measuring time because therapy is helpful, but distressing, and these two things squashed together make me uneasy. All the pressure to be honest and self-reflective, no thanks. And the codes of conduct—they're too restrictive. Is it wrong to giggle when I should be deeply contemplative? Is my full attention truly necessary for the therapeutic process to, whatever...fix me? And this place, it's not calming. The chairs are hard, cardboard-beige, and bleeding the essence of Big John's Furniture Palace.

Why isn't a furniture palace ever named after a woman?

I pull a stray thread from my sleeve, ball it up and push it into my jean's pocket. My elbow is itchy. There's sand between my toes. Think I'll get a cat from the animal shelter. Not only did I lose my dad, but I've also been divorced since last December, so the single life looms large. Maybe a kitty with blue eyes. Or not. The last blue-eyed animal living in my house was Dylan, my ex-husband, and he didn't work out too well. I absolutely kind of loved him the day he proposed. Less than a year later, I absolutely kind of realized he was a lying sack of shit.

I'll skip the blue eyes.

Another woman enters the waiting room. Face down, her identity hidden behind thick, white-rimmed sunglasses and a flowing cloak of blonde curls. She sits a few feet away. I wonder what her deal is. Is it like mine, or does she have something more serious going on than a messy divorce, a secret family history, a dead dad, and a mother who becomes more confusing the longer I know her?

I pull the thread out of my pocket, unwind it, and wrap it around my thumb. We sit together. Separately. Silently.

"Katy, you ready?" Dr. Jonas' voice pulls me from the stupor.

I follow her through the hallway to her office, which remains as plain as the last time I was here in February. She's exchanged the plastic ferns for two live spider plants. One on her desk, the other on the bookshelf next to the window.

She sits across from me, with an iPad perched on her knees. "Welcome back. It's been a minute since your last appointment."

"Thanks. I got home from France last week, but work's been busy. What's the iPad for?"

"Keeping up with the times. I should have gone to computerized notes years ago. This is better. More secure, and HIPAA compliant."

"No more yellow lined paper?" I ask, remembering what a freak show I was during my first few therapy sessions, obsessing about what she wrote on those pages, and convinced the consent forms I'd signed were a ruse to steal a vital organ.

"No, Katy. Everything will be in The Cloud."

"What if your cloud gets hacked?"

"I don't think it will."

"What if it gets sunny?" I ask.

Her eyes narrow. "Sunshine has no effect on data storage."

"Hm." I try not to stare at her skinny ankles and orthopedic sandals sticking out below the hemline of her flower print skirt.

"Tell me about your trip," she says.

"Paris is nice in the spring. It's cool and rainy and I love my uncle's apartment. It's fun pretending I belong there, and my French is getting pretty good. And there's the chocolate."

She grins. "And the cheese and bread. How's your mother?"

"She's grieving in her own special way."

"Which is what?"

"Telling strangers her husband took off to Thailand, had an affair with a prostitute and then dropped dead."

"Oh no." She grimaces. "Sounds as if your mother might benefit from some counseling."

I snort. "Never in a million years."

"Did you bring up finding the briefcase with her?"

"I was planning to."

"And?"

I rub my fingers together. "I didn't."

"Timing is everything, and you know her best." She twists the top off of her water bottle. "How was coming home?"

"Sort of lonely."

"How are you coping with that feeling?"

"I dunno." I glare at the tissue box next to me and imagine the damage I could do with some steel-toed boots. Not everybody gets weepy during therapy. I don't. Well, I have, but I didn't enjoy it. And do I tell her about the French *episode* now? Dropping like dead weight, drooling on the floor, then coming to with my mother glaring at me.

"Katy?"

I turn back to her. "I cry sometimes, curl up in a ball and feel sorry for myself. Then I get over it. I've got Jesse and Russ here, and Ethan in Denver."

"A great support system."

"Uh-huh."

"And your dad?"

"I miss him, and I get triggered by the dumbest things—like someone my age walking through the grocery store with their dad. I actually get jealous. Which is nuts, right?"

"Not nuts at all. It's a very normal response. Can we talk about it a little more?" she asks, giving me the shrink-look. The, *you're the one who has shit to work out,* stare.

"I'd rather not." I pull on my ponytail. What's to talk about? He died. It was the worst day of my entire life. But like I said, things are getting better. Well...they *were* getting better.

"Are you sure?" she asks again.

"Yeah. Not today."

"Fair enough. Are you in touch with your brother?"

"I spoke to Ethan a couple of days ago. Guess his mom keeps crying about our dad."

Dr. Jonas lifts the water bottle to her mouth and takes a sip. "Another secret your family kept for a long time. All of it coming out must have opened the emotional floodgates for her."

"She did keep her son's paternity quiet for over thirty years." I look at the spider plant near the window. "Those things are almost impossible to kill."

She smiles. "It's why I bought them."

"Uh-huh." I put a hand on my right knee to stop it from bouncing. "Should I get a cat?"

"We're changing the subject?" She looks at me for acknowledgement, then continues. "That's a *you* decision."

"I guess. Do you think it's a bad idea?"

"Do you?" She leans back in her chair.

I shrug and switch up again. "Dylan's not in Florida anymore."

"How do you know?"

"Russ told me. He said a friend of a friend saw him in Savannah."

"Sounds like gossip about your ex-husband."

"Dufferin Beach isn't a big town, Dr. Jonas. We're all up in each other's business."

"Let's assume it is, and he's left the state. It's one less thing to worry about."

"I guess. But it's me, so I'll just replace it with something else."

"It shouldn't be a personal challenge to seek out stress. It's the same as a virus. It'll find you." She twists a silver bracelet around her thin wrist. "Unless you've already gone searching. Is there something you're not telling me?"

I look away from her.

"Spill it, Katy."

I look back. "I had a huge argument with my mom, and then I might have had a panic attack." I toss the words out quickly. "It was bad. I thought I was dying."

"Tell me what you felt right before."

"Anger. I got light-headed, my heart was beating way too fast, and then I blacked out."

Her eyes go wide. "You passed out?"

"For a minute. My uncle took me to his doctor. He checked my blood pressure and said I was too excited, so I should have an espresso and calm down."

Her lips pucker. "That's one way to go. You said you were having words with your mom?"

"We were having many words. But I've fought with her before. I'm not sure where the panic attack came from."

She asks, "Have you ever had one before?"

"Just the time with Jesse last year, but I earned that one."

She squints, as if narrowing her eyes will make anything I say more understandable. "How did you earn a panic attack?"

"It's a long story, and it wasn't the same."

"I'm going to send you an app with some exercises you can practice. It will help when you sense anxiety coming on. In fact, let's try it now."

I sit up on the couch. "Right now?"

"Absolutely. I want you to close your eyes and picture a bowl of soup."

"What kind?"

"It doesn't matter," she says. "Your favorite."

I squeeze my eyes shut. "Tomato. Am I supposed to picture the bowl, too? Because the bowls at work have little flowers on the edges."

"Katy..."

"And at home, I have tomato soup from a coffee mug. Like those big ones you get at a gift store or from a museum or a zoo or something."

"The mug. Picture the mug. Focus and inhale for five seconds."

I open my left eye. "You want me to smell soup that isn't here?"

"Yes, and close both eyes. Slowly inhale through your nose, hold it for five seconds, then blow out through your mouth. Cool the soup down."

I follow her directions, trying to conjure the tangy, savory scent of my imaginary soup. Inhaling, holding my breath, blowing it out. I open my eyes. "Am I doing it right?"

"Yes. Wonderful, but keep practicing. Learn your soup."

"What's the point?" I ask.

"It's called grounding. Centering your mind and body. Even counting to ten or fifty can work. It forces your brain to think of something other than the panic you're feeling."

"A distraction?" I ask.

"In a sense. I sometimes think of it as discharging the energy. I want you to keep practicing the soup exercise, but let's go back to the situation with your mom."

"It was stupid. We were talking about my life. What I was going to do moving forward."

She shuffles in her chair. "Okay."

"She kept pushing me about getting out and dating. The clock's ticking. When am I going to have kids?"

"That upset you," she states, not as a question, but as confirmation.

"It's the way she said it. Like I owe her a plan or an explanation for all the stupid things I've done. And instead of telling me she's proud of me for getting a divorce and standing up for myself, it's like she's disappointed, or like I should be over it already."

"She's not hearing you."

"She doesn't want to hear me," I say. "Or she can't. I have to play by her rules, which are emotionless, or stuffed into some airtight compartment. It's probably why I can't bring up the whole Jewish thing, which has also been confusing, by the way. All the religious stuff. My family doesn't even go to a normal church, and a Jewish church would be specialized or something."

"Synagogue," she says. "A Jewish church is called a synagogue."

"I know, but you get the point. I don't understand anything about religion."

"It's a process," she says. "Several new situations have presented themselves in your life. It's no wonder you're confused and overwhelmed about things. It may have contributed to the conversation escalating."

"No kidding. She told me I was being stupid and the only thing I should worry about is finding a new husband." I bite my lip. "So, I told her she should have tried a little harder to hold on to hers."

She cringes, "Oh. Ouch."

"Yeah. It wasn't my best move. She pretty much turned into a human flamethrower at that point, and my poor uncle was completely freaking out."

She taps on the iPad, then looks up at me. "How long did it go on?"

"No clue. We yelled at each other until I started crying. Then I couldn't breathe, and I blacked out."

"How was she when you woke up?"

"Still pissed. She told me to go back to Florida and then locked herself in her room."

"Have you spoken to her since?"

"Nope. I flew home the next morning."

"I'm sorry. It sounds extremely stressful. Are you okay pushing into this a bit longer?"

"I can try." I stare at my bare ring finger. "Everything is different. My parents were always around, now Dad's gone. Do I keep the restaurant open? What am I supposed to be doing next? And my mother, I don't know how to handle her. I don't even know if I can."

"How about letting things work themselves out organically?" she suggests.

I frown. "I hate that word."

"Hate? That seems aggressive. Why do you hate it?"

"Well, when I think of organic, I think of a farm where someone's done a lot of work to make the corn, or whatever, grow without pesticides. They've swatted off the bugs for months and used some magical poop-infused potion to make their crops grow into something edible. Consumable."

"Poop-infused," she repeats. "Okay, I'm with you. Go on."

"Well, I don't think it's what you mean when you say organically. When you say it, it means I should sit around and let things happen."

"True. But we can go with your version. How would it apply to your future?"

I blink and wonder if I've stepped on her toes, which are probably sharp and pointy, like her nose and cheekbones, and there it is, that weird, oozy place in my brain where thoughts multiply but never add up. I try to focus. "There's the problem. I've got no idea what my version of the future looks like."

Her fingers drum on the armrest. "Do you remember the discussion we had last year about using your energy in situations you can't control?"

"Yeah. I was freaking out about all the things that could go wrong with Dylan and the divorce."

"Right," she says quietly.

"And you said the outcome wouldn't change even if I worried myself to death. You said worry sucks the air out of people."

She smiles. "Pretty close. We worry, things turn out fine. We worry again. Things are still fine, or not, but the worry didn't help, didn't hurt, didn't contribute to the outcome."

"I get it." I slide my phone from one hand to the other. "Taking things day by day, minute by minute. Maybe it'll keep me from having another panic attack."

"Relax, Katy. Feel the world around you. Don't dread it."

I push my lips together, trying not to laugh. She comes up with some strange sayings. What if she's right? I should chill out. Mom is still in France, which means I can avoid her by way of geography. Things are rosy, or at least a palatable shade of pink. I should stop worrying so much. All the bad stuff is behind me.

CHAPTER 2
SIR

I repeat Dr. Jonas' mantra throughout the day. "I'm feeling the world around me." And I do. It's humid. I'm sweaty. My scalp is itchy, probably because I'm too lazy to rinse all the shampoo out of my hair. I *feel* work too because I'm back at the restaurant, prepping, cooking, burning my fingers and sliding across the perpetual slick spot in the walk-in fridge.

After closing, I begin the first round of training for my new server. We're in the dining room wiping down the tables and chairs, sweeping and mopping when Jesse bangs on the front door.

"Mrs. Katy," Cricket says. "There's someone yelling out front."

I unlock the door, and Jesse brushes by me. "I wouldn't have to wait if I had a fucking key. Who is this?" she asks, motioning to the teenager.

I move the mop from my right hand to my left. "Cricket, this is Jesse Tanner, my best friend, and the most ass-kicking lawyer on the planet."

Cricket holds a pale, freckled hand out in greeting. "Cricket Calliope Punch. Third year at Dufferin Beach High School. Nice to meet you, sir."

Jesse's right eye twitches. I hold my breath.

"I was supposed to be a boy baby," Cricket continues. "Mom said she panicked when I came out a girl baby, so she named me after my dead great-granny Cricket from the hills. Mom said she was a cheating, lying, man-chasing drunk who should've been put down like an old Coon Hound." She stops to come up for air. "I don't know where the hills are in case you were wondering. Are you really a lawyer, Mr. Tanner? My uncle Cordel-Dale in North Carolina is a lawyer, too. He's really super rich. Are you super rich?"

Jesse's lips part, her teeth bared in a vampiric grin. She turns to me, momentarily speechless.

"Cricket." I hand her the mop. "Start behind the bar and work your way to the front."

"Alrighty," she says with a quick curtsy.

Jesse watches her walk away. Her eyes twinkle in a way that's not magical at all.

"Don't be mean, Jess. She's a little odd."

"I want to hurt her, but I would feel remorse. It's not a sensation I'm familiar with."

"I get it. But I didn't hire her for you to mess with."

She grunts. "She wouldn't know it's happening. Got food?"

"In the kitchen," I say, glancing at Cricket, who's shaking a wine bottle over her head.

In the back, Melissa is finishing up. She drops a handful of dish towels into the laundry bag, then pulls her apron off. From the office, Russ asks why we left the new girl alone.

"She's mopping," I tell him. "Sort of."

Jesse peeks over his shoulder. "Never thought I'd see you work on a computer. Did you learn Excel?"

"I did, darlin'," he says. "It's my new image. Upper management and all. Don't it make you love me more?"

"I couldn't possibly. Are you recording data?"

While Russ shows off his new skills, I pull a container filled with homemade chicken soup from the fridge. "We're updating the menu," I say. "Will you be pissed if I microwave this? I don't want to clean the stove again."

"My other option is SpaghettiOs eaten cold from the can, so no, I won't be pissed. What brought all this about?"

Russ swivels toward her. "Katy wants to try some new recipes. We're tracking what the customers order." He tucks his blond, shoulder-length curls behind his ears. "And what they don't."

"What are you finding?" she asks, repositioning herself next to the microwave.

"We've been wasting money and time on food nobody wants." I offer her a spoon. "We're trying some new dishes. Remember the mac and cheese I used to make in college?"

"Yes!" She nods slowly for dramatic effect. "Please make the magical ham and cheese. I could swim in that shit."

Two minutes pass. The microwave beeps, and I place the warm soup in front of her. She dives in, moaning in a way that makes even Russ blush.

"Have you not heard of Miss Manners?" I drop a kitchen towel on the growing puddle next to her size ten feet.

"My grandmother read her column. Queen of etiquette. It's no way to live." She burps, then wipes her hand on her shirt.

"Isn't that silk?"

"It is," she says. "And I have ten more like this at home. I enjoy expensive clothes while scorning civility. It's freeing. You should give it a try."

"Try what?" Cricket asks, hugging three bottles of wine close to her chest. "Something's wrong with these wines, Mrs. Katy."

"Care to explain?" I pry two bottles loose from her grip.

"There's dirt inside." She turns her remaining bottle upside down to demonstrate. "See the tiny pebbles? People shouldn't drink from these."

"It's not dirt. It's sediment. Perfectly safe."

She examines the dark green glass. "Well, I've never seen wines like these in all my life."

"You're seventeen, Cricket. Your life hasn't been that long."

Jesse beams. "She's right, Kiss. Your wine is full of fuckery. Whatever will you do?"

I turn to her, the woman who saved me from a terrible marriage. "Why are you here, Jessica? Is there something you need other than a microwaved meal?"

She stares at me. "Indeed. I'm here for a reason."

"Which is what?"

"It's about the message I sent you."

"Was it a text message?" Cricket squeezes between us. "I never text anyone but my mother. I find it to be very impersonal."

I look over her frizzy, red-haired head toward Jesse. "I was busy. I haven't read it yet."

Cricket raises her hand to speak again. "My mother purchased me a cellular phone after I took my driving test. I passed the fourth time. Pretty good, right? Mom still doesn't want me driving, though. How many times did you have to take your driving test? My instructor was a big fat man, and he had a hook instead of a right hand."

Jesse steps backwards and bumps into Russ, who's trying to leave without being noticed. "An actual hook?" she asks.

"Yes, sir. A big metal one."

"Damn," Jesse says, pulling a knife off the butcher block and swinging it left to right. "Did he point the hook to give you directions? Oh my God, were both of his hands hooks?"

"Only the one, sir. And he used his mouth for instructions."

"Jesse!" I take the knife away.

"What?" she cackles. "We need to talk about Quinn."

"Not interested. He was an asshole to me right after Dad died. So, no thanks."

"Is Quinn the man you divorced?" Cricket cranes her neck toward me. "And if I didn't say it earlier during my interviewing process, I'm very sorry about your daddy passing. Mom says she'd fall straight into the drink if Dad croaked." She takes her phone from her pocket. "Speak of the devil's eggs, Mom's here. Can I be clocked out now? Should I throw the wines into the dumpster?"

I blink, trying to find words. "Please don't. And yeah, you're good to go. Leave the wine and post your hours on the portal."

"Okey dokey pinokey." She peels off her apron and gives the bottles another disapproving look on her way out.

"She's going to be a handful," I say, locking the door behind her.

Jesse tilts the bowl and slurps up the last of the soup. "Where did you find her?"

"Her mom cuts my mom's hair. I ran into her at the store last week and she asked if I'd give her kid a chance. I was trying to be nice and figured someone her age wouldn't be nuts yet."

"Guess you were wrong," she says, pulling out a cigarette.

"Possibly," I admit. "And not in here with those, Jess. You promised to quit."

"I smoke half, then throw the rest away. It's a process."

"Uh-huh. Why are you hassling me about Quinn? There's no way I can deal with him and my mom." I untie my apron, stained by today's menu, and toss it on top of the dirty dish towels. "Do you think I should get a cat?"

"What do you need with a cat?" She places the unlit cigarette on the counter. "What's the issue with your mom? You guys have always driven each other nuts. What's the big deal?"

I sigh, in no mood to tell a second person about the war that broke out between us in France. "The big deal is that Dad was the buffer. The guy who cleared the landmines between us. Now he's gone."

"You two have always butted heads. For what it's worth, I think she means well, even if her delivery is a little indelicate." She flashes a sleazy, lounge lizard smile. "Perhaps Quinn could make you feel better."

"Not his job." I push the cigarette toward her. "I know you made him say that shit to me last year, but he was too convincing. It's stuck in my brain."

"Get over it. I forced the speech down his throat. Made him practice, in fact."

I grab my backpack from the small office, shut off the lights, and walk to the dining room. "I'll let you out from the front."

"Did you hear me, Kiss? I made him practice. It took three times for him to get it right."

"Great." I step out onto the sidewalk. "He's a slow learner."

"He was upset." She follows me. Her cigarette bobs up and down between her lips as she speaks. "I think he might have started crying."

"He cried?" I turn my face toward her as I twist the lock.

"I didn't acknowledge it. Wouldn't want to humiliate the guy."

"I know how much you hate doing that. Anyway, I shouldn't be dating yet."

"I call bullshit, Kiss."

"Uh-huh," I mumble, because she's right. I've been talking to Nickety-Nick on the phone once a week for the past three months. We're not officially dating, but if Jess found out, she'd take my head clean off, then use the bloody stump of my neck as a decorative stamp for the invitations to my funeral.

"Call Quinn," she says, unlocking her car.

"I'll think about it."

"You know you love him," she says.

I lean on the hood of her Prius. "Love is stupid."

She winks at me. "Not if you want to be *happily*."

"Do I, though?"

"You truly do," she says, throwing her bag into the passenger seat.

"How do you know?"

"Because, you dumbass, if you didn't want to hear from him, you would have blocked his number."

CHAPTER 3
FIREFLIES

Jesse's right. I could have easily cut off Quinn's phone calls and texts. But like all things man-related, the reason I don't is a source of constant bewilderment.

Especially on Sundays, when it's obvious that I am so very single. And alone. During the work week I'm too exhausted to think about it, but on days like today, I'm *Little Orphan Katy*. Back when my parents were around, we'd pack a picnic lunch on the weekends and head out on our boat, *The Happily*, named in honor of my grandmother's annihilation of the English language while wishing all forms of happiness upon me.

These sentiments, "You vill be happily ven you big girl," or "Go finding za happily," were always accompanied by a sweet smile and her fingers, the jaws of life, squeezing the blood out of my cheeks.

Things are different now, and my weekends are wide open. Not so happily. I've adopted my dad's Sunday morning routine of reading the paper version of *The Times*, spread out on the deep red Persian carpet in my living room, while consuming a quadruple shot of espresso with equal amounts of whipped cream. After the coffee, things get dicey. I lose focus, fidget, and for something new and exciting, have panic attacks.

I've taken on many of these new traditions to keep from staring into the gaping maw of my new life. It's all fine though, perfectly fine, but also the reason I'm searching the internet for small pets. Rabbits, gerbils, a guinea pig? I move on to cats because Mom would freak out if a rodent became my new roommate. My phone rings. Her ears must be burning because she's the one calling.

"Hi Mom," I answer warily. The last time we spoke I was laid out on the floor in my uncle's apartment in Paris like a lamb about to get its throat slit.

"Hello, dear. Why are you sounding nervous?"

"I'm not nervous. I'm just cleaning up around the house. How are you?"

"I am very well. How is the restaurant?"

"Fine. Busy."

The line goes quiet.

"This is all you do?" she asks. "Work and clean your home."

I'm currently chewing on the pink skin around my thumb, but this isn't the information she's looking for. "I dunno, I'm hanging out. I spoke to Grandma about an hour ago."

"How is she?"

"Good."

"Good," she repeats. "You sit inside all day. How will this get you the new husband?"

My eyes squeeze shut. Has the trauma of losing dad kicked her need to micromanage my life into high gear? It's time to troubleshoot. My eyes pop open. "I've been talking to Nick."

"Nick from university?"

"Uh-huh," I squeak. What have I done? Nick's been my secret since New Year's Eve, in a lock box where nobody can tell me I'm stupid or wrong or making another mistake.

"I see." Her tone lightens. "I have always liked this boy. He comes from the good family."

"We've just been chatting on the phone. Don't get all excited. I haven't seen him or anything."

"But you will?"

"Sure," I promise as a car pulls into the driveway. I know the driver. He's been here a thousand times. "Mom, someone's here. I need to run."

"Who is it?"

"Russ," I lie. "We've got some work stuff to do. I'll call you later, okay?"

"Igen," she says, then hangs up without another word.

• • • • •

I watch Quinn get out of the car. My ex-husband's ex-best friend, who last winter informed me that our one-night stand was to be taken literally. One night, in his words, to see what it would be like. His delivery was glacial and more humiliating than any breakup I'd endured in high school or college.

Since then, I learned his speech was concocted by Jesse to stop me from getting distracted by one man while divorcing another. It worked, but his act was too well-played, and impossible to forget. Now he's standing at my front door on a lonely Sunday afternoon. I don't need this. I've got Nick back. Sort of. I haven't actually seen him. But there's the whole phone thing.

"Please let me in," he says through the screen. "You can't avoid me forever."

"What would you name a kitten?" I stare into his honey brown eyes. Damnit, genetics do not play fair. How can a man look this good?

"Buttons. Open the door."

"Buttons? Cute, not very original. Got anything better?"

"Will you let me in if I do?"

"You were an asshole to me." I say, trying to ignore his wide shoulders. He's wearing one of those *Untuckit* shirts, dark green, slim fit. Perfect fit.

"Did you read my texts apologizing?"

"What about Faucet?" I ask, trying to appear stern, arms crossed. Of course I read his texts.

"That's not a name," he says. "It's something you buy at a hardware store. Please unlock the door."

"No," I tell him. I can barely juggle my existence. What would I do with two men? He is pretty, though. And what about Nick and our long, late-night conversations about the old times? I repeat myself. More for me than him. "No way."

"Why not?" He takes a step back and mimics me by crossing his arms.

"Because," I sputter. I'm low-level discombobulated. He's a man, an actual man, and his aura is glowing with waves of bioluminescence. A swarm of fireflies at dusk. Whatever—I haven't had sex in months. "What did you ask me?"

"Give me ten minutes, and five extra for coming up with a good cat name. Then you can kick me out."

"Uh-huh. Who decides if the name is acceptable? What if you think it's good and I think it sucks?"

"You decide."

I look over my shoulder. The house is in order and will remain this way for approximately twelve hours. "Okay," I say, rotating the deadbolt. "Ten minutes and a good name."

"Thanks." He steps inside and looks around. "Like what you've done with the place."

"Had to have it professionally cleaned after Dylan moved out."

"I heard. Nice paint color."

"It's called Goat. Kind of boring."

"Goat? No, it's off-white. Who comes up with these names?" He moves past me. The faint scent of his cologne makes me tense, makes me inhale, trying to draw it in. "What are you up to?" he asks.

"Stuff. You know, feeling the day around me." I say, sitting far away from him on the couch and hoping he doesn't ask about what I just said. Distance is good, as are his hands. I know this from personal experience.

"How are you doing?" he asks.

"I dunno. Fine, I guess."

"Yeah. I hear you. Sorry about your dad. It must have been rough." He clears his throat. "I mean, it must still be. I remember you guys were close."

"Yup." My voice falters. "It wasn't great."

"If you ever want to talk about it. About anything."

My head moves to convey that the message has been received. He's here, feeling remorse and pity, guilt…curiosity.

"I'm also sorry about last year," he continues. "What can I say to make you understand? It was a shit situation and Jesse is persuasive."

"I'll give you that. How did she tell you to do it? To embarrass the hell out of me?"

"Jesus," he winces. "Not sure I could have felt any worse, but now I do." His jaw clenches. "She scripted it. Gave me the right words to push your buttons. Told me to keep it short and closed-ended."

"You said I wasn't your type."

"You're not, or I didn't think you were. The closer you stick to the truth, the better the lie."

"But I'm your type now? You changed from swiping on hot beach babes to being a nice boy who's into weird girls?"

"Only the one I'm looking at. And you're not weird, even though you want to name a cat Faucet. Okay, you are a little…interesting. But I've changed, and it's been enlightening." He looks down, then back up at me. "The last few years haven't been my best."

"Probably because you spent them with Dylan. Guess I could say the same. Still, how many women have you been with since that night, Quinn?"

"None."

"Bullshit." I need an ice bath, please. He is so damn hot. Am I supposed to believe he's rebuffed the multitude of women who have undoubtedly thrown themselves at him? He walks into a room and heads turn. Hearts beat faster.

"We're not all like Dylan. At some point, you need to trust people again." He scoots a few inches closer. "How about Pixie?"

"I've got three friends with cats named Pixie."

"Tallulah," he offers.

"Nuh-uh."

"What would be in it for me to keep texting you? To apologize over and over if I didn't mean it?"

"How would I know what gets you off?"

He grins. The fireflies flutter.

"What the hell, Quinn? Don't look at me like that."

"Are you blushing?"

"No." Who am I kidding? My face is on fire.

"Give me another chance, Katy."

"What's in it for me?" I ask.

He sweeps wisps of hair from his face. The gold tones catch the late afternoon light coming in through the window. Oh my God, this is terrible. I think about the night we spent together. I never had a chance.

"A future with a great guy," he says. "A kitten. No breeders, you need to adopt. They're full at the shelter almost all the time."

"How do you know?"

"I volunteer there. I grew up with animals, and I love them, but my apartment has a no pet policy. I travel too much anyway.

The shelter is my weekly fix, and it's nice to give back, you know? Pay it forward."

"Damn it." I slump into the seat.

"What?" he asks.

"You're being nice. I don't know what to do with that." I slide my phone over to him. The screen is filled with pictures of cats from the shelter. "Check it out."

He scrolls through the images. "They named this one Smudge. This is Francesca, Zeus, Ivan, Muddy. This is Albert." He shows me a picture of a huge, long-haired Persian. "They asked me to name him. He's hyper. Chews on catnip like it's meth."

"Wow. There's an image. But it's not a bad name, I guess."

"Does it get me an extra five minutes?"

"I need time, Quinn. The ink on my divorce is barely dry, my dad just died, and my mom's still out of the country."

Also, I don't add out loud, I'm having secret conversations with Nick. *My* person, who's currently in Berlin or London or Geneva.

He sighs and stands up. "You have some things to work out?"

"We both might like me better if I do," I say. This is a factual statement.

"I'll wait. At least you're talking to me now."

I hold my breath as he comes close, gently takes my right hand, and kisses my fingertips. Holy shit. Nobody can remain functional under such duress. I try not to blink. Jesse's getting a call the nanosecond he walks out the door.

CHAPTER 4
DICK & JANE

Jesse is thirty minutes late for our emergency meeting. I don't know what big plans she has on a Sunday night, but she's made it clear I've interrupted them.

"What's your deal, Katy? And why did you want me to come here?" She strides down the slope of my parents' backyard to the canal. "You have eight minutes, and then I'm leaving."

"I needed to get out of the house, and it's peaceful here at night." I straddle the dock and the boat as she steps on board *Happily*. "I made fresh sangria."

"Keep talking." She walks gingerly to the nose of the twenty-five-foot sailboat. "I don't understand how people get sea legs. You prance all over this thing like you've got Spidey webs on your feet. Why don't you ever fall off?"

"It just takes time," I say, carrying the pitcher, two glasses and a bag of potato chips. "Also, I've been waiting tables since I was twelve."

"Congratulations." She sits down and takes the wine glasses from me. "So, what's wrong?"

"I've got a man problem."

"Me too. Waiting for me in my bed." She holds her glass up to me. "Pour it to the rim."

"You're seeing someone?"

"I don't see people, Kiss. I do them. Two in this case. As soon as we wrap this up."

"Ew, Jesse. Gross."

She pulls a chunk of watermelon from her drink. "This is excellent. You should bottle it."

"Thanks. Tell me about the two people."

"You can't handle it. You're a prude."

"I can totally handle it." I shove chips into my mouth. "Tell me everything."

"What do you want to know? One is Dick, the other is Jane."

I try not to choke. "Oh, God. Really?"

She snorts. "No, not really. Who knows what the hell their names are? One's a man, the other is a woman. They're both hot, fully functional, and willing to leave my home in a timely manner."

"You are truly offensive. But…like, how does it work?"

"You want the details?" she asks.

"I don't know. Do I?"

"Probably not. Suffice it to say, I get a lot of attention as the newest participant." She takes the bag away from me. "Shall I continue?"

"Maybe not."

"Great. Now what's happening that can't wait until my sex day is over?"

"Your sex day?"

"Yes. Sunday, day of sex. It's a rule, or an amendment or something. Now tell me what's up or I'm out."

I take a swig of the sangria. It really is delicious. "Quinn showed up."

"To your house?"

"Yes."

"Longer sentences, Katy."

"Fine. He arrived at my home earlier today, knocked on the door and apologized. I let him come inside for a couple of minutes."

"And now you love him again?" She empties her glass.

"I don't love him. But he is really cute."

"Cute is the word you want to use here? Are you fourteen?"

"Extremely attractive," I counter.

"Great. Go on a date with him. Fall in love and get on with your life."

"I have a bit of a conflict," I tell her, fishing a slice of orange from the wine.

"Conflict?" She refills her glass.

"Yes."

"Again, Kiss, longer sentences."

"Okay, but don't get mad."

"Gonna kill you in a minute. I've got two butt-ass naked people sliding around my new silk sheets waiting for me."

"Did you do this crap in college?" I ask, trying not to sneer.

"Quietly toward the end. You were a mere babe, and I didn't want to freak you out. Now tell me the thing that's going to piss me off."

I bite my lip, then admit, "It's Nick."

"What about Nick?"

"Remember when he texted me on New Year's Eve?"

"Yes. You said you didn't return it."

"Did I?" I bite into a maraschino cherry and wash it down with more sangria.

"Did you call him back?"

"I dunno." I say with the stem between my teeth. "Possibly."

Her nostrils flare. "You've been speaking to him?"

"Yeah. Almost once a week since January."

She leans on the thin aluminum railing. The boat dips gently. "Have you seen him?"

"No."

"Are you going to?"

"Probably."

She rubs her fingers on her forehead. "You know how I feel about this."

"Yup."

"He wasn't good enough for you."

"Dr. Jonas said I wasn't clear about my intentions with him. You know—back in the day."

"So." She clears her throat. "Had you been clearer, things would have turned out differently? He would have married you, been a fucking knight-in-Nick armor, and treated you like..." she trails off, rolling her eyes.

I shrug. "I dunno. She said I needed to demand more from the relationship. Or stated that I wanted more."

"Hm." She stares out into the darkness.

"I think he's changed, Jess. He has some big job in Europe."

"So, being on someone's payroll turned him into a decent human being? What's the job, mouthpiece for the Little Sisters of the Poor?"

"No. Some kind of currency consulting with banks."

Her lips turn upward in a sour grin. "Where do you fit in?"

"We're working on it."

"Do you remember college, or have you blocked out those four years of your life?"

"I remember."

"You recall how you said he was your person?"

"Yes, counselor."

"Not your lawyer anymore. Then you'd get drunk and make out and he'd say he has important personal goals, and you should only be friends."

I watch a moth dart past the light on the deck. "Yeah."

"And then you'd cry."

"I kind of remember that."

"Yet we're still not on the same page?"

"You liked him too, Jess."

"And I still do. He's funny as hell, smart, interesting. Also a narcissistic asshole. You fell for someone who dropped all the right words in front of you, then pulled them away like one of those strings a cat plays with."

"That's not how I saw it."

"Clearly," she says. "You let all the things you grew up wanting cloud your judgment."

"What's wrong with wanting a normal life?"

"Nothing, but you need to pick a better playmate for the fairy tale your parents pushed down your throat. Princess Katy finds a sweet, hard-working dude, makes fat pink babies, and lives happily ever after. If that's what you want, you should look elsewhere. Nick isn't your guy."

"But he's my person."

She stands up, leans to the left and right to keep her balance. "Then you don't understand what it means to have a person."

"Hm," I mumble, pushing her words away. What if she's right? She's always right. But maybe not this time. I lick the sweetness of the sangria off my lips. The mast sways underneath the stars. A thin layer of clouds filters the light from the moon.

"What do I do about Quinn?"

"Give him a chance," she says. "He might be the real deal. But you're too stubborn to take my word for it."

"No, I'm not." I look over as she makes her way to the stern of the boat. "Hey Jess, you know your shirt's on inside out."

She pulls on her collar. "Left in a hurry. And sure you are. You're going to let Nickety-Nick twist you into a ball and then wonder why your heart's getting torched like a marshmallow. Now let me off this barge so I can go get laid."

CHAPTER 5
NEW BROTHER ETHAN

I'm in the middle of my workday when Jesse sends a text about being tired and needing a nap. My response is swift. *Are you looking for sympathy from a prude? Shoulda rested but you sexted.*

"I like rhyming words," Russ says, looking over my shoulder.

I slide the phone into my pocket. "I'll keep that in mind."

"Do you even know what sexting is, Katy-Bell?"

I cringe. "I'm not sexting. I'm giving Jesse some crap about yesterday and I needed a word that rhymed."

He tugs on my ponytail and heads into the office. "I don't think I want to know. Let's do some work on the menu updates."

I follow him and carefully lower myself into an ancient folding chair. "I have some ideas."

"Like getting new office furniture?" he asks, sitting down in front of the computer. His left and right index fingers hover over the letters f and j. On the screen is the file he's named "New food grub."

"I'll take it into consideration. However, I made some tasty sangria last night."

He says, "I'll have to take your word for it."

"Oh, hell. I'm sorry. It tastes like dirt and earthworm jerky." I high-five him. "You're a sober rockstar."

"I know, darlin'. Is the booze good enough to put on the menu?"

"I wrote it down here." I take a small notepad off the desk. "Hungarian brandy. Apricot specifically, red wine, fresh squeezed orange juice and lots of fruit. A dash of ginger ale."

He types it into the grub file. "Does it have a name?"

"Can't it just be sangria?"

He leans back and stretches his arms over his head. "Let the customers name it. We'll have a contest."

"Great idea. We'll post it on the website and Instagram." I write some notes and toss the pad of paper back onto the desk. "Also, the casserole Jesse was talking about."

"Groovy." He begins typing. "What did she call it?"

"Magical ham and cheese. It's the shit, man."

He looks over at me and grins. "Little cocky, aren't you?"

"Don't you trust me?"

"With my life, sweet-pea. Cook up a batch and I'll take it for a test drive."

• • • • •

At 4 p.m., I pull a large Pyrex baking dish out of the oven. It contains a mountain of the good stuff. Pasta, small cubes of ham, cheese, and my grandmother's secret sauce. My eyes burn from the heat, and the smell of broiling cheese fills my nose. Russ is circling before I set it on the counter.

"What in the hell?" He lowers his face and inhales. "Smells incredible."

"I told you. Let it cool or it'll burn your taste buds off."

He takes a step back. "Your pocket's ringing," he says.

I place a sheet of tinfoil over the dish and pull my phone out. Caller ID glows on the screen. *New Brother Ethan.*

"Hey!"

"How are you, sister?"

"Great. What's going on?" I smile. I am someone's sister.

"What are you doing tomorrow night?"

I watch Russ peek under the foil. "I'll be here at the restaurant. Why?"

"Wanna fly?"

"Always. Where are we going?"

"Denver, for a day and a half. Can you swing it?"

"It's really short notice," I say, watching Melissa and Cricket walk in to begin their shifts. "How is this supposed to happen?"

Cricket drops her backpack outside the office door. "Mrs. Katy, are you actively on the telephone?"

"Yes. It's why I'm holding it up here by my ear. Can you check the dining room floor? Give it a once-over."

"Who are you talking to? Is it one of your men?"

"My brother." I nod at Melissa, who frowns, then directs Cricket out of the kitchen.

"Sorry," I whisper. "That's my new server, Cricket."

"Peculiar name," Ethan says.

"Fits the owner. So flight benefits finally kicked in and you're not going to make me fly commercial again?"

"We flew commercial last time because I wasn't on the payroll yet."

"Fair," I acknowledge. The perks of his new job hadn't begun when I went back to Denver with him right after New Years. "Tell me the details."

"We're dropping someone in Sarasota, which means we're empty on the return flight to Denver tomorrow night. I have permission to put you on the empty leg."

"I can't believe I get to fly private. Wait, how do I get home?"

"Same way. You're the only person onboard to Florida. Paying passengers on their way back to Denver. We would have parked the jet there for a couple of days, but we have too many trips in between."

Russ feigns interest as I chat with my brother. He taps his right foot, waiting, then finally shovels a large square of mac and cheese onto a plate. I watch him pull a section of crunchy broiled Monterey Jack off the top. His eyes flutter as he chews.

"What time would I be back in Duff Beach?"

"Thursday arrival into SRQ at two p.m. You'll be home by three."

"What's an SRQ?" I look around the kitchen and decide I'd be sorry if I don't go.

"Actually, I don't care what it is. I'm in." I smile as Melissa and Cricket return to the kitchen.

"Great," Ethan says. "I'll text you the details. And SRQ is the airport code for Sarasota."

"Ooh, I learned something about aviation! What should I wear?"

"Something respectable. No ripped jeans or tank tops."

I end the call by thanking him for the free ride and set the phone on the counter as the girls sample the pasta. Melissa takes a spoonful, says, "num-num," and hops a few times to show her enthusiasm.

Cricket fills her dish slowly, leveling the food off with great care. "I can have this, Mrs. Katy?"

Russ shakes his head. "It's already on your plate, girl. Why are you asking?"

I push the foil back on the baking dish. "I want you to try it so you can recommend it to the customers."

"What if I don't like it?" she asks.

"Then don't recommend it. And Katy. Just call me Katy."

"Okay, Mrs. Katy." She takes one bite. Then another. "What about the other menu items? I haven't sampled those."

"You're welcome to try anything we make. Just eat before your shift begins or after the dinner rush."

"Do I have to pay for it? Mom says I should eat at home to save my money."

I take a rolling pin from the baking supply drawer. "Nope. On the house."

"I don't pay?"

"No. On the house means it's free."

"Hm." She raises her eyebrows, picks up a single noodle, then pops it into her mouth.

I fight to keep my *inside* face, the one with the sneering WTF expression, contained, and sprinkle flour on the large wooden board my dad bought years ago. For a minute, my stomach sinks, thinking of him standing in this exact spot, singing, or lecturing as he'd fold and roll dough. He would have removed Cricket by the scruff on her first day. He was a good man, but patience wasn't one of his virtues. I dust off my hands, look up and notice she's staring at me while Russ stares at her. Work comes to a full stop because nobody has anything better to do than watch everyone else.

"Cricket, can you stack the dishes for plating?"

She blinks and adjusts her thick glasses on the bridge of her nose. "Okie dokie, lolly-poppy."

"Uh-huh," I say and continue cutting four sticks of butter into pea size bits on a chilled marble slab. The knife blade hitting the surface is soothing. The clickety-clack relaxes me.

What's the weather like in Denver in the spring? What will I wear to travel? I drop the butter into the electric mixer with a cup of sour cream. Do I bring snow boots or shorts? Dishes clatter, water boils, the A/C clicks on. What I take with me doesn't matter. It's going to be an awesome adventure. I can hardly wait to go to Colorado.

CHAPTER 6
BABY TOY PLANE

It's Tuesday evening. I cut out of work early and head home to select appropriate traveling attire. Not. My wardrobe consists of jeans, shorts, tank tops, and yoga pants. To be clear, I don't buy yoga pants in order to do yoga. Quiet focus and intention are too stressful for me, as is bending myself in two, or three, and sorting out why the earth is only under my feet when I'm stretched out in a way that looks a lot like a sex video.

Forty minutes later, I'm driving north on I-75. I've had a brief conversation with Jesse to let her know where I'm going, and a much longer one with my mother. She had many questions. Mainly about how safe a "toy" plane could be. She doesn't approve, and now I'm under orders to text her the second I land in Denver.

My phone navigates me to the private terminal where I'm supposed to meet Ethan. I park my wee sad Toyota among the big kid cars. At the reception desk, a friendly woman welcomes me, asks if I'd like a designer coffee, then directs me to a seating area tastefully decorated with gray couches, off-white cushions, and a glass table.

Pilots walk by and dip their heads in greeting. Their slight bows remind me of the three days I spent in Bangkok last

November when my dad had a heart attack. I try not to think about it too often, but it's always these unexpected images that trigger memories of endless bowing, and watching Dad wither in a hospital bed. And meeting Ethan, who I knew only as a stranger at the time, nosing into my family's worst nightmare.

I'm composing a text to Nick when four women walk in from the tarmac. They're dressed in designer clothes, carrying Louis Vuitton purses. Behind them, a young man with a badge identifying him as hangar ops, struggles to carry their nine-hundred shopping bags from Bergdorf Goodman, FAO Schwarz, and Saks. I glance at my business casual pants and the white button-down shirt I ironed this morning. The women grace me with fake smiles as they float past. They probably think I'm here to clean the bathroom.

I finish the text to Nick and hit send. *Guess where I am?*

After thirty seconds of waiting, I get antsy and walk to a large window facing the commercial terminal. I watch the smaller jets, tucked between larger aircraft, roll by in the glow of runway lights. They do look like toys. I hate it when Mom's right.

"Passenger Kiss?" I swivel around and find my brother. "Ready to fly?" He hugs me and takes my carry-on. "Come with me. You have to sign a waiver."

I follow him into a room with several computers and a wall-sized map. "What's this place?" I ask.

"Pilot room. It's where we do our flight planning." He pulls a document from the printer and hands it to me. "Read it, sign it."

"Why?" I focus on a line about not pressing charges in case of death. What?

"It's a liability waiver. You're flying as a guest. You have to promise not to sue us if we crash."

This seems more serious than the papers I signed in Dr. Jonas' office. Those were about confidentiality and insurance.

These are about hurtling to the ground in a fiery test tube. Suddenly I don't feel so good.

Ethan notices my hesitation. "It's fine. These jets are maintained a hundred times better than any car on the road, and we have thousands of flight hours. I promise to keep you safe."

"Pinkie promise?" I ask and hold out my hand.

"Absolutely." We shake fingers. "You think I'd let anything bad happen to my little sister?"

A few minutes later, we're out on the tarmac. Another pilot is standing in the glare of a fuel truck's lights at the side of the jet.

"Katy, this is my co-pilot, First Officer Butcher."

Pilot Butcher tilts his glasses up and looks me over. "You didn't tell me your sister was hot."

"Stand down, Butch. She's too good for you." Ethan winks at me and leads me to the stairs and into the jet.

"Sorry about him. And yes, he is wearing sunglasses at night. He thinks it's cool. Welcome onboard."

"Thanks," I say, then notice he's staring at me. "What did I do?"

"Nothing. I'm curious about what you think?" He pushes my bag into a slot near the cockpit.

I study the cabin. "It reminds me of the baking pans we use for our Yule logs. Kind of arched at the top and flat at the bottom."

He snorts. "Ridiculous. A baking pan doesn't have leather seating."

"True. But I feel a little claustrophobic in here. Like I'm in a tunnel."

"It's nice though, right?"

"Yeah, beautiful. Not like any plane I've ever been on." I search for items to compliment. "Cupholders. Handy. And the seats are a pretty color."

"Mocha with cream." He runs his fingers over a headrest. "It's the actual name of the color."

"Nice," I say, remembering Quinn's comment about the paint on my walls. "And there are seat belts. Probably a good thing, right?"

"Same rules apply here as on a commercial jet. Keep it on unless you're using the lav. Want to see the cockpit?"

"Sure. Should I know how to land in case both of you drop dead?"

He raises his right eyebrow the way my dad used to.

"The learning curve might be a bit much. But check out how cool it is."

His hand brushes across the instrument panel as he explains each component. The throttle, control wheel, or "yoke", he says, and the rudder pedal. I smile and nod as my brother elaborates on every switch and dial. Is there alcohol on this jet? How can this many knob thingies work in tandem? What if one breaks?

He leans close to me. "You seem anxious."

"Only a bit. But it's all really cool, so thank you for doing this, you know, flying me around, in case I didn't say it earlier." I grin and continue to babble. "It's all kind of new. Whoever thought I'd get to fly on a private jet?"

"Whoever thought you had a long-lost brother?" He swivels me ninety degrees and gently pushes me into the cabin. "Almost go time. Sit anywhere you want and buckle in."

"Okay," I tell him, and head to the seats closest to the front. "Is this all right?"

"You look good to me," First Officer Butcher says, stepping onboard and pulling the aircraft door shut. "You ready, Katy Kiss?"

"Uh-huh."

"Are you a good kisser?" He grins and rubs his hands together.

I need a minute here to keep my face from distorting; from morphing into Medusa so I don't turn this fucker into a stone block. "I dunno. Are you good at cutting meat?"

His eyes go blank. "Why would I be good at that?"

"Oh God," I mumble. "Never mind."

His grin gets wider. "Sit tight, doll. I'll check on you in a few."

I push into the seat, buckle the belt, and lean my head against the window.

"He's a dick, isn't he?" Ethan says a few minutes later. He sets a drink on a small, polished wood table next to me. "You can smack him when we land, but I need him to fly."

"Is this a Greyhound?" I ask.

"Yes, it is. Grapefruit juice and vodka, right?"

"How did you know?"

"I remember from last December. Also, you seem like you might need it."

"Thank you. Is he a good pilot?"

He smiles and takes a few steps toward the cockpit. "Surprisingly, yes. So, don't worry."

"Uh-huh." I take a sip of the Greyhound and silently judge the canned grapefruit juice. My brother is the best brother. Ever. The aircraft rolls a few feet backwards. Ethan is on the radio saying something about our departure and Sarasota Tower. A Delta airliner taxis near us as we rotate away from the building. I love Delta. Their planes are big and sturdy, not at all like a cake pan.

CHAPTER 7
WELCOME TO DENVER

Three and a half hours later, we're preparing to land in Denver. I've had four tiny packages of organic cashews, two alcoholic beverages, and several offers from co-pilot Butcher to show me around town. I'm ready for this flight to be over.

Nobody mentioned small planes get tossed around more than the big jets. Ethan said they can change altitude quicker than the larger jetliners to avoid turbulence, but still, one has to consider the weight of a lighter aircraft and all that aerodynamics bullshit. I'm only saying, I would have liked a heads-up before getting on this roller coaster ride.

"At least the landing was smooth," he yells from the cockpit.

"Yup!" I answer in my most enthusiastic voice. Outside, the Rocky Mountains are visible from the snow reflecting in the light of the moon. To the east, a series of hangers slide by as the aircraft slows on the runway. I turn my phone on. There's a text from Russ saying he's finished off the magical mac and cheese for second-dinner, and can I please make some more? I scroll to the message I sent Nick. No response. He could at least disable his read receipts. Then I'd feel better about myself. I groan quietly and stare at the blue lights lining the runway. "Why didn't we land at the normal airport?" I ask as we turn and taxi.

Ethan answers, "Big airports don't much care for small airplanes, and DIA isn't any different. We clog up commercial traffic, create delays and generally get in the way. Centennial is our home base. Third busiest general aviation airport in the U.S."

"Interesting." I mutter under my breath. Not at all interesting.

He radios something to the tower, then promises we'll be on the road in fifteen minutes.

• • • • •

Promise kept. I've never gotten out of an airport so fast. The benefits of private travel are significant. Too bad they're only available to the rich and famous who demand that we do as they say while they do as they please. Well, mostly. I take in the landscape as Ethan chatters about the area on our drive home. Over here is REI, his favorite place on Earth. Over there is Park Meadows if I need to shop, and there's IKEA, if I want Swedish meatballs or furniture that comes in a thousand separate pieces. We're taking the University exit, and the University of Denver is a few miles down the road.

"You showed this stuff to me in January," I tell him.

"It was covered in snow then. Now it's green, well, getting green. Except in the mountains. The snow hasn't melted up there yet. Anyway, we're almost there."

"Are we going back to your mom's?"

He cusses quietly at the car in front of us, then swings past it in the left lane. "Nope. I moved into my own place two weeks ago. Don't judge. There are still boxes all over."

"Was she upset when you left?"

"Not really. She's ten minutes away and agrees her thirty-something-year-old son should not be living in the spare bedroom."

"You don't want to be that guy."

"I'm not," he says, with a flash of defensiveness in his voice. "But I've been working in Bangkok for the last two years, and she was lonely." He looks over at me. "And the whole thing with your dad."

"Our dad."

"Our dad," he repeats. "It really took her for a ride. I didn't want to leave her alone right away."

"The dutiful son." We pull into the driveway of a one-story brick bungalow. "Is this it?"

"It is. Mom's already here. She's excited to see you again."

My stomach does some more acrobatics. I was here a few months ago, meeting his mother for the second time in my life. I don't remember the first time because I was three when my family showed up for what must have been the most awkward *friend* visit ever.

I step out of the car into crisp, dry air. It's all so different from Florida. I want to say I hate it, but I kind of don't. It's fresh and clean, energizing. I fight the urge to do a cartwheel on the soft grass in his front yard.

"Katy!" Ethan's mom rushes to embrace me. "Milyen csinos ez a lány."

He pulls my bag from the back seat. "Yes, Mom. She's very pretty. Try not to embarrass her."

I thank her as she squeezes my cheek. Why am I always so surprised to hear other people speaking Hungarian in America?

"You must be starving." Her smile is wide, genuine. How can a woman who was cast out to hide a pregnancy be so kind to the daughter of the man who knocked her up?

"Thanks. I could eat." I give Ethan a playful shove. "Your son got me drunk."

Ethan kicks his shoes off inside the door. "You're not going to puke in my house, are you?"

"It's possible. Why didn't you tell me the flight would be so bumpy?"

"Why did you have so many drinks?" he asks, grinning.

"I only had two. Why didn't you have some real food on board?"

His mom giggles. "You are bickering like brother and sister. I must say this makes me quite glad." She takes my arm and walks me into the kitchen. "I made soup."

I sniff the air and recognize the scent of chicken, carrots, and sweet parsnips. It's the fragrance of my grandmother's apartment in Montreal. My childhood. Warm, safe, and filled with love. "It smells delicious, Mrs. Sindall."

"Lena, please," she insists. "I would not mind if you call me Mom, but I do not want to be rude to your mother."

"That's a low bar lately. I thought your name was Magda."

"Yes, Magdalena. I have been using Lena for years."

I stare into the pot. "Is this matzo ball soup?"

"It is. Your father showed me how to make this years ago." The last few words barely make it out of her mouth. She sucks in air before speaking again. "I'm sorry. I am still emotional about his passing." She wipes the sudden tears from her eyes. "His recipe was like the science experiment. Very precise."

"My dad taught you?"

I watch her stir with a wooden spoon. She's short and a little round; the softhearted fairy tale godmother. A huggable maternal archetype.

"This is your family's recipe." She points at me. "I believe your grandmother, Juci's."

"I don't think I've ever had it."

She glances at me, then knocks the spoon on the rim of the navy Le Creuset pot before dropping it into the sink.

"It's strange right?" I say sheepishly. "I'm twenty-six. Do you think my parents avoided making this soup because I'd figure out that we're Jewish? And then I'd freak out? Or they would." I look away. "I don't get it."

"I did not know your family was keeping this many secrets." She turns the faucet on. "I cannot say I agree with their decisions."

"What do you mean by this many?" I ask. "Is there something else I don't know about?"

"Paranoid much?" Ethan walks behind me, picks up the pot, and carries it to the table.

"No." Lena hesitates, then waves her hands in front of her face. "Nothing for you to worry about. Have soup, dear," she says, ladling the golden liquid into our bowls. "You will feel better."

"Thanks. This looks amazing." I dip my spoon into the steaming soup.

"I do not put in the parsley until the end. When we smell this, we know it is ready." She smiles. "How is your mother? I hear you have been in Paris visiting her."

"She's hurting. More short-tempered than usual."

"Did you talk about these things with her? About your family's…" She stops to glance at Ethan.

"About our history?" I shrug. "And my parents lying to me about everything I am and what they've been through? Nope, she wasn't up to it, and I'm not ready to pull the pin out of the grenade."

I stop short, force myself to smile and taste the soup. It's warm, salty, and delicious. For a minute, I consider trading out my anxiety soup to matzo ball. I take another spoonful. Wish Dad would have passed this recipe down to me directly, along with the fact that we're Jewish, that I have a brother, and how a chunk of my family disappeared during the Holocaust.

Her voice brings me back to the conversation. "They did this to protect you, and I understand it." She touches Ethan's hand. "My son knows of his heritage, but we do not tell others."

"You don't?"

"No. Why would we?" she asks. "What good comes of it?"

Ethan's posture stiffens. I can tell he's uncomfortable with the conversation.

"The world is crazy," she continues. "We never know."

"Never know what?" I ask.

"Tell her, Mom," Ethan mumbles.

She taps her pudgy fingers on the table. "When it happens again."

"Seriously?" I ask. "You can't possibly think those things could happen in America in this day and age?"

Her bright green eyes dim for a moment. "We do not speak about this tonight." They brighten again, and in her smile, I see a glimpse of the kindness my dad might have fallen for all those years ago. "You are here with us now, Katy, and this time it will be a wonderful vacation."

Our late-night dinner ends with a Hungarian portion of dessert topped with a dash of tension about things unspoken. Lena kisses both of us on the cheek and heads home.

CHAPTER 8
GIRL DIES IN BASEMENT

When I'm at home, I take extra care to lock all the windows and doors before I go to bed. I activate the alarm and slink from room to room, searching for wayward danger. Last night, in my brother's house in Denver, I fell asleep without a care and slept like a baby in the cool spring air streaming through the open window. Nothing bad happened. I don't even remember dreaming.

This morning I feel refreshed. Someone's mowing their lawn nearby, and the scent of cut grass stirs up memories of the time my dad bought an electric lawn mower, ran over the cord, and shocked himself repeatedly until Mom pulled the plug and asked him point blank if he was having a stroke.

I'm still tucked under the blanket when I hear a loud thump followed by Ethan yelling, "I'm fine." The sound continues as I get up and walk to the kitchen. He's standing at the basement door, pushing boxes down the stairs.

"What the hell are you doing?" I ask as he launches another cardboard box.

"None of it's breakable. Towels and linens. Nothing to see here."

"You remind me of Dad," I say. "The way your sentences get kind of clipped. Like, end of story, no counter-arguments will be accepted at this time."

"Oh, yeah?"

"Yup. Genetics are so random. A blind date between an egg and a sperm." I scan the kitchen counter. "Got any coffee?"

"I've got a press. Know how to use one?"

"I own a restaurant, Ethan."

"But do you own a press?" he asks again. "Anyway, I was just trying to have some fun. Coffee's already made." He picks up the last box and starts down the stairs. "Oh, my back! It's so heavy!"

"Should I call 911?" I ask as my phone chimes. It's a text from Russ.

Quinn dropped by last night after you left. Said something about talking you into going to the animal shelter.

I return the text. *He came into the restaurant?*

What's his play? What does he want? What do I want? I'm older, wiser, in therapy for fuck's sake. Shouldn't I have all the answers by now?

Russ texts again, *Yep. Cricket lost her shit and asked if he'd ever been to prom.*

Oh hell. We've gotta muzzle her. Nice of him though - huh?
He's the man.
He's A man. How's work? You okay?
Groovy baby. How's it a mile high?
Whatever, Russ.
Whatever you. gotta work.

I drop my phone on the counter and pour half and half into my cup when Ethan calls up from the basement. "Come down here!"

"Why?" Cream first, coffee second, the way my parents taught me so I wouldn't need to stir. Save a spoon, save some water, save the world.

His voice drifts upstairs. "I want to show you something."

I peer into the dim light of the staircase and shiver. There aren't many basements in Florida. I don't want to go down there. I want to stay here in the low-oxygen Denver daylight.

"Katy!"

"Okay." I put my bare foot on the first step and descend into the darkness. This is terrible. Who built these stairs and why is there a gaping hole between each slat? Don't they have building codes in Colorado? The hair on my arms stands up as I grip the old wooden banister for dear life. Each step squeaks and moans under the pressure of my weight.

"Ethan?" I call out, wondering if a panic attack is going to send me tumbling downward. I stop moving, close my eyes, and smell my tomato soup. What if my brother is an ax murderer? Is he even my brother? I should have demanded a DNA test. What if I'm about to get killed? What if I'm the next story on some true-crime podcast? Florida girl gets chopped-up by a young man impersonating her secret brother… the long con. What if this story isn't exciting enough for a podcast? I open my eyes and take another few steps. What if my death is too pathetic to make front page news? Florida girl goes to Denver and dies. Big deal, see story on page twenty-three underneath the ad for oatmeal soap.

"Ethan?" I call out again.

"Yeah." His voice sounds distant.

"Where are you?" I reach the bottom step and shove a box out of my way. The corner is torn open, and a pile of blankets has spilled onto the floor. "Your baby blanky is trying to escape its container."

"In here." He pops his head out from a room to the left of me.

It's dusty, gloomy, and a hundred degrees colder than on the main floor. Please don't kill me. Please don't kill me. Okay, maybe ten degrees.

"What's wrong with you?" he asks. "You're pale as a ghost."

"Am not."

"It's just a cellar."

"We don't do cellars in Florida. Can't you store your shit above ground?"

"I guess I could," he says, disappearing into the room. A lightbulb swings over my head, casting shadows on the floor. I search for a vent. Nothing.

"Ethan, this lightbulb is moving on its own."

"Probably haunted."

"Shut up," I squeak. "I feel like I'm in *The Amityville Horror*."

"It's just a house," he says.

No, it's a subterranean space where nothing good could happen. The walls are gray cement-block, decorated with old pipes twisting and turning like a road map to nowhere. Morning light squeezes through a tiny window above a metal rack stacked with tattered wicker baskets and plastic containers.

"Where did you find this place?" I step over a scattering of rusted tools.

"My stepdad owned it," he says, leafing through a box of pictures. "Mom got it in the divorce. Guess she uses the space down here for storage and rents the upstairs to kids who go to DU."

Hesitating by the door, I ponder if this will be my last unwise decision before my so-called brother drops me into a hole and feeds me insects for the next thirty years. I shouldn't have come to Denver. I should have stayed home and saved a kitten with Quinn.

He waves a photo album in the air. "There are pictures of you in here."

"Of me? And what's DU?"

"The University of Denver. Come in here. Look at this."

"In there?"

"Yes, in here. The room won't bite. Grab one of those folding chairs."

In here is a damp, narrow room filled with things I have no interest in. On the far end is an ancient space heater and another window below ground level, set in a window well full of overgrown weeds.

"But it's creepy, and I'm pretty sure the heater's a fire hazard."

He looks around. "I'll toss it. And it's not creepy at all. Check out the artwork." He points to some drawings tacked to a cork board. "I like that one with the orange flower."

The board is set on a toddler sized desk next to the wall. I move closer and study the drawings. Three crude pictures of flowers on top of stick figure bodies. Two colored in pink crayon, and one in bright orange. "Good stuff. Yours?"

He shrugs. "I don't think so. I drew robots and cars and planes. Maybe the previous renters had kids."

I wipe prehistoric dust off the folding chair and sit down. It's frigid down here. My fingers are tingling, on their way to going numb. "How do you know it's me in the photo?"

He turns the album toward me. "Because mini-you is standing between your parents. The hair, the eyes." He smiles. "It's a hundred percent you."

I study the picture. "I remember the coat. I think Mom still has it. I used to dig my hands into the pockets because they were lined with fake fur. Dang, I was a pink roly-poly."

"With pink earmuffs." Ethan turns to another page. "You were cute. Round, but cute."

I look at the images taken near a mound of snow. My parents were so young. Mom was stylish, elegant, with the same short, layered haircut she has now, and Dad seemed happy. His cheeks were bright red from the cold, and his hair was a thick clump of dark curls.

"Who's this dude?" I ask, pointing to a picture of a man standing near his mother.

"Shit," he snaps and pulls the picture out of the album.

"Let me see. Is that your stepdad?"

He rips it to pieces before I get a good look.

"Wow, Ethan, you really do hate him." A piece of the photo flutters to the floor. A section showing the man's eyes. Dark, stern. My ears begin ringing, acid sloshes in my stomach. "I need to eat something."

"I'll make waffles in a minute."

"Great," I say, bracing my legs on the floor. "My head feels strange."

He stares at me. "Are you okay?"

I don't remember anything after that.

CHAPTER 9
NOW IS TIME TO EAT

I wake up, laid out and disoriented on the couch. The sight of Ethan's mom gaping at me adds an extra layer of humiliation as she tries to discern what style of damage would make a healthy young woman drop like a sack of potatoes.

There's no mystery here. I got dizzy and blacked out. It wasn't a panic attack. I didn't hyperventilate, and Mom wasn't yelling at me about her version of my future. It's probably the altitude, oxygen deprivation, and a basement that's the gateway to the underworld.

The smell of food makes my stomach rumble.

"Oh hell. Head rush." My punishment for sitting up too quickly. I close my eyes. The aroma of food from the kitchen is sharing space with the scent of the freshly cut grass outside.

Lena sits next to me and rubs my shoulder. "Are you feeling better? We are making waffles."

"You didn't need to come over. I'm fine."

"It is not a problem. I work only a few miles away at the school."

"It was a food thing, or an air thing. I swear I'm good."

"Please do not go to the downstairs again," she says.

"You don't have to ask twice. I'll steer clear," I promise, trying to read her facial expression.

"Good." She hesitates, looks away from me, then back. "I'm sorry you are being freaked out. The downstairs should be cleaned, but I never have the time."

I smile at her pronunciation. Her Hungarian accent isn't as strong as Mom and Dad's, but American slang isn't rolling off her tongue either. "I must be a little claustrophobic. It felt like we shouldn't be down there." I blink a few times. "I'm over it though."

She doesn't look convinced and touches her hand to my forehead. "No fever."

"Probably not dying today."

"This is not funny." Her eyes well up. Once again, I've hit the nerve connecting her to my dad, the father of her only child.

"Oh gosh, I'm sorry. Please don't cry." I stand up slowly. "See?" One step sideways to balance myself.

"I do not see," she says, steadying me. "But now is time to eat.

• • • • •

An hour later, I'm getting the toned-down, *Katy's a wimp* tour of Denver. Ethan and I walk to Washington Park, known to most people in the city as Wash Park. It's 165 acres of green space bordered by multi-million-dollar homes. During the summer, the locals use the park for all manner of recreation: picnics, frisbee, volleyball, and tennis. They stroll through the flower gardens, or watch their children burn off energy at the playgrounds. Most of these same activities happen in the winter too, because, well...Denver. People here want to be outside.

I absorb snippets of Ethan's geography lesson on the walk over. The houses get larger as we get closer and change from modest homes built a hundred years ago, to new construction that could be displayed on the cover of Architectural Digest.

He points to a river of flowers cascading from a remodeled Tudor's Juliet balcony. They have star-shaped blooms, petals inside of petals, layered in purple, white and yellow.

"Those are Columbine, the state flower of Colorado. They're blooming a little early this year." He nudges me off the sidewalk of South Franklin Street. "Let's cross here, by the lake."

"Can you swim in there?"

He snorts. "Hell, no. You can rent paddle boats. I think it's a tourist thing. Let's get to the trail. Keep your eyes open for bikes and rollerblades." After a few more steps, he says, "Sorry about the stuff Mom said last night. She can get pretty intense. I'm glad she reined it in."

"She was acting a little strange." I try to keep pace with his stride. "What did she mean about this time it'll be a good vacation? Does she think I didn't have fun when I was here in January?"

"You did spend a lot of time wrapped in blankets. But I don't know. She probably thinks you don't want to talk about the Jewish thing."

I step out of a woman's way as she races past us with a jogging stroller. Her baby is dozing under a powder blue blanket.

"Damn," I mumble under my breath. It's hard not to notice her long legs, powerful strides, blonde ponytail bobbing rhythmically as her feet hit the ground. "I don't do running."

"I'd run for her." Ethan watches her lope into the distance.

"Of course you would. Why are men so easy?"

He dips his head to the side and grins. "What about her looks easy?"

"Fair point," I agree. "Anyway, I guess you always knew about your family?"

"About us being Jewish? Yeah. Absolutely."

I step over a clover-filled crack on the sidewalk. Everything here is blooming. Filling up with color.

"You've got to talk to your mom," he says. "I know it's a complicated situation, but even if your parents' intentions were good, you deserve an explanation."

"She's not ready, and I don't want to push her buttons."

"What about your buttons?" He stops and stares at me. "Don't they matter? I don't get how you never suspected anything. In all this time."

"Well, I didn't. But I'm curious about what my grandmother will say tomorrow night when we Facetime her. Wonder if she'll stick to the same company line."

"Our grandmother," he corrects.

"Ours. Right. Sorry. Either way, we didn't do anything religious. I told you last year, I thought Easter and Passover were the same holiday. All those pastel colors and Easter eggs and stuff."

He starts back on the path. "Wow. Is it bad that I just pictured a rabbi and the Easter Bunny walking into a bar?"

"No," I say, smiling. "Anyway, what does it matter? I'm agnostic." I trot behind him. "Hey, slow down. My legs are shorter than yours."

"Agnostic means what to you?" he asks.

"It means I believe something is out there, but I'm unsure of what it is."

"Out there?" He slows his pace. "Lurking?"

"No, not lurking. It's about doing the right thing because it's the right thing to do, not because you're afraid some floaty dude with a beard is keeping score."

"There's an image," he says. "Now the floaty dude's walking into the bar, too."

"Nice. Coexistence." I stop, pull out my phone, and snap a picture of a clump of dandelions. "One man's weeds, but they look like flowers to me, and they feed the bees in the spring. You shouldn't pull them out."

He stands next to me. "An example of doing the right thing? Leaving food for the bees?"

I begin walking again. "I guess. Just doing the good thing, and hoping all our positive energy, alive and... well, departed, is enough to keep the world spinning the right way."

"Lovely thought," he says. "I wouldn't call it religion."

"I never said it was. It's what I believe. Like when you hold the door open for a stranger, even if you have to hang out a few extra seconds, and the smile on their face says you might have done the first nice thing they've experienced that day, or in weeks. And then they hold the door for someone else."

He kicks a rock off the path. "Paying it forward."

"In a perfect world," I say, remembering Quinn's words about the animal shelter. "Good begets better. People should behave. None of us are important enough to be exempt."

"I hear you," he says. "Promise me you'll have a chat with your mom."

"I told you I will."

"And by a chat, I mean a real conversation."

"Yes, I understand. I'll sit her down and demand to know why, when, and where."

He nudges my arm. "Or why not or never."

"Or that," I say, watching an elderly couple walk toward us. "Look how cute they are, holding hands."

"They've been coming here for years." Ethan greets them as they approach. "Lovely morning for a walk."

They smile and tell him it is, indeed, a lovely morning as they pass by.

I glance at them over my shoulder. "That's the freaking sweetest thing ever."

"They walk in the park every day unless the snow gets in their way."

"Must be nice," I say. "Bet they know exactly where they came from. Does it seem like I need an instruction manual for my own family?"

"Families are complicated." He stops talking, distracted by the woman with the long legs and the stroller running past us again. "She lapped us." He turns to me. "Let's get you some more food, but then I want to go to the zoo."

I pull on a sweatshirt as we cut through a meadow near a group of kids playing frisbee. Their dogs, running alongside them, are in on the game. I'm still trying to keep up with Ethan, but my lungs are burning, and I'm getting a headache.

"You're a wimp." He looks back at me with a smile. "Denver's kicking your ass."

By the time we get to his house, glittering rays of sunshine are breaking through the clouds, illuminating their outlines like an ethereal spotlight. For the first time in months, I feel relaxed, actually kind of stoned. I flop down into a lawn chair in the yard and giggle. Who would have thought a Rocky Mountain High is a real thing?

CHAPTER 10
NOT A POET

Ethan feeds me leftover matzo ball soup with thick toasted slices of sourdough bread. Our original plan was to head to the mountains to climb St. Mary's Glacier, then come back down into the city for a brewery tour. After my blackout in the basement, he's changed the itinerary to the "kid-glove" experience. We begin at the zoo, where a thousand school kids swirl in screaming hordes, and the animals stand behind protective metal and glass, wondering how they're more dangerous than the wild things on the other side.

No matter where we go, I'm struck by how much bigger the sky looks here. In Florida, except for the beach, a glance upward is filtered through the twisted branches of the live oaks, or leafy fronds of the palm trees. Here, the entire sky is wide open, framed only on the distant horizon by mountains.

"Something up there?" Ethan asks. He's holding two ice cream cones in front of me. "Chocolate or mint chip?"

"The answer will always, always be chocolate." I take the cone as a cluster of sweaty children walk by us, immediately followed by a chorus of "We want ice cream!"

He hands me a napkin. "What were you grinning at?"

"What do you mean?" I ask.

"You were staring up and smiling. What's that all about?"

"Oh, the sky is so big, I was thinking how different it is here than back home. Humans are little dots on a planet that's a little dot." I look at him. "It's all perspective. Big sky, tiny unimportant humans."

"True," he says. "I noticed it in Bangkok, too. All you can see there is a sliver of sky trying to squeeze through all the utility lines and buildings. Here...well." He turns his face toward the sun and closes his eyes. "It's better. Even if I am tiny and unimportant."

I taste the ice cream. "Kinda feels like God used finger paints to make Colorado."

He opens his eyes and squints at me. "Don't grow up to be a poet, kid. Ready to hit it?"

I ask if I can finish my cone first, then promptly drop the scoop of ice cream onto the ground.

Ethan laughs, then takes a bite of mint chip. "Nice one. Want some of mine?"

"No thanks." I stare at the melting blob on the concrete.

"It's okay," he says. "Don't worry about starving to death. We're getting hot dogs next."

CHAPTER 11
SAD TREE

A hot dog is a hot dog, though not if it's from a Denver institution, Mustard's Last Stand. So says my brother as we roll into his driveway. Our plan is to spend the evening lounging in his backyard, eating, drinking, and hanging out with his best friend, Noah.

Ethan checks his phone. "He's on his way. Let's throw some drinks into the cooler."

I follow him into the kitchen. We search for paper plates and napkins and find them in a half unpacked moving box. He gives me a canned seltzer with vodka and lemon, then we head outside as his friend arrives.

"You're Katy?" Noah asks from well above six feet. He has a kind face and the purest gray eyes I've ever seen.

"Guilty. Nice to meet you."

"How goes it?" He shakes my hand before I drop into a forest green Adirondack chair.

"Dude," Ethan says. They bump fists. "Right on time."

"I finally meet the mystery sister." Noah smiles at me.

"I think you were out of town when I was here in January."

"Conference." He swings a large paper bag onto an old picnic table and begins unloading. "Got everyone the works.

Chicago Dogs, a shitload of fries and every sauce they'd give me." He sits down. "Was the lot across the street for sale last time I was here?"

I follow Ethan's gaze to the *for sale* sign on a plot of land consisting of dry dirt, rocks, patches of yellow grass, and a sad tree, more dead than alive.

He lifts his sunglasses, lowers them back down. "No clue. I never see anyone over there." He smiles at Noah. "Want to buy it? We can be neighbors."

"I'm not touching that," he answers.

"It looks haunted," I add. "There couldn't have been a house there because that poor old tree is smack in the middle. Holy crap, I bet there's a tunnel from the lot to your evil basement."

Noah asks, "You have an evil basement?"

"According to my sister." He winks at me. "Mom ripped my head off for letting her go down there."

I turn to him. "When did she do that?"

"When you were on the couch. She was pissed. Think it's the Hungarian formality kicking in. It's not properly decorated or filled with Persian rugs and a thousand books. Guests don't belong down there."

"I'm not a guest. I'm your sister."

Noah swats at a cloud of gnats. "Why were either of you in the cellar?"

Ethan lobs a beer at him. "I was unpacking boxes and found a photo album with some old pictures of Katy and her parents. It wasn't a big deal. I wanted to show them to her."

Noah shrugs, sits down, and everyone digs in. We make food sounds, chewing, slurping, and drinking. The setting sun casts pink and gold rays between the clouds. The breeze is cool on my skin.

"This is delicious," I announce as a dollop of sauerkraut from my hot dog falls onto the grass. "How long have you guys known each other?"

Noah finishes his beer. "Best hot dogs around. Kindergarten, right?"

"I stole his lunch." Ethan clears his throat. "A lot."

"Which was kind of odd," Noah says. "Because all I had was peanut butter and jelly. Guess he wasn't into the salami his mom packed for him."

"Salami is good." I take a bite from a crunchy pickle. "It can be a little much for school lunch. My mom did the same thing, and I remember being embarrassed by the smell." I lick my fingers. "What was Ethan like as a kid?"

Noah snorts. "Before or after his parents split up?"

"What do you mean?" I ask and notice my brother's face cloud over.

"I mean his dad—" He stops short and looks at Ethan apologetically. "Stepdad, sorry. He was an asshole. We were both scared shitless of him."

"He was mean to you too?"

"He had no filter," he says. "Didn't matter who was in the vicinity."

Ethan pulls a second beer from the cooler. "I still remember how much everything changed after he left. It's like there was this peace, you know? All the tension went away. Think it was in second or third grade."

"What was it like before?" I ask.

Noah bites into a hot pepper. "Chaotic. We didn't hang out at your house much, did we?"

Ethan balances his beer can on the arm of his lawn chair. "Not if we could help it."

"Wow. That sucks," I say, pulling my knees to my chest.

"Everyone was nervous around him," Ethan says. "Walking on eggshells. You had to weigh every word, every action. I could say, 'Hey, Dad,' and he'd be fine. Fifteen minutes later, the same two words would set him off. He was jealous. Psycho controlling with Mom. Anytime we were in public, he'd have a hand on her like she was his property. He made sure everyone understood that she was tethered to him."

"God, I'm sorry. He sounds awful."

He shrugs and studies the label on the beer can.

"Do you ever hear from him?"

"No. He's probably in jail. I'm sure something he's done warrants it. Or he's terrorizing another family. Or he's dead."

Noah folds his hotdog wrapper into a neat square. "I keep offering to check if he's locked up."

"How would you find out?" I ask. "Are you a cop?"

He swats at the gnats again. "Not a cop, but I work in law enforcement."

"Doing what?"

"Whatever an undergrad in sociology and a master's in forensic psychology gets you. Profiler, loser in a dark office sifting through evidence and records and data."

"I think it sounds cool. Better than what I do."

"Restaurant, right?"

I nod. My phone buzzes. My heart skips a beat. "Gotta take this." I leap out of my chair and race-walk into the house, where I make a wide circle around the basement door and lock myself into my room.

I savor the anticipation of Nick's text, slowly rereading the message I sent before we left Florida. It was a lighthearted sentiment, not needy at all. *Guess where I am?*

His answer, two days later.

Where?

Seriously? Can't he come up with something more creative? Lower Zimbabwe, the northern tip of Iceland, the heel of Italy? I contemplate an appropriate response to his pathetic one word text.

I was about to get on a private jet! Now I'm in Denver.

Someone comes in from the yard. A door slams shut. The toilet flushes.

The read receipt pops up. He's seen it. I kick my sneakers off, lie down on the bed, and lick a spot of mustard off my finger.

Music filters through the walls. Amy Winehouse.

I watch the screen and wait.

CHAPTER 12
ETHAN OR EE-TEN

And wait. For another hour, until Ethan knocks on my door and asks if I'm ready to Facetime our grandmother in Montreal.

"Oh, crap," I mumble, having forgotten all about our scheduled call.

I join him at the kitchen table where his iPad leans against a stack of books.

"Are you kidding, Ethan? Did you shave?"

"Possibly."

"And comb your hair and change your clothes?"

He adjusts the collar on his white shirt. "So what? I don't want her to think I'm a slob."

"Oh." I smooth my wrinkled tee shirt. "I guess that's reasonable."

"Ready?" he asks.

"Let's do it."

The phone beeps in Denver, and rings in Montreal, where my grandmother's smiling face fills the screen.

"Do you see her okay?" My cousin turns the phone on herself, waving. "Hi Ethan. I'm Nori. We're cousins. Nice to finally meet you!"

Ethan grins. "Nice to meet you, too."

"So nice," she says. "Hi Katy-Baba. Miss you, sweetie."

"I miss you all, too. When are you coming to Florida?"

"Who knows? Work's so busy. You guys should come up, eh? Okay, talk to Grandma. She's super excited."

My grandmother pulls the phone near her face. "Let me seeing him!"

I try not to laugh as she points and pushes her finger on the screen. "Oh, very beautiful." She claps. "Ee-ten, I am very happily to meeting you!"

Ee-ten, Ethan, smiles, and waves.

"You are looking so like my Robi. Let me seeing him." She brings the phone close enough again to see the deep furrows on her forehead and pretty hazel eyes hidden under heavily wrinkled lids.

"Ee-ten," she continues. "I am very excited to seeing you in the person. I like for you to coming to Montreal."

"I'd love to, ma'am," he sputters. "I mean, um. Can I call you grandma?"

"Oh my gosh!" Nori blurts out. "Absolutely. Right Katy?"

I nod. "I'm trying to get him used to it."

"Yes! You call me grandma."

"Are you sure?"

"Igen!" she yells. "And we talk, you and me. I want to hear all the things about you. How your Mami is?"

Nori rolls her eyes and tells her not to be so loud. "Holy cow. She's going to break my eardrums."

Grandma takes the instruction with her usual good humor. "Okay, okay." She switches over to Hungarian. "Tell me what these big questions are."

"She wants to know what big question you need to ask," Nori repeats in English for Ethan.

"You don't have to translate for him, Nori. He speaks Hungarian. But yeah, okay…here's the thing."

I stop and look at my brother for support. He winks and tells me to go for it.

"Okay, Grandma. I found some stuff last year in Mom and Dad's closet."

"Igen."

"Stuff about our family."

I immediately recognize her expression. The conspiratorial grin I grew up with when she'd hand over the mixing bowl with the last of the whipped cream or slide over an extra sugar cube to dunk into her espresso. When Mom and Dad said no, Grandma came to the rescue, and always with that devious "I got you" smirk on her face.

"You know what I'm talking about, don't you?"

She pats her cheek, still half-smiling, probably calculating the consequences of her response. Nori looks from her to me, her brown eyes round with curiosity.

"My grandfather's briefcase?" I ask.

"Tudom," she says. She knows.

"You too?" I glare at my cousin.

Nori's lips pucker.

"Damn it! Why does everyone know we're Jewish except for me? And why did we have Christmas? Why didn't we do any of the Jewish holiday stuff?"

"Don't be dramatic," Nori says. "My dad's Catholic, eh, so we picked Christmas. I've always known Mom's side of the family is Jewish, but we didn't participate in any of the holidays, either." She touches our grandmother's shoulder. "Mom told us when we were little, right? Nobody kept it from us."

My grandmother clears her throat, then confirms that Nori is correct. The family decided to be "passively" Jewish. Quietly, and on the down-low. The other cousins were told about their history, but my parents, for reasons she was asked to respect, decided it would be better for me not to know anything at all.

I rock back in the chair. "Why wouldn't they tell me?"

My grandmother continues in Hungarian. It was part of the reason they moved to the U.S. They wanted their past erased. A fresh start, neutral ground, without the need to explain anything to anyone at any time. Ever.

"Wow." I cross my arms. "Did they ever worry I'd find out?"

"Yes," she flips back to English. "They knowing this may happen."

"Did Dad tell you about the letter he left me in the will?"

"Igen." Yes.

"Does Mom know about the letter?"

"No!" she proclaims with all her ninety-year-old might, then tries to explain what Ethan, Nori, and I have never experienced. Rage about the past, the murder of millions of Jewish people, and the fear of it happening again. Fear strong enough to make families change their last names or hide behind the veil of other religions. Thousands of men, women, and children, willing to give everything up, including their history, in order to melt into the safety of the crowd.

"Grandma," I ask after she stops speaking. "We also found some letters about Grandpa's dad."

"Yes," she says slowly. "Kiss Bela."

I glance at my brother. "Do you know what happened to him when they took him away from the textile factory?"

"Happen?" Her tone has an edge I'm unfamiliar with.

I lean closer to the phone. "Ethan's mom said he never came home."

"They take him and some others. Varadi." She points to Ethan because Varadi was a part of his mother's family, then recounts the story in Hungarian. We listen silently as she tells us about the ten men who were rounded up like cattle to the slaughter and marched off by foot. "No train. No car. They made them walk," she says. "Bela, known for his kindness, helped two of the older men who weren't able to keep up the pace at the back of the line. The SS didn't care, didn't embrace a single drop of humanity. They shot all three of them."

"Christ," Ethan whispers. "They killed him for trying to help?"

My grandmother nods. Nori looks away from the camera, and I stare at my fingers, which have gone ice-cold.

"I don't understand," I say, looking up. "He was helping."

One sour snort of laughter comes out of her. "So what?"

"So what?" I repeat. "Weren't there rules or something? They weren't doing anything wrong?"

"No, they were not, and Bela was a good man," she continues, still in Hungarian. "This was a long time ago, and things are better now. Why are you so curious?"

Ethan speaks first. "I want to know about the family. Mom told me about ours, but I don't know much about yours. I mean..." He stops for a few seconds. "You know what I mean."

"I understand," she responds. "And Katika, sweetheart, you are always searching. What do you need from me?"

My eyes well up before she finishes the sentence. "I'd like to know why nobody ever tells me anything."

"Oh my dear." She looks down for a moment, and I see the thinning hair on her head. The dark brown color, long gone, but the curls are still tightly set in place thanks to her weekly visit to the beauty salon. She looks back up to respond. "You're right to ask this question. I don't know why they thought this was better. Maybe they were trying to protect you."

I use the bottom of my shirt to wipe my teary eyes. "I don't need protection."

She laughs and reverts to English. "Okay. You the big girl now. Let me thinking about this, but I needing to rest. We speaking soon?"

We thank her, but I'm left feeling guilty for forcing her to recall such a terrible memory. If this is overwhelming for Ethan and me, it must be much worse for her. We promise to chat again soon, and after catching up for a few more minutes, end the call.

I ask Ethan if he's okay. He's just met his paternal grandmother for the first time.

"It was great meeting her, but that story. I can't process it," he says. "How about you? I saw you got emotional there for a minute."

"Got caught off guard, I guess. Dad never talked about it. Not a damn word." I stand up and stretch my arms over my head. "I don't understand why I had to be kept in the dark."

He slouches in his seat. "She made it pretty clear. They wanted a clean slate. I have to tell you, the more I hear, the less I question their decision."

I open the fridge, stare at the options, and pull out a ginger ale. There's a lot to think about. The slate, no longer clean. My history, no longer an amorphous mystery. I pop the can open and wonder how difficult this discussion will be with my mother. Will she ever be ready to open up, or will she go nuclear? Again. Or is there a third option of pretending she knows nothing in the hopes that I'll play along and shove away the past like she and my dad did?

CHAPTER 13
THE SAXOPHONE WAS INVENTED WHERE?

The return flight to Florida the next morning is smooth until we descend under an angry gray layer of clouds, lightning, and booming thunder.

I text Mom when the wheels hit the runway. *Home. All is well.* No need to include the part about the storm, the wind whipping water across the tarmac. Or the conversation with our grandmother.

"Sorry," Ethan says ten minutes later. He pulls a large umbrella from a bin by the front door of the terminal. "Gotta turn and burn. We're running late. I'll walk you to your car."

A plastic bag from Publix blows past us as we sprint through the parking lot. I give him a quick hug and jump into my Toyota. "Let me know when you get home."

He gives me the thumbs-up and runs toward the building. His umbrella flails in a gust of wind.

It's two-fifty, Thursday afternoon. I'm dripping wet, and Nick has just returned the text I sent last night.

I have a few minutes. Want to talk?

I dry my hands and arms off with the beach towel from the passenger seat, then turn the ignition on. The engine revs like an electric scooter. Parked around me is a collection of BMWs, Mercedes, Teslas, and a Land Rover. How did I not get towed?

I text him back. *Yeah! I'm in the car. Call me.*

Rain lashes the windshield. I answer on the second ring, set the phone on my thigh, hit speaker, and pull out of the lot.

"Sweet Katy." He sounds so pleased. I imagine his goofy grin, ear to ear.

"Hi Nick."

"Where are you?" he asks.

"Leaving Sarasota. On my way to work. Where are you?"

"Guess."

I slide to a stop at a red light. "You want me to guess where you are on the entire planet?"

He chuckles. "Where was the saxophone invented?"

"No clue. Memphis?" The light turns green. I wait a beat. A supersized SUV barrels through the intersection.

"Not everything comes from America. Guess again."

"I'm driving through a monsoon, Nick. Not sure I have the bandwidth."

"Think Europe."

"Saxophone…Saxony? Germany?"

His sigh is audible. His smile, probably fading. Disappointed because I won't play the game. Then he says, "Adolphe Sax invented it in Belgium in 1840."

"You could have said the best chocolate in the world." I wipe the water dripping down my cheek.

"Too easy. But now you know. I'm in Brussels. Guess what I was thinking about this morning?"

"Really, another guessing game?"

"I was thinking about the night we met."

"Uh-huh." I can't see past the hood. Traffic slows to a crawl.

"Do you remember?" he asks. "It was raining then too. We were stuck in the dorms all day and ended up at that party on the sixth floor."

Of course, I remember. The millisecond he stopped in front of me, tilted his head and smiled as though I was the secret he'd been keeping his entire life. Meeting a stranger who doesn't feel strange. A person who connects with you for no understandable reason, no history, no people in common. The memory is embedded in my brain. The beginning of an epic relationship. I run my fingers through my damp hair. Nick is still talking.

"And I got into a fight with Jesse about politics," he says. "How's she doing?"

"The same, but more. You almost took each other's heads off."

"She won the first round. I was distracted."

"By what?" The rain slows. Steam rises off the asphalt.

"By you. Everything about you."

I blush, all alone, driving on the slick roads toward Dufferin Beach.

"Bring back any memories?" he asks.

I check the rearview mirror. Catch a glimpse of my own goofy smile. "A few."

"I stole you away," he whispers.

"Stole me away, huh? Aren't you being a little theatrical?"

"I swept you off your feet, Kiss. We didn't leave your room for two days."

A truck passes me on the left and sends a wall of water onto my windshield. "Fuck!"

"Sounds like you need to focus on the drive."

"It's crazy out here. And yeah, two days. Kind of hard to forget."

"Yup."

His tone is clipped suddenly, but I'm the one answering senseless questions and struggling to keep my car on the road. "Sorry, can you give me a second?" I ask.

"I'll let you go. We'll talk next week."

"Are you sure? The rain's clearing out."

"Don't worry. I'll call you soon."

He hangs up before I can respond. His abrupt exit leaves the same old pit in my stomach, like it's me who's done something wrong.

A few blocks from The Point, I stop at a light waiting to turn left. My phone beeps. Maybe it's him texting again.

I read the message from Quinn telling me to stay safe in the rain and offering to help at the office. To help with anything. I still don't trust this—his good behavior. His words from last year replay in my mind. *It wasn't love or anything.* I pull into traffic, the phone slides off the seat, and by the time I park behind the restaurant, I've forgotten all about him.

CHAPTER 14
POST & HASTE & EGGS

Thursdays at the restaurant are often more packed than Fridays. The soggy weather does nothing to slow the influx of hungry diners. People slog through their week, put food on the table, go to work, fight traffic, do laundry. Friday may be a day to celebrate the coming of the weekend, but it's on Thursday night that everyone is saying to hell with it. They're burned out and want somebody else to feed the masses.

We're too busy to discuss my trip, and I'm running as soon as I get through the door. Melissa waves with an armful of tablecloths. Russ kisses my forehead and tells me I look like a wet rat.

"Welcome home," he says, dumping a heap of potatoes into the sink.

"Thanks for taking the reins. Again. Anything disastrous happen while I was gone?"

He nods. "All good darlin'. Gonna get our asses whooped tonight. I can feel it."

I tie an apron around my waist. "I'm ready. Cricket's on at four, right?"

He grunts and looks over my shoulder. "Must be four. She's here."

"Three-fifty-two, Russell." She drops her dripping backpack behind me. "I try to always be eight to eleven minutes early to any obligation. It makes me seem like I care."

I turn, surprised I didn't hear her come in. "Isn't it better to actually care?"

"Same difference. How were your travels, Mrs. Katy?"

"Very successful. Thank you. Can you drop the Missus and call me Katy?"

"Yes ma'am. You visited your half-brother? The one you never knew about before your daddy died?"

I nod and drum my fingers on the cold stainless counter.

"Do you like him? Was it weird to meet someone you've been secretly related to your whole life but didn't know? I have a brother too. His name is Bud."

"Bud?"

"Bud Punch. Mom says he's as bad as a rotten apple in a Christmas pie." She shoves her hands into her pockets. "He's ten years older than me and lives way up north in Orlando. Is it all right for me to begin working now?"

"Preferable even," I assure her. "Want to check the register? Make sure we have enough ones."

"Alrighty-mighty-flighty."

"Oh, gosh," I mumble. How does she come up with these phrases, and what in the hell is a Christmas pie? Russ adjusts his earbuds. The sound of Alabama Shakes bleeds through. Crazy sweet voice. Janis Joplin from the tail end of the aughts. I drop two dozen eggs into a pot of water on the stove.

Russ's head bounces in rhythm with the music. Melissa stomps into the kitchen, says, "Welcome back. I'm going to smack that chick." She slams her hands on her hips, takes three cleansing breaths, then heads back to the dining room. I consider intervening, but there's too much to do before everyone shows up, bangs their knives on the tables and demands food.

Work gets done. I spoon mayonnaise and sour cream into a bowl, stir in sugar, small chunks of Granny Smith apples, and a large can of peas and carrots. Russ walks by with an open container of black pepper. I bend over and sneeze into my shirt.

"Bless you, baby!" he shouts.

"Thanks." I wash my hands, store the bowl in the fridge and check on the eggs bouncing in their pot. Once they're hard boiled, I'll peel them and finish off the deviled eggs, or what Hungarians call Kaszinó Toyás.

The night goes on. Food goes out, payment comes in, tummies get full. Cricket eats away at our sanity while scoring bigger tips than Melissa. None of us understand, but Russ suggests it's the entertainment she provides. Ignoring my rule about crowding the customers, she does the opposite. She has no boundaries, and everyone seems cool with it.

At eight-thirty, Ethan texts. He's landed safely back in Denver.

At ten minutes to ten, the restaurant is emptying out. Russ and I clean the kitchen, and girls pick through the leftovers.

"Mrs. Katy, can you make macaroni and cheese again?"

"I can, Cricket. Think it should go on the menu?"

"Sure as shit," Russ says, swinging a kitchen towel over his shoulder. "Posthaste."

I slowly twirl the broom in my hand and stare at him. "Posthaste. Really?"

"Doing the word of the day thing." He grins. "I even know what it means."

Cricket clinks her fork on a glass to get everyone's attention. "Those are two words, Russell. Not one. Post is one word, and then haste is the second. Mrs. Katy, did your old husband steal from your family?"

Melissa abruptly stops eating. Russ sighs in a way that sounds a lot like a growl.

I stop moving the broom. "I think it's actually one word, or it's hyphenated. And why are you asking about Dylan?"

"A round lady with big teeth and white hair was telling me about him. Did he also cheat on you with a waitress?" She glances at Melissa.

I clutch the wooden handle. "He did steal from us, and he did cheat. But it wasn't with Melissa. Obviously."

"Why is it obvious? Why is your face all red like a cherry lollipop?"

"It is?" I touch my cheeks. Hot, and I can't feel my fingers. My ears are ringing. What the hell? The broom slides out of my hands and hits the floor with a sharp thwack. This isn't like the panic attack I had in France. It also doesn't feel like the blackout from Denver.

"What's happening to you, girl?" Russ is next to me in an instant.

"I'm fine. It's just hot in here." I turn away from him. Maybe it's an air pressure thing. Thick Florida air, thin Colorado air. I've gone from a very high city to an even higher sky, then down to sea level in a tiny toy plane. And there was lots of rain, and wind, and Nickety-Nick reliving our past. Ear ringing is a consequence of altitude change, isn't it? Either way, this is no big deal. It's my body's attempt to reacclimate, and it's nothing a good night's sleep won't take care of.

CHAPTER 15
WORK-HOME-WORK-HOME

I get that good night's sleep, and all my fingers feel just fine Friday and Saturday. My ears stop ringing, my temperature regulates. Sunday morning, I'm sniffing a bag of espresso beans when my mother calls. I wait until the third ring to answer.

"Hi Mom." I pour the shiny beans into the grinder. "What's going on?"

"You are sending me one of the texting messages since you get back to Florida and this is all?"

"You track me on your phone and see where I am every second of the day."

"And the night. You are very dull. Work, home, work, home."

"Hold on." I put her on mute and pulverize the beans.

"What is happening?" she asks.

"Making coffee. How's Paris?"

"We have moved Josephine into the hospital for lost minds. How was this terrible airplane to Colorado? I was so excited the entire time you are flying. I almost have the nervous breakdown."

"Perhaps you could see someone about that."

"About what?" she asks. "How are Ethan and his mother?"

"Nice deflection."

"The mother's job is to worry, no?"

I roll my eyes. "I'm sorry about Josephine. How's Uncle Martón handling it?"

"Tired, and of course, very sad. He spends every day sitting with her." She pivots. "How is your new brother?"

"He's good. The trip was short but fun. We went to the zoo, and just kind of hung out."

"This is all you do for two days?"

The coffee drips into a small glass carafe. "It was one and a half days. He showed me a really cool park near his house."

"Washington Park?" she asks.

"You've been there?"

She clears her throat. "His parents took us once. It was very beautiful."

"Yeah, it still is. We found some pictures of you and Dad and me from when we were there."

"What kind of pictures?"

"The three of us standing in the snow. I have that little jacket on. The one with the fuzzy pockets." I rinse a mug, fill it a fourth of the way up with whole milk. "I was a sausage roll. What the hell were you feeding me?"

Radio silence. "Mom?"

"All babies are plumb."

I add the dark roast into my mug of milk, swoosh it in a circle. "Plump, mother, not plumb. Either way, it was cool seeing what we looked like back then. And Ethan's new place is nice."

"I thought he was living with Lena."

"He's still close by, but he moved into his own house. It's cute, though the basement is such a nightmare, I kind of passed out down there."

Her voice gets louder in my ear. "What does this mean? You fainted?"

"I blacked out for a minute. Or a bunch of minutes. Ethan brought me upstairs, fed me some waffles, and I was fine."

"Why didn't you tell me?"

"It wasn't a big deal." I bite my lip. She wasn't concerned the last time I hit the floor. Why is she freaking out now?

"I do not understand. Did something happen? Did something scare you?"

"Scare me? No, I was hungry, and the altitude got to me. You know altitude sickness is an actual disease...event? Well, whatever. It's real."

A screenshot of a kitten pops up on my screen. A text from Quinn follows.

She needs a home. Your home. Meet me at the shelter.

"Hell," I mumble, looking at his message. "Anyway, it wasn't a thing. I went downstairs because he was going through some old photo albums. Oh my God, I saw a picture of his stepdad. He looked insane. Do you remember meeting him?"

She doesn't answer.

"Mom, are you there?"

"Yes. I am here."

I text Quinn back and tell him my day is jam-packed. Which it is not. "What else is going on in France, Mom?"

"Nothing, dear."

"Nothing. Okay. You're the little chatterbox today."

"Katy."

"Yeah?"

She sighs. "It is that I miss your father."

I catch my breath. She's not prone to such statements, but these few words roll over me like a freight train. My tears come in an instant. This is how close I am to tumbling down the rabbit hole of grief, any day, any hour, any minute. I wipe the wetness from my cheeks.

She sniffles and blows her nose. "I think now is time for me to come home."

CHAPTER 16
ANKLE OR CREW?

Another hour of staring at the walls, the floor, the empty space. I email Nori and my grandmother a list of questions about my great-grandfather. Where were they killed after being taken from the factory? How long had they been walking? How did the families get the news? I don't ask the other questions I have, but keep wondering, morbidly, who was shot first? The able-bodied man or the elders he risked his life to help? What did they think in their last moments? What the hell is wrong with the human race?

• • • • •

Later in the afternoon, Jesse meets me in the sock section at Target for lazy Sunday afternoon shopping. Trillions of fun things to pick from. Millions. Okay, maybe thousands. Patterned socks, fuzzy socks, athletic socks, tights. I love this place.

She glances at me. "Ankle or crew?"

"Ankle, definitely."

She picks the crew length. "How was the beautiful state of Colorado?"

"Great. The flight was a bit turbulent. Did you know small planes get bumped around more than big ones?"

"Don't care. Let's go to Birdies after this."

"Isn't he shut down for renovations?" I turn my cart away from her. "I need a new pillowcase."

"I need trail mix," she counters. "And he's open to the locals. I'll be up front in ten minutes."

Fifteen minutes later, she finds me in the pet supply section.

"What's the situation, Kiss? Why are you buying cat food?"

I show her the text from Quinn asking me to come to the animal shelter.

"Cute kitty," she says. "You're going to need dishes, some toys, and probably a cat tree."

"Uh-huh." I wave a wand with a string and pink feather tied to the end of it.

"You're going to meet him?" she asks.

"No," I say, still waving the wand. "I'm going to put all this stuff back. I was just trying it on for size."

She leans on the handle of her cart. "You don't mean that, do you?"

I take another cat toy off the shelf and smile at my best friend. "I don't know what I mean."

CHAPTER 17
MUDDY

Behind the reception desk of the animal shelter is a fabulously large portrait of the auburn-haired woman who left her entire estate, several million dollars, to the lost animals of southwest Florida. Namely, to Duff Beach. Everyone was grateful, with the exception of her two auburn-haired children.

The facility is spacious and clean. Oversized pens house stray dogs and puppies, and the Cat-Hab crawls with kitties. This is nirvana for every animal tossed out of cars, homes, or the lives of people who don't fully understand the definition of commitment.

Quinn leans against the entrance to the Cat-Hab. Holy crap. Who looks like this? Tall, lean, faded jeans, and a black tee shirt with the shelter's logo printed on the front. His hair is messy in a perfect way. I swallow my embarrassment because I'm the opposite. "Mussed." This is a word Russ used to say when he was still drinking. I'm wearing torn jeans, an old tank top, and my sneakers are stained green from mowing the lawn this morning.

"You ready?" he asks.

At least I took a shower. "Uh-huh."

"Your shoe's untied."

"What?" I ask as he crouches in front of me. It's an effort not to run my fingers through his thick hair. *No, Katy...don't touch.* Over his shoulder, a kitten watches us from inside the hab. Meowing, pawing at the glass. Big blue eyes, dark button nose. "Oh my gosh, look at this baby." I bend forward and lose my balance.

Quinn grabs my flailing arms to keep me from crashing into the enclosure. "Let's go see." He straightens up, wiping freshly cut blades of grass off his hands. "Before you kill me."

A volunteer, a teenage girl, beams at Quinn, then gives me the once-over and tells me to sign the guest book. She inspects my name, squeezes a dollop of disinfectant on my fingers and barks instructions. "Get under your nails," she demands, before letting us inside.

The room is built out with shelves, steps, and cubbies filled with blankets and toys where the cats can roam or chase their tails amid the distractions.

"My baby," I whisper. A woman and her young daughter are now passing the kitten between them. "*Nooo.* What if they take her?"

"They won't." Quinn sits on a plastic bench and pats the empty space beside him. "You're always so stressed. Stop spinning out. Just let it be."

"Funny." I drop down next to him. "You sound like my shrink lady."

"Your shrink must be a genius." He gently bumps my knee with his. "What does she say?"

"That I should let things happen organically. Not to worry so much."

"I agree with her," he says. "You can't control everything."

"You really do sound like her. But then why did you show up at my house and plant yourself by my front door? Why didn't you wait for me to come around?"

"All fair questions." A wry smile spreads across his face. "I don't have a great answer. You must have needed a nudge."

"Uh-huh," I mumble and try not to notice how good he smells. Warm, inviting, with a hint of something that makes me picture him in the shower. Oh my God.

"So," he says, saving me from myself. "Other than working and painting your house, what have you been doing for the last few months?"

"Stuff. Are we really going to sit here and talk about my daily routine while my cat is whisked away?"

"It could happen." He rubs a gray and white tabby's ears.

"Great," I say. "I was just in Denver with my brother. Did you hear about him?"

"Jesse told me. How did you find out about each other?"

"Long story," I tell him, remembering the morning I saw the little gold heart on Ethan's necklace and put all the pieces together. "He lives in Denver. Flies planes for a living."

"Cool. Does he work for the airlines? Air Force?"

"No," I say as a rotund white cat circles my legs. It must sense that I'd be a consistent source of unhealthy food scraps laden with sugar and sour cream. "Private aviation company in Colorado."

"Very nice."

"Yeah. I've been there twice already. I got to fly on a private jet this time."

He turns to me. "No shit! For free, I assume."

"Free, definitely. It was fun." Fat cat loses interest. "And I was in Paris with my mom for a week."

He nods. "How's she holding up?"

"I'm not sure. We had a disagreement. Well, it was more of a fight. But she's coming home finally."

"Want to tell me about it?"

"The fight? No. It was nasty. No need to relive it."

"Are you glad she's coming back?"

I sigh. "Yes and no. I'm nervous about the two of us ripping each other's heads off. Dad was here to mediate before. I never realized how big of a job it must have been."

"Understood. You're both hardheaded."

"I'm not hardheaded at all. She is."

"Of course," he agrees. "What was I thinking?"

A middle-aged woman with long straight hair comes in. She has a volunteer badge on. We sit quietly while she scoops up a cat that looks a hundred years old.

"How old is that poor thing?" I ask. "All of its fur is gone."

"Hi, Quinn." She smiles at him like the teenager did. "He's only three. It's a Sphynx cat." She holds it close to her chest. "He's getting moved to a Sphynx rescue. They're super sweet but require a very special person to care for them." She gazes at Quinn again, her eyes moving from his face down to his shirt, then lower. Damn. I've never seen a woman leer so brazenly. She must think he's one of those very special people.

I lean forward to get a better look. "He's adorable in a gross way."

She nods. Her eyes flash to my right. "Muddy's watching you."

"What?"

"Muddy." She points to the blue-eyed kitten sitting next to me. I didn't notice the mother and daughter moving on to another kitten on the far side of the hab.

"She's a sweetie," the woman says. "Definitely a runt."

I turn on the bench and hold out my hand. Muddy purrs and steps onto my lap. "Hi sweet baby."

Quinn reaches over and rubs her head. "Is she a mix?"

"No, she's a Tortie Point Siamese. Seal Tortie."

Muddy pushes close, bops my nose, rubs her cheek on mine. Game over. I'm in love.

Quinn gently tugs on her tail. "I've never heard of a Tortie before."

The Sphinx lets out an unnatural sound. The woman tightens her grip on him. "Like a tortoise shell. Her color will get more mottled. The cream coloring will get darker as she gets older. Beautiful cats, and Siamese are smart, vocal. Full of personality. She likes you."

Muddy turns in three circles, pushes her baby claws into my thighs, then curls up on my lap. She purrs and drops her head into my open palm.

Quinn stands up, careful not to scare Muddy, and smiles. "See how easy that was? All you needed to do was stop spinning."

CHAPTER 18
A PROPER LADY

After eight-hundred and sixty-two questions about my character, housing situation and ability to raise a three-pound kitten, Muddy is released into my care.

I bring her home, where she tests her new surroundings in stealth mode, creeping along the ground like she's searching for unspent munitions. Her explorations come to an abrupt end when I peel the lid off a can of kitten food. Her ears perk up, she gallops to her dish and devours the meat-like paste. Afterwards, she licks her cream-colored paws clean like a proper lady, then climbs my leg, claws first.

Wincing from the pain, I pull her into my arms. "This is what I get for bringing another blue-eyed animal into my house." She bops my nose again with hers, sniffs my eyelashes, and snuggles into my neck. I snap a selfie, send it to Jesse and Nick. I consider sending it to Quinn, who begged off coming home with me. I was relieved until he hugged me. Until the scent of him was up close and personal, and I felt the muscles under the tee shirt.

Muddy, forever name yet to be decided, sleeps on the bed with me. She kneads my hair, twirls into a circle, and lies down. The sound of my sweet kitten purring knocks me out in less than a minute.

CHAPTER 19
LET'S TALK ABOUT SEX

It takes twenty-five seconds to get into Dr. Jonas' waiting room today because I hold the door for three exiting patients. A gaunt faced woman and her twin boys, DNA replicas of their long-suffering mother. Twin one bumps into the door. This is an eye-glued-to phone related injury. His stunned face twists into fake agony as he lets out a low moan. Twin two punches his brother in the shoulder before screeching about needing a hamburger. NOW.

Two words pop into my mind while the boys run circles around their mother on the sidewalk. Birth control.

"You ready?" Dr. Jonas watches the trio of doom.

"Not for that." I say, staring out the window.

"Mm," she mumbles, leads me to her office, and motions me to the couch. "How are you doing? Any panic attacks?"

I push into the stiff cushion. Just once, I'd like to lie down, stretch out from one end to the other and ask why any of this matters. Would Freud have been so obsessed with psychoanalysis had he considered how insignificant we are, spinning on a pretty blue ball, rotating around the sun? Let's be honest, we're a cloud of celestial dust thick enough to give God an asthma attack. Dr. Jonas clears her throat and waits for my answer.

"Nope. Must have been a one-time thing." I say, immediately feeling the heat of my off-white lie.

She blinks. Her sharp knuckles tense.

"I was in Denver with Ethan. I got to fly on one of his private jets, but it was only for two days. So, all we did was go to the zoo, drop ice cream, and have hot dogs with his best friend."

"This all happened last week?"

"Yes." I nod. "And yesterday afternoon I met Quinn at the animal shelter and adopted the cutest kitten. Her name is Muddy, because she looks like she's been hanging out in the mud. It doesn't suit her, though. She might look like a Penney."

"Congratulations on making a decision about the cat. Who's Quinn?"

"It's kind of complicated. Also, my mom's coming home next weekend."

She smiles. "We only have fifty minutes. How about we pick a topic?"

"Which one?"

"If you're confident the panic attack was a one-time thing, we don't have to dwell on it."

"I'm pretty sure," I say, averting my eyes.

"Okay. Then let's talk about your mom coming home. She's been gone for a while."

"Since last August."

She sneezes, apologizes, then sneezes two more times. "Sorry, always in threes."

"Are you allergic to cats?"

"I didn't think so." She sniffles and dabs her nose. "What emotions are you having, knowing your mother is coming home?"

"Not sure. It's going to be rough for her. Walking into the house without my dad being there. I know all those firsts were hard for me last year when it happened. She might be upset.

Probably she'll spin off some attitude because she's not comfortable showing any weakness."

"Katy."

"Uh-huh?"

"I didn't ask about her feelings. I asked about yours."

"Oh." I stare at her angular face, the severity of her cheekbones, the squareness of her jaw. "Nervous, apprehensive, I guess. Especially after our fight. What if she pretends it didn't happen?" I look at my fists, bunched into tight balls. "Avoidance is what she does, but I don't want to play her game. And what if she tries to roll over me at work?"

"Do you think that might happen?"

"I've been telling her all the stuff we're doing at the restaurant, and she seems fine with it. But what if she comes in and starts treating me like a kid?"

Dr. Jonas stares at me while I stare at her. Alas, this must be one of those therapeutic learning moments where the patient is forced to pull enlightenment out of their own ass.

"Honestly," I continue. "I'm nervous that it'll be like moving home after college, and whatever growth I've had will be squashed in the shadow of her domineering personality."

"Ah," she says. "There we go."

"That's what you wanted to hear?"

"Not about what I want to hear, Katy. It's what I want you to be able to say."

"Wow. It's real? Thinking this stuff is legitimate?"

"Of course it is. You've stepped up spectacularly by my calculation, and now you're worried that you'll be forced to step back."

I nod. Her acknowledgment of my fear is validating. It makes me feel like an adult, instead of a child fussing and stomping their feet.

"You've successfully run the business," she says. "It's fair to stand on that ground, but difficult if you two can't communicate."

"Because I'm the only one talking. How am I supposed to communicate when all she does is hide in her turtle shell and hurl insults?"

"Does it hurt you when she, as you say, hurls those insults?"

"It's just what she does." I pull on the ponytail holder wrapped around my wrist.

"But does it hurt you?" she asks again.

"I don't know. I've never thought about it. I mean, I guess it does, but she doesn't mean it. It's just, you know, a defense mechanism."

"Why does she need to defend herself against you?"

I blink. Pull the ponytail holder some more. Blink again.

She takes her cue from my silence. "You look a bit shell-shocked. You may not be able to change your mother, but you can change your end of the equation."

"How do I do that?"

She looks at her iPad for a few seconds, then back at me. "That's the trick, isn't it? You might have to do some talking. Get your words out. Be honest, even if you think it might be upsetting."

"That seems one-sided and frustrating. What if she yells at me?"

"Yell back." She stops and smiles. "Nicely. And push a little. Mothers are complicated, and from what you've told me, she has some extra obstacles. But having a healthy relationship is important, especially now that your father is gone. If you feel up to it, dig in a little."

I groan. "Dig into solid lead?"

"Hopefully, yes, while managing your expectations. You're trying, but you can't control other people. You can only control how you respond to them."

"I guess." I bite my lower lip. "Can we talk about something else?"

"Of course. Want to talk about Quinn? Actually, whatever happened with Nick?"

I stare at my blue flip-flops. "Can we stick to Quinn for now?"

"We're still avoiding the discussion about Nick?"

"We are," I say, wondering how much detail I need to give her. "Quinn was Dylan's best friend, and I, um, might have slept with him last November."

"Okay," she says.

"It was only once. And I thought he was using me, but Jesse says he wasn't." I pull my fingers through a tangle in my hair. "And now he keeps bugging me to see him."

"Bugging you successfully then, since you saw him recently."

"He helped pick out my kitten at the shelter. And he looked good." I watch my shrink work very hard to keep a straight face. "I mean, you know, it's been a minute since I've, um…"

"Had sex?" She finishes my sentence.

"Gosh, so direct." My cheeks heat up. "He's seriously attractive. But I don't like him that way. He's just…" I tap my fingers on my legs. "Hot. Which means I'd be using him, and that's not a me thing."

Eudora Jonas nods and again says nothing.

"And right," I add. "There's the Nick thing. We've been talking. Guess it's something you should know. I texted him after Christmas, and he texted back."

"Really?"

"On New Year's Eve. Jesse found out and lost her shit."

"Why? You were all friends in college, if I remember correctly."

"Yeah. I mean she and Nick were good friends. And me and Nick were in between, like I said last year. Sometimes friends, sometimes a lot more."

She rubs a red splotch on her neck. "Why did Jesse get upset when he returned your text?"

My phone vibrates next to my thigh. "I dunno."

"No idea at all?"

I push my lips together before answering. "She doesn't think he's good enough for me. But she doesn't get it. She isn't there when it's just the two of us."

My phone vibrates again. "Sorry, I have to make sure The Point isn't burning down." I punch in my pass code and see the message from Nickety-Nick. He's probably responding to the picture I sent of Muddy.

Guess where I am now?

My shrink clears her throat. Time's a wastin'. I drop the phone next to me.

"The Point is not burning down," I tell her and smile. "What were we talking about?"

"Nick."

"Nick," I repeat. "It's complicated. There's so much going on in my head, I don't know what to think. I got a kitten. Did I mention that?"

"You did."

We stare at each other again. Me judging her wicked sharp collar bone and choice of flat shoes. She, probably judging the cat hair on my shirt, or the way my brain is a mess of bouncing ping pong balls.

"Katy," she says. "I really want to push you on Nick here."

"Why?"

"Because you avoid talking about him at every turn."

"So?"

Her eyebrows knit together. "It's important. It's about your progress."

"You think I can't get better until I spill my guts about him?"

She sighs.

I sigh.

"This is kind of pissing me off," I grumble. "I'm not ready to talk about him, and it's all you ever want to hear about."

She folds her hands together. "I'm sorry you feel that way."

"It's fine," I say. "This isn't working today. Do you mind if I cut out early?"

"I'm not going to hold you hostage," she says with a steady stare.

"Okay." I jump up from the couch. "I can't right now." In the corner of my eye, I try to read her expression as I pull the door open, and just like on our very first visit, slam my face against the edge. I continue walking, squeak, "I'm fine," and hurry out of the building in twelve seconds flat.

CHAPTER 20
EGOMANIAC

I can't get home to Muddy fast enough. Jesse's kneeling in front of the sofa, waving the pink feather toy over the pillows.

"Check it out," she says. "I can make her crash into shit."

I watch the cat chase the feather from one end of the couch to the other. Each time, she tumbles headfirst into the padded armrests. She's not getting hurt, but this game doesn't seem particularly humane. I rip the toy out of Jesse's hand.

"What the fuck?" she asks.

"You're fired from pet-sitting." I drop the toy on the counter, take a bag of frozen peas from the freezer and push it against my cheek. "Why are you torturing my cat?"

She stares at me. "What's your problem? I was playing with her. And what's with the peas?"

"Little accident with a door." I scoop the kitten up. "What if her skull is still soft? You could be giving her brain damage."

She rolls her eyes. "You're an idiot. Did something happen in therapy? You were in a good mood when you left the house."

Muddy rubs her face on my cheek, then swipes at the bag of peas. Her tiny nails dig into my arms. "Dr. Jonas," I mumble. "She keeps harassing me about Nick."

"Good," she says, taking a pop out of the fridge. "Someone should."

"Did you tell her to bug me about him?"

"You're still not understanding client confidentiality, are you, Kiss? I'm not Eudora's friend. We have a professional relationship. There would be no chance in hell that, one, I'd tell her to discuss something with you, and two, she would entertain such a conversation." She slurps soda from the can. "Why did Nick even come up? If you don't mind me asking?"

"I thought it might be minimally pertinent information in the therapeutic process."

"Wow. Quite the statement." She frowns. "You know how I feel about it. He's not the one for you."

"I didn't say he was. Whatever, he always seems disconnected. I sent him a picture of the cat and his response was for me to guess where he was."

She cocks her head. "That's not disconnect, it's narcissism. Let me see your phone."

"Why?" I ask, backing away from her.

"I want to talk to him."

"Text him yourself, Jessica."

"Hand me your phone. I want to give him some shit." She steps toward me, grinning, with her arms stretched out.

I clamp down on Muddy. "No. Fuck off."

She stops short, her playful smile evaporates. "What's going on with you? You're acting like I'm going to hurt you."

"I am not," I say, then realize I'm squeezing the cat too tight. "Oh, hell." I drop her gently to the floor. She shakes and scampers away.

"Christ, Katy, you're all sorts of weird, but I've never seen you do that before. You should have seen your expression. It's like you were actually afraid of me."

I drop down on the couch. Is this a good time to smell my tomato soup? This doesn't feel like a panic attack.

"Can I sit with you?" she asks. "Or should I stay over here?"

"I'm fine. You can sit."

"What happened just now?"

Muddy gallops across the floor, finds a shoe, and shoves her head inside of it.

"No clue," I tell her. "Could it be an anxiety attack?"

"That was fear, woman, not anxiety."

I slide my phone over to her. "Here. Text him if you want to."

"Are you sure? You're not going to stick a knife into me, are you?"

"I will not. And he'd probably love to hear from you."

She scrolls through our messages. "Ew, nasty, what's this about when you guys first met? Looks like you two had your own sex day."

"That's not how it was," I mumble. That's totally how it was.

"Whatever." She stops talking and composes a message.

I lean toward her. "What are you writing?"

She sends the message and holds the phone out for me to see.

Hi you fucking dick. It's Jesse. Why are you bothering my girl? Don't you know we're together now? And btw, no, I don't give a shit about where you are.

I try not to laugh. "Nice. I'm sure he'll answer right away."

She winks at me. The phone chimes. He's texting back.

Hello Jessica Tanner. You love me too. Give me a couple hours and I'll convince you.

"He really is a dick." She types another message. *Not a chance, you baby-faced egomaniac.* She hits send.

The phone chimes again. *Do you want to know where I am?*

Jesse looks at me. "Do we?"

I shrug.

She types a question mark in response.

The text bubble pops up, three dots... *Heading home to the States.*

CHAPTER 21
WATER WITH GAS

Leaving Muddy home alone fills me with anxiety. But I have to work, and cats are self-sufficient and self-entertaining. I spent half the night agonizing about the details of Nick's return, and the other half imagining the horrible things that could befall my new fuzzball while I'm away making sugar-laced pastries and cutting the fat off chicken thighs. She could strangle herself on my computer cord or drown in the toilet. She could eat a pesticide laden cockroach. What if she's writhing in pain while I'm prying open a jar of jam or assuring a customer there are no peanuts in the roasted potatoes?

Russ tells me I look tired. I tell him to screw off. Parenthood is complicated. Evidently, not all fun and games.

"It's a cat," he says, mopping up a sticky spot on the dining room floor. "She'll be fine."

I pull a chair out of his way. "I know. I'm just freaking out."

"No kidding. Wait till you have one of them human babies. You'll need to be medicated."

"Perhaps." I shuffle the menus. Inspect them for cleanliness. One of my pet peeves. How clean is the restaurant's kitchen if the menu is sticky? "Mom's coming home."

He stops mopping. "When?"

"Next weekend."

"Gonna be weird, Katy-Bell. We've been in charge for almost a year."

"Tell me about it. But maybe it'll be good?"

"Is that a question, darlin'?"

I shrug and head to the kitchen. It'll be what it is, but right now I have other things to torment myself about. Like Nick. When exactly is he returning to the States? Is it now? Is he already here? Could he walk into The Point later today? I texted him after Jesse took off yesterday, but he didn't respond.

On the mental list of items to talk to Dr. Jonas about, I add my need to obsess over random things. And people—who leave me perpetually waiting for a reply. Why can't someone wait breathlessly for me?

Quinn sends a text asking about the kitten. I stare at it until the oven timer goes off. Food to prepare, people to feed. There are already four customers standing out front, waving to be let in, pushing their sweaty foreheads against the glass. I make a second mental note to buy more Windex.

• • • • •

At three, we catch our first break after the lunch rush. I send Russ to check on Muddy while I place orders for cleaning and paper supplies. My eyelids feel heavy as I enter numbers into boxes on the computer. I push the laptop away and rest my head on the desk. Just a short nap. Twenty minutes.

Long enough to have a nightmare where it's deathly dark. I turn in a circle searching for light, but there's nothing. No end or beginning. No people. It's desolate, cold, and I'm terrified.

"Hello?" I whisper. "Where am I? What's happening?"

The panic rises. I shiver, feeling the goosebumps on my cheeks, anxiety creeping into my chest. Twisting around again, I'm afraid to take a step, afraid I'll get swallowed by the void. I hyperventilate, try to speak, but my tongue is a useless lump. I can't form any words. Hot air comes out of my mouth. My legs are stuck, glued in place.

"Katy, wake up!" Russ shakes my shoulder. "Girl, what the hell? You were moaning."

"What?" I wipe drool off my lips.

"And not in a good way, honey."

"That was not restful." I rub my eyes. "I was making noise?"

He nods. "You were breathing real hard. Were you having a nightmare?"

"I guess. I don't remember."

He pushes my hair out of my face. "You a freak, woman."

"Thanks, Russ. How's my kitty cat?"

"Cute as a button." He shows me the short video he took on his phone. "She's snoozing on your pillow."

"Aw, Muddy. Thanks for checking on her."

I hear the back door slam shut. Russ's posture stiffens, his jaw clenches. Three-forty-five, Cricket's right on time. She marches into the office.

"Good afternoon, Mrs. Katy and Russell. I trust the day is proceeding well?"

Russ mumbles something under his breath and slips past her. I gaze at her purple jeans, trying to find a rational response, but my brain is still in a fog.

"It is. How about yours?" I ask.

She sits down and fishes a tube of lip balm out of her pocket. "It was very pleasant. I had two tests, which I believe I scored at least ninety percent on." She pops open the tube and sniffs. "Cherry-lime. Want some?"

"No. God no. That is not a sharing thing."

She shrugs. "Very well. I did not enjoy P.E., however. That's physical education, if you didn't know."

"I know what P.E. is, Cricket."

"Oh. Well, I figure it's been a long while since you were in high school. Anyway, we had to run a mile and jump over hurdles, and I am not physically equipped for this type of activity. Miss Bobbolo, my teacher, has much longer legs than I do. She doesn't understand how it's not possible for me to leap over these contraptions. Mother wrote a letter, but Miss Bobbolo won't hear it. She says I have to keep trying or I'll get a zero. Anyways," she says, "I'm ready to begin work now."

She leaves without waiting for my response. Poor girl, I wonder if she has any friends, or if she lives her life surrounded by stunned onlookers who can't decide if she needs a slap or a hug.

I swivel back to my desk to finish placing my order for napkins and toilet paper. An email pops up from my mom.

Katika,

My time here in Paris is almost at the end. Your uncle and I are having many good days together in the city. Josephine is on the top of our minds, but life is going on. I tell you all about this when I am getting home. I am very nervous about returning, and now you have divorced Dylan, so I do not even have a grandchild to look forward to. Do not worry, I will not be in your way or ask for too much of your time. But please have Miss Lisa clean the house. If you can, open the windows to let the air in. Also, please go to the store and buy these things. Rye bread, make sure it is fresh, and milk, apricot jam, you know the good kind I like. Sugar, sliced Gouda from the woman at the counter, please, not the one which has been sitting for days, flour, butter, two waters with gas, and check if I having any good toothpaste at the house. Okay, this is all I ask of you. My flight number is below. It is arriving in Tampa at five-thirty-five Sunday afternoon.

I will be happy to see you and finally come back, even though I am alone, and a widow now and probably my feelings will be very sad. But this is my problem. Do not worry. I will not take your time. Also, have the bug man spraying before I am arriving. And make sure Miss Lisa changes the sheets and the towels. This is all. See you soon.

The email reminds me of my parents' instructions on my last day in Thailand about being the *advance of it team*. Russ leans over my shoulder and reads the email.

"What's water with gas?" he asks.

"Carbonated water. Club soda." I look at her list again and take a deep breath. "Fuck. Me."

"Oh darlin'," he says. "You got that right."

CHAPTER 22
IT BEGAN WITH A DUMPLING

The rest of the week flies by. Sleep deprivation is setting in because Muddy is nocturnal, and by association, I am as well. Odd things happen in the early hours of a new day. The world gets quiet. TV shows get *more*—more violent, more spicy, infomercials are especially informational, and staying awake keeps me from having another one of those nightmares.

By Friday I've unintentionally broken lots of glassware at The Point, poured salt into cake batter instead of sugar, and flooded the kitchen once. Much like the cat, I take delicious naps during the day. Unfortunately, some of those are while I'm standing close to an open flame.

A wall of exhaustion hits me after closing. Melissa is counting cash. Russ is stacking bowls, and Cricket is eating a late dinner, pushing a pile of dumplings around her plate.

"Mrs. Katy, what's in these little white blobs?"

"You deliver them to the customers all night long. How do you not know what they are?"

"I know what you call them," she says. "But what exactly do they consist of?"

"Flour, eggs, water, and a pinch of salt."

She skewers one on the prongs of her fork. "Why don't you make them more nicer to look at?"

"More nicer?" I repeat, yawn, and lean against the counter.

"I'm just saying you could roll them out and make them more prettier and not as blobby."

I can't find any words. Instead, I grin and grip the metal cabinet handle like a sloth until Russ turns off the lights and ushers everyone out of the building. This is great. I'm completely spent, and one-hundred percent sure that no nightmare or panic attack will interfere with my body's need for rest.

• • • • •

I was wrong. Dylan used to say he knew when he was dreaming. He could control his actions and the places his mind carried him to in the wee hours. I never believed him because he was a man pig who lied as easily as he breathed. I, on the other hand, am not aware that I'm dreaming. I am in the moment, and my reality shifts without permission.

And so another nightmare begins. Cricket morphs into a dumpling, skinny arms protrude from the folds of her doughy middle, and she asks to be salted. I climb onto a wooden step stool and season her up. She gets a few shakes of pepper and some fresh sprigs of parsley.

"Thank you, Mrs. Katy. I'm ready to be served now."

Russ appears from nowhere. His eyes are blood red, and his teeth are rotting with a thick layer of tartar caked to his gray gum line. "I'll take care of her Katy-My Bell-Bell-Bell." His words echo as he rolls her away, taking the light with him.

And now it's dark again, I'm alone. The air smells musty, like an antique store. A blast of icy wind brushes the nape of my neck. Someone's behind me.

"Who's there?" I cross my arms protectively. "What the hell is going on?"

"Don't be a baby, Katy."

I'm startled by the deep voice and swivel around. "Who are you?"

"Baby."

"Get away from me!"

"Baby!" The voice booms in my ear.

I thrash in the darkness and wake up, sweaty, with my heart pounding hard enough to feel the blood rushing through my head. Muddy's watching me from the nightstand, ears perked forward, sweet little head tilted to the left. I scratch her cheek. "Did I scare you, munchkin?"

She lifts a tiny paw up, puts it down, then pounces on me. The guilt of displacing her keeps me in bed for another few minutes, but I have to move. I need light. I need to be sure this isn't still part of my nightmare.

"Sorry sweetie." I nudge her off and check my phone. Six-ten a.m.

She follows me through the house as I switch on every light, the TV, and start the coffeemaker. The doors are locked, the alarm is armed, but outside isn't what's spooking me. It's what's inside my head. Can panic attacks morph into nightmares?

I tug on her furry tail. "Think I should tell Dr. Jonas about the dream?"

She meows. I meow. Oh yeah, I'm going crazy. And how did Russ get thrown into the mix with glowing eyes and meat cleaver teeth? What in the hell is wrong with me?

I feed the cat, sneak out of the house to avoid hurting her feelings, and walk to the beach. The sun is pushing the night sky to the west, and the cool sand tickles my feet. I inhale deeply in an effort to expel the terrifying dream. No luck. The dread remains front and center.

The clouds shimmer over the gulf. Three seagulls shriek and chase each other at the water's edge. I'm not having the nightmare again. I'll have a sleepover with Jesse, or somebody, anyone but Russ and his crusty teeth, because I'll be damned if I'm spending another night alone.

CHAPTER 23
DRINK TILL YOU DROP

A few hours later, I have another excuse to leave the house. It's the annual Duff Beach Drink Till You Drop Art Festival, and we're on the hook to bake hundreds of bite-size desserts. Specifically, our crowd favorites, Zserbó and Kiss Brownies. Yes, I know brownies aren't Hungarian, but my parents are, and they created this recipe shortly after they created me. Made in America with Hungarian roots. Chocolate, walnuts, rum soaked raisins, a little love, and a whole lot of sweetness. Mom and Dad said I was almost as sweet...until I turned thirteen. Not so much after that.

Cricket is waiting for me at the door. "I'm ready to make pastries now."

I wince. Didn't she say something about being ready in my nightmare? I nod, unlock the door, and let her in. Russ sleepwalks in behind her, carrying a liter bottle of Mountain Dew.

He tips the bottle, drinks, wipes his lips, burps.

"Blessings," Cricket says to him.

"Cool." He shakes his head and puts the soda down. "Where do you want me, boss-lady?"

"You're on brownies. I'm on Zserbó. Cricket will prep."

Cricket adjusts her thick glasses. "What does prep mean?"

I drop a five-pound bag of whole walnuts on the counter in front of her. "It means you're going to chop these into small pieces." I slide a butcher knife near her. "Do you feel comfortable using this? Can I trust you not to take a finger off?"

She picks it up by the heavy steel handle. "I'm cutting the nuts with this?"

"Only if you're comfortable with it. Want me to show you how?"

"No need." She rotates her shoulders and neck, then lowers herself into an ungainly lunge. "I practice my knife play at home every Monday and Thursday evening from ten to eleven p.m., while I watch my crime shows."

"Knife play?" I ask.

"Yes, I'm quite adept at it."

"I see," I tell her, and once again try to maintain my poker face. "I'm counting on you. Go slow, be careful. We don't want chunks of Cricket mixed into our desserts."

She giggles, turns her back to me and begins working.

At the other end of the kitchen, Russ is brewing espresso and melting chocolate.

I begin my own prep, cutting chunks of butter into pea size bits. I'm on my third stick when Jesse texts.

Morning my love. Need assistance?

I snicker at her message. *Sure. Want to bake?*

Fuck no. Offering only emotional support, sitting next to you at the booth support, and eating your profits support.

I lick butter off my fingers and return her text. *How about bringing us food?*

Perhaps

I put the phone down, then pick it up and send one more message.

Have you heard from Nick?

A text bubble appears. *No.*

I shove the phone into my pocket and get back to throwing flour into the mixer with sour cream, sugar, and a little ice water. For the next three hours, Russ sings along to his extensive playlist featuring Hozier, Led Zeppelin, and Weezer on repeat, while I teach Cricket how to turn butter, chocolate, raspberry jam, and sour cream into something you'd give up an extremity for.

Jesse arrives at eleven-thirty with fried chicken, french fries, and coleslaw.

"Look at this deliciousness," she says, eyeing the trays of pastries lining the counters. "I gotta have me some."

"Mr. Tanner," Cricket blocks her way. "Each piece costs two dollars, or two tickets according to the festival rules."

"Uh-huh." She ignores her. "Are these the brownies with the wasted raisins in them?"

"Yup," I say, tearing into a chicken wing. "Thanks for bringing food."

Russ shoves fries into his mouth. "Gonna check to see if they set our table up out front."

I nod, eat more chicken. Cricket carefully spoons coleslaw onto a plate. "Mr. Tanner, did you participate in the festival last year?"

Jesse and I lock eyes. Last year at this time, spring, I was unhappily married to Dylan, my dad was alive, and Jessica Tanner had long since ducked out of my life. Since my wedding, to be exact. It wasn't until my parents took off on their "seeing the world before one of us drops dead" tour, that I worked up the nerve to crawl into her office, grovel for forgiveness and beg her to help me get a divorce.

Jesse looks away first. "I was busy that day."

"How about the year before?" Cricket turns to me.

"Who can remember that far back?" I answer. "Can you check on Russ? There are already crowds of people wandering the streets. He may need some help."

"Okie dokie smokie." She's blissfully unaware of the tension and skips out toward the dining room.

"Awkward." Jesse pops a brownie into her mouth.

"Not for her. Are you going to hang out with me or make the rounds?"

"Both. Most of the art is shit, but once in a while you can find something interesting. I heard Jimmy is running a booth with beer and hard lemonade."

"I need some of that," I say, picking up a tray of desserts.

"Everyone does," she agrees, and follows me out front.

• • • • •

Drink Till You Drop is well attended. People have come to town from Fort Myers, Sanibel, Captiva Island, Sarasota, even St. Pete. The desserts are beginning to sell out, with festival goers returning for seconds and thirds. We've printed flyers with our website, Facebook, and Instagram accounts, and added a fifteen percent off your first meal coupon to the bottom of the leaflet.

Russ has been excused for the day, but checks-in occasionally with an assortment of heart-unfriendly food. He nurses an enormous water bottle, his constant companion since he stopped drinking alcohol. Cricket is also clocked out, but not before causing a stir for demanding payment for partial pieces of pastry, including crumbs. Jesse is, as promised, eating the profits, but she's just delivered my second hard lemonade, so I don't care.

I take the drink from her. "Thank you, Jessica."

She comes around the back of the table and sits next to me. "Drink this one slower."

I slump in the plastic chair, enjoying the scene, the smell of fried food, the rhythmic sound of drums and horns from the high school band playing in the distance, and the thought of having a rare Saturday night off. "You know Mom's coming home tomorrow."

She turns to me. "Russ mentioned it earlier. Are you ready for her?"

I shrug. "It'll be fine."

"Is that the booze talking?"

"Ask me in a week. Want to do something later?"

She licks the chocolate topping off the pastry. "Sorry. I have plans."

"Gross, Jesse. No need to be so graphic."

She cackles, "No need to be a prude."

"Whatever. I had a bad dream, and now I'm freaked out."

"That's why you want to hang out? What was the dream?"

I tell her about it, sipping my drink between sentences.

"So," she reiterates. "Cricket is a dumpling, Russ is the devil, and then you were alone somewhere cold?"

"Freezing cold. Doesn't sound so awful when you say it like that. But it was eerie, like someone bad was in the dream with me."

"You have been acting weird lately. Telling me to screw off the other day. Are you having a psychotic break?"

"No."

"Are you doing drugs?" she asks.

"No."

"Are you living a double life? Do you creep around late at night and kill people?"

"Uh-huh." I hand four pieces of the zserbó to a group of sunburned tourists. "We're joking." I assure them.

Jesse grins as they hurry away. "You should talk to your therapist about it."

"It's anxiety because my mother is coming home, and I'll have to tell her I know we're Jewish and play along when she ignores the fight we had in Paris. What do you think Nick meant when he said he was coming to the States?"

"God, Katy, the way you change subjects," she huffs. "It's really irritating. He didn't say it in code. At some point, he'll show up. It's not brain surgery."

I grab my phone, swipe through his texts, and drink more spiked lemonade. "Jimmy makes the best drinks. Think I'll marry him."

"That's one option," she says. "What about this guy?"

"What guy?" I ask, still hunched over the screen, scrolling.

"This one," Quinn says, standing in front of our table.

I put my phone down and look up. Christ, he's pretty. The sun is behind him, outlining his frame like a hot, ghostly apparition.

He grins and holds out a five-dollar bill. "I'll take whatever this buys me."

"How about we barter?" Jesse leers with the purpose of causing the greatest amount of embarrassment.

"Jessica only has pornographic wares to exchange." I tell him. "Take what you want. You don't have to pay."

"I wasn't talking about me," she says. "Perhaps Quinn can entertain you tonight."

"I'm not busy." He drops the crumpled bill on the table. "How about a couple of brownies now and dinner later?"

"I need to get home to my cat."

"I'll bring dinner over."

"I have to clean up here."

He grins again, all smooth, like he already knows I'll give in. "I'll help you clean."

From the corner of my eye, I see Jesse shaking her head. What does this man want from me? He's already messed with my head, had sex with me, humiliated me. Is he going for round two? "I don't actually have to clean anything."

His enormous brown eyes narrow. "I didn't think so. How about we meet at your place at seven?"

"Seven seems reasonable." It takes work to focus only on his face, and not let my gaze drop to his chest, or lower. Damn it, I shouldn't have judged the woman at the shelter so quickly.

"Great. See you then?" he asks, backing away from us.

"Yup. Guess I will."

CHAPTER 24
BEAUTIFUL ANIMAL

Drinking, dropping, and buying art ends precisely at five-thirty. Ocean Avenue quickly empties of the drinkers, and the buyers who have dropped money for art that seemed spectacular while intoxicated but will probably end up in the garage sale pile by the end of the year.

Russ swings back around, this time with a dark-haired beauty on his arm. "This is Marisol." He holds her hand and introduces her to me.

"Hi Marisol. Nice to meet you."

She nods and I fight the urge to put Russ into a headlock. To tell her he's slept with almost a hundred women. To tell her to run. Instead, I accept his offer to clean up, so I can go home and get ready for dinner with the guy who, six months ago, broke my pride by saying, "it's not love or anything."

• • • • •

Muddy slumbers as I thrash about the house, shove three weeks of mail into drawers, vacuum, and clean the half bath. The full bathroom, I leave messy as a personal deterrent. The only way to get in there is through my bedroom, and Quinn is not welcome in this area of the house.

Nori texts and says Grandma is still working on the response to my email. An email with one main topic: Why has everyone kept me in the dark? She adds her own question to mine. Why was I the only one left out of the loop? Why do all the first-generation Canadians know more than me? The one and only first-generation American.

By the time I shower, shave my legs, and wash my hair, it's six-fifty. I run my fingers through my dripping curls, scrunch them, rearrange them. No matter, I look like a wet poodle. I fish through a cabinet searching for makeup and find a tube of old mascara. The doorbell rings, I jump, the mascara wand rams into the bridge of my nose.

"Damnit!" I rub the dark brown smudge off with my fingers and hurry to the door.

"Wow," Quinn smiles and steps inside. "You put makeup on for me?"

"No!" I sputter. "I mean, I didn't do it for you." Sure I did. Any other Saturday night I'd come home from work, take a long hot shower and slither into bed like an earthworm.

His smile widens. "Well, you don't need it. You're a natural beauty." He holds up a large paper bag. "Hit Whole Foods on the way over."

Beauty? This word has never been used to describe me. Sweet, friendly, entertaining. Never beautiful. "Thanks," I say, taking the bag. "Something in here smells great."

He follows me into the kitchen. Muddy follows him. We are a line of beautiful animals.

"What did you bring?" I ask him.

"This and that." He tickles the cat's ears. "Did you name her yet?"

"No." I pull plastic tubs of food from the shopping bag, a large loaf of crusty sourdough and several packages of cheese. "There's no way we're going to eat all of this."

"When's the last time you went grocery shopping?" he asks.

I glance at the fridge, which is all but empty. "I dunno. I bought a bunch of food for my mom yesterday."

"Plates?" Quinn asks.

"Over here," I say, and pull two dishes off the shelf. "I didn't rearrange the kitchen after Dylan left. You know where everything is."

He swivels, opens a drawer, and finds the cutlery. "Guess I do. Is your mom home?"

I remove a few more items from the bag. Two cupcakes piled high with icing; a coffee bean buried halfway into the cream. My mouth waters. "Tomorrow afternoon." I hop on the counter, legs dangling as Muddy swipes at my bare feet. I point at the plastic tray holding the cupcakes. "Can we eat those first?"

He pulls one out. "You want this?"

I search his face for the things I've accused him of, find nothing, then silently berate myself for not cleaning the bathroom. What I want is the man holding *this*. I scoot back on the counter, hoping he can't hear my heart pounding.

He steps closer, gently pushing himself between my legs, laying a hand on my thigh. "All you have to do is ask."

I'm not sure I'm breathing at this point. He takes a bite out of the cupcake, then brings it close to my mouth.

I lick the frosting, stare into his eyes, fixate on his lips.

"More?" he asks.

I let out a quiet sigh. "Not of that."

CHAPTER 25
PENNEY

Two hours later we revisit dessert. Muddy is loafing next to us on the couch.

"I think we corrupted her." I pat her head and concentrate on the dessert. The mocha frosting is perfect, not too sweet, rich, and full of strong coffee flavor.

"Not sure I can look at her." Quinn leans close to me and kisses my cheek. "Are you going to give her a real name?"

"I'm narrowing it down."

"To what?"

I brush my fingers through his hair. "Evie."

He grabs my hand, holds it tight against his face.

"Hazel," I offer.

"She's not a Hazel."

"Lucy?"

His eyes narrow in concentration. "I dated a Lucy."

"Of course you did. Did you date a Sawyer?"

"No," he whispers. "But she's not a Sawyer."

"Willow?"

"Go on." He kisses my nose.

"Frankie?"

"Mm," he says.

"Goldie?"

"She's not a Golden Retriever."

"Sabrina."

"Cute." He runs his fingers down my neck and over my collarbone.

I scoot closer to him. "Violet."

"Getting warmer." His hand travels lower, skitters across my hip.

"Penney." I flinch at his touch. "Penney might be the one."

"I like it." He pulls me on top of him. "Think we're about to corrupt her some more."

• • • • •

This goes on all night. Sex, food, sleep, repeat. By morning, I announce I might not be able to stand up or walk.

"Sorry," he says, wrapping himself around me. "Did I damage you?"

"Horribly." I pull his hand to my face. His skin is a soft, warm, form-fitting blanket of deliciousness.

I feel his muscles tense. "Did I hurt you?"

I swivel inside the pocket of Quinn. "I mean, I'm a little sore, but not in a bad way."

He relaxes, brushing his fingers through my hair. "I'm sorry about last year."

"Uh-huh." I bury my face in his neck.

"No, seriously. The day at the ice cream parlor, I keep replaying it in my head, wondering if I could have done something different."

"Jesse made you do it."

"I could have said no or told you why. I promise I'm not that person."

I bite his lip and wrap my leg around his lower back. "Okay," I mutter. My brain has become one-dimensional. There are no thoughts, only electrical impulses, heat, sweat, pleasure. I want more of him, and I'm going to get it, no matter how good it hurts.

CHAPTER 26
MOTHER UNIT

I push Quinn out of the house Sunday at noon. Mom's flight arrives at Tampa International in a little over five hours, and I need every second to pull myself together. To wipe the smile off my face.

Newly named Penney is on the kitchen counter, staring at me.

"Don't look at me that way."

She meows.

"You shouldn't have seen those things." I kiss the top of her furry head. "All the fooling around, and you know...legs and arms and body parts and stuff."

Another meow. Either she's very offended...or she's a cat.

"You get to meet Mom soon."

She tilts her head, and it reminds me of the way Dr. Jonas works so hard to maintain a nuanced neutrality about the whacked-out things I say.

I stand under the shower, a bit sorry to wash the scent of Quinn off me. He's ridiculous in bed, like he was last year, but without the fear of getting caught or taking a risk. During the last twelve hours, I waited for the enthusiasm to wear off. But it never did. He is all-knowing without the attitude. I shiver and dial the water temperature to hot-as-fuck.

At three, I'm at my parents' house, making sure everything is in order. Mom will still find something wrong, but it's clean, the fridge is stocked, and the windows have been open for thirty minutes in a feeble attempt to chase away the musty bouquet of emptiness. Of a family eviscerated. I've even purchased sunflowers and neatly arranged them in the kitchen and her bedroom. It's fresh, clean, and welcoming—an ironic backdrop for the loneliness and misery she'll slam into as soon as she walks through the door.

Alone. Without her husband.

I text Jesse before pulling out of the driveway.

Heading to Tampa to get Mom.

You've got this. Did you have any nightmares last night? She finishes her text with a smiley emoji wearing dark shades.

There was no time for REM sleep to kick in, but I'm not sharing this factoid with my best friend.

Nope, no dreams at all.

Cool - saw Quinn was still there this morning.

What the hell Jess, r u stalking me now?

Drove by on my way to the office

It's Sunday, Jessica.

All play and no work makes Tanner a bitch. Catching up on cases.

Liar, I text at a stop sign.

Bit me. Bite...sorry. Tell me about the duck, ducking. F-ING later. Say hi to ur mom.

I drop my phone on the passenger seat and drive north through Sarasota and Bradenton, then east toward 275 and the Sunshine Skyway Bridge into Pinellas County. On my left is Indian Key, and because the weather is clear, I can see the place I married Dylan. The Don CeSar resort, sitting on the soft sand of St. Pete Beach like an enormous pink wedding cake.

The drive is smooth, and I pull into airport parking at exactly five-ten. Mom texts as I shut the engine off.

I have landed.

Welcome home! I'm here! Meet you outside customs.

"Hell," I whisper. I can handle this. Mom can handle this. In the elevator, a young couple grope each other as if it's their last time ever. The man is lanky, thin and tall. He paws at the woman, grabs her ass and growls like a Great Dane in heat. We travel three floors together in this uncomfortable configuration. The two of them all but doing *it* in the elevator, and me staring hard at a cast-off luggage tag on the ground.

In the large waiting area, she texts again, saying the line is *horrifying*.

No worries, I write back, then realize I haven't thought about Nick since yesterday.

This is a conundrum. I love Nickety-Nick. He's my soulmate, my person. What does that make Quinn? What does it make me, for doing what I did last night?

I am, once again, confused by my own behavior. Nick is...well, Nick. Our history is more than a collection of memories from college. It's rain and sun and shadow, an emotional weather system washing over me each time I think of him. A tactile sensation of all the things I felt in our best moments—or our worst. I scrape clear nail polish off my fingers and picture his eyes, his pale skin, and wavy blond hair.

My phone beeps. Mom's on her way out. It beeps again. Quinn, asking how the ride to Tampa was.

I move to the front of the crowd. A few people have signs or flowers, and almost everyone is smiling, searching the faces trickling out of the security area. I watch the reunions, the hugs; vicariously participating in the communal joy, and it occurs to me how an airport is one of the few places we can gawk at others in a socially acceptable, non-creepy way.

Then I see my mother rolling two large suitcases behind her.

"This was the most terrible flight." She kisses my cheeks, then checks me over like I'm about to walk the runway at Fashion Week. "You have lost more weight. How will you find a man with the bones everywhere?"

"And here we go," I mumble, taking a last look at the crowd. Is anyone watching us?

"I do not want to go anywhere, dear, only to home. What is this shirt? Did you forget how to use the iron? You cannot be seen this way." She pulls me by my waist and tries to tuck it in.

"Mom!" I step away from her. "Stop it, I'm not seven. Also, when you say things like that, it hurts my feelings." I take another step back. Dr. Jonas told me to be honest. She didn't tell me if I'd need to duck and cover.

She bats her eyelashes. My words have gone into one ear, rattled about, and promptly exited the other ear. "You are prettier when you are seven because I am picking your clothes out every day before school." She smiles. "You let me do this again, and we can find the new husband."

"Didn't know it was a joint project," I mutter, trying to stay calm. "Give me one of your bags so we can get out of here."

• • • • •

Two hours later, we're pulling her suitcases out of the car. The forced conversation about friends and the restaurant on the ride home has stopped dead. No mention of our argument in Paris, or the face-plant on my uncle's floor. Guess we're not going to talk about it.

Now it's end-time and go-time all at once. The end of her life as she's known it. The safe, comfortable marriage evaporating in a hospital room in Bangkok; propelling her into a mysterious future where the rules will need to be redrawn.

The color drains from her face as she walks from room to room. She forces a smile at the arrangement of flowers on the dining room table.

"Very beautiful, dear. Thank you. I would not think the Sunflower is so pretty because of the low cost."

I swallow her backhanded compliment. I can't fully understand what she's going through. What's it even like, folding two lives into a singular unit, then having it blow apart? Dylan and I blew apart, but our ending was my doing, not some sick joke at the hands of an unfair universe. My parents didn't ask for this, and now my mother is left with nothing but a pile of shrapnel she'll have to arrange into something livable. Purposeful.

I wipe a few stray tears from my eyes. I miss my dad, and I love my mom as much as I loved him. It hurts to imagine the pain she's in right now.

"Do you realize I have not been driving a car since we left on our trip?"

"Who'd want to drive in Paris?" I ask. "I filled your tank, though, and had the oil changed. It's good to go. And the bills are all up to date. I bought some food. Are you hungry?"

"No." She peers out at the yard. "How is the boat?"

"*Happily* is good. I haven't taken her out."

"Not at all?" She looks surprised.

I follow her gaze outside at the blue and white boat that hasn't seen open water in almost a year. "Doesn't feel right yet, you know, with all the changes."

"Changes?" Her big brown eyes go wide. "There is only one change, and of course, it is nothing to be coughing at."

"Sneeze," I say quietly. "Sneeze at. Not cough."

She shakes her head.

"And what do you mean, only one change, Mom? Everything is different."

"Your father is dead," she declares matter-of-factly, then kicks her heels off.

"What about Ethan?"

She picks up the shiny black shoes and walks toward her bedroom. "Your brother is new information for you, not me."

I trail behind her. "But his existence changes things."

"Your life." She pulls the closet door open and runs her hand across her husband's shirts. "What will I do with all of this?"

I drop down on the bed. "I don't get it. How can you be so clinical? Our lives are completely different now."

She turns to me. "Robi is gone, and you are having this extra brother." She grimaces. "And you have no man anymore. Other than this, what is different?"

I look past her, knowing my grandfather's briefcase is tucked into its usual place. "Stuff."

"Stuff," she repeats, moving the hangers, inspecting blouses, pants, and dresses she hasn't had access to in almost ten months. "We will be fine. I have put my thoughts into this while I was in Paris." She bends over and grabs a handful of hangers. "Why are the shoes in such a mess?"

"I didn't do it." My response is automatic. Eight-year-old Katy is never far away. "I wore one of your skirts to court last year. I must have been in a rush to get rid of that last man."

"Mm. You think you are very smart."

"Sorry," I mumble.

She says nothing, and neither do I, though I want to ask a hundred more questions. Why is there a briefcase loaded with our family's secret history shoved into the back of the closet? Why wouldn't you tell me we're Jewish? Why won't you apologize for freaking me out in Paris when I passed out in front of you?

I stand up and take a few steps closer to her. "Mom, are you going to be okay?"

She lifts the sleeves of my dad's shirt to her face, inhales. Tears roll down her cheeks. "I will be very well, dear. We have survived the worst of it. Now only the blue clouds are ahead."

CHAPTER 27
REMNANTS OF AN ELEVATOR

Mom sends me packing shortly after I tell her that skies are blue, not the clouds. She blames the time change and promises to call first thing in the morning.

Back at my place, Penney is happy to see me—and my discarded right shoe, which she immediately stuffs her head into. She twirls on the floor, little fuzzy face hidden, then ejects herself and gallops to the other side of the room with her tail high in the air.

Quinn sends a follow-up text to the text I forgot to answer, asking how it went. Is my mom okay? Am I? I respond with a smiley face, then prepare a healthy dinner of Froot Loops. Penney is interested in the milk, but neither the Froot nor the Loop. Spoon in one hand, phone in the other, I scroll through messages and an automatic reminder from Dr. Jonas' office about our appointment tomorrow.

I update Jesse that Mom's safely home and suggest we meet for lunch later in the week. Next, I leave a voicemail for Ethan, but he's on his way to San Diego, then Mexico City, and back to Denver. Such is the life of a private aviation pilot.

I expend copious amounts of energy pretending to be busy, trying to ignore the fact that Nickety-Nick still hasn't told me when his big return will be. Should I reach out? Another message would put me two texts ahead of him, with no response.

"I'm stupid," I say under my breath. Who counts how many texts each person sends? There's no rule about a single text equaling a single reply. We're all adults here, and I'm only attempting to make future plans, as would any normal human, when an arrival is impending. Imminent.

I poke at an orange Froot Loop, trying to drown it in light pink milk. It goes under, then pops back up like a life preserver. "Fuck you, sugary cereal. Stay down."

• • • • •

Five hours later. Time for another nightmare, courtesy of the lovebirds making out in the airport elevator. I'm crouching in the corner of a metal box and there they are, lovebird one and two, sticking their swollen tongues into each other's mouths.

"Can't you do that somewhere else?" I ask.

They tower over me. Look down at me. "Want some?" they ask in unison.

"Want some what? No, go away. Get a room."

"Need some?" The man asks. He's so tall, wisps of his dark hair sweep against the ceiling.

I stare as they go at each other again. The woman licks his lips, moans, then turns to me.

"You need to pee, don't you, Katy?"

I can't be hearing right. "No!" I yell. What I need is to disappear. Fold myself into invisibility.

The man slides his index finger between the woman's teeth. It reminds me of the tongue depressor my doctor uses. "Katy needs to pee," he says.

"Shut up!" I yell again.

"Baby. Try to hold it. Try."

He pulls his fingers out of the woman's mouth, then slams her into me. I scream, feeling the weight of her warm body collapsing on top of mine, sweaty arms and legs twitching like a dying cockroach. The light goes out, and I wake up with two thoughts running through my brain.

1. What the hell is happening to me?
2. I really need to pee.

CHAPTER 28
THE PRISM OF IMPROVED VISION

Once again, I cross paths with the twin boys and their sad-sack mother. They're more subdued this morning. One kid has his face in his phone, the other is twisting a pencil up his nose. Mom is pale, her hair is dirty. I hold the door as they exit the building.

"Are those little monsters your clients?" I ask after sitting down on her couch. "Oh never mind. I know you can't tell me."

"I can neither confirm nor deny," she says, then tilts her head down and stares at me over a pair of square-framed reading glasses. I smile, wondering if round frames had been suggested to soften her sharp-as-hell linear features.

"New glasses?" I ask instead.

"Unfortunately. Age marches on. My vision isn't what it once was."

"Mm. They look great," I tell her. But no, they don't.

"Thank you. Should we pick up where we left off last week?"

My stomach rumbles. Breakfast is an important meal. One I often forget. "Where were we?"

"We were talking about Nick. Actually, you got a bit upset."

"Oh yeah. Sorry about getting huffy. I don't know what to say about him yet, and anyway, Mom came back yesterday."

She glances at her iPad. "Right. Did she get in without any issues?"

"No time issues. Other issues." I roll my eyes. "I had the house all cleaned up for her, but I didn't hang out long because it was almost seven by the time we got home, and she was tired."

She studies me, now through the prism of improved vision. I hope my poor attitude doesn't become more visible.

"I asked if she was okay and tried to talk about Dad."

"How did she respond?"

"She said she'd been thinking about it, and it'll all be fine." I cross my feet and scratch my knee, even though my knee isn't itchy. "And I didn't want to push about the other stuff, the Jewish stuff. I figure we have time."

She rubs her nose. "You didn't want to push when you visited her in France, either."

"No. Is that silly? I wanted a break and to wander around Paris. Maybe I should have said something right away, but it was nice to disconnect for a minute. And if I'm being honest, I was avoiding the stress of how a conversation would go."

"It's not silly at all," she says. "I understand why you'd feel that way. You will be bringing it to her attention, though, won't you?"

I sit up straight. "Of course. It's a huge deal. Ethan and I organized all the pictures we found. He thinks we should do a DNA test, but I'm nervous because then they'll know I'm here. Like, what if the Nazi shit happens again, and there I am, announcing my Jewishness online?"

She nods. "I won't do those tests either. But I'm glad you're embracing the situation."

"For sure. We spoke to my grandmother in Montreal, and I sent her an email with a thousand questions. I'm waiting to hear back."

"I'm glad you've begun the conversation. If not with your mother, at least with others in your family."

"Uh-huh," I say, then stare at the carpet weave.

"And the fight you had in Paris. Did you bring that up with her?"

I look up. "God no. I don't want to pass out again."

Her eyes narrow. "Is that the only possible outcome of an argument with her?"

"I don't know. If she wanted to chat about it, she would have."

"What if you want to chat about it?"

"You don't know her. And what's to talk about anyway? She's pissed that I got a divorce and thinks I'll end up being an old maid or something." I tap my feet. "Though she said milky-maid. Her English can be off sometimes. Anyway, do people still say old maid?"

"I'm not sure. But let's stay on track here. Your relationship has changed. It's the two of you now, with more pressure to face each other directly."

"Right. My dad's not the buffer anymore."

"You keep talking about him as the go-between," she says. "Perhaps you need to work out why you needed a buffer in the first place."

"That's a reasonable question." The room gets quiet, and I feel pressure to continue talking. "I had a nightmare last night. Actually, I've had a couple."

"Would you like to tell me about them?"

"They're stupid. Think I'm stressed about Mom getting home and the Dad stuff it'll bring up."

"Are the dreams similar?" She pulls a tissue from the pastel blue box meant for despondent therapy patients. "Have you had any more panic attacks?"

"No panic attacks," I answer. "The dreams are different in some ways, but it's always dark and someone keeps calling me a baby."

"Sounds unpleasant. Any other details?"

"I don't remember a ton about them." I purse my lips. "That's strange, right?"

"Not really. We can forget the details of dreams quickly." She blows her nose.

"You must be allergic to my cat."

"Perhaps." She sniffles. "I want you to write down anything you remember from each episode. Are you comfortable with that?"

"I'll try," I say, studying the framed diplomas on the wall. "I slept with Quinn."

"Oh. Guess we're changing subjects. Was it enjoyable?"

"Enjoyable, how? I mean, yeah, it was great." I stare at my knees, which are still not itchy. "This is embarrassing."

She adjusts her glasses. "There's nothing embarrassing about healthy sexual activity. You're consenting adults, I assume?"

"Yeah. But there's the whole Nick thing." I lean back. "I'm not a slutty person, but I pretty much attacked him."

"Okay," she says.

"I mean, he did too. The attacking was mutual."

"Then it's a good thing, Katy."

"But I love Nick."

"Alright."

"So why did I sleep with Quinn if I love someone else?"

Her right eye twitches, like she's winking at me. But she's not, because that would be weird. Has she had too much coffee? Does she have a disease, and if so, what ailment makes your eyelid flap up and down? Where is the off-button for my brain? I smile like I'm normal until she has mercy on me and begins speaking again.

"Sex and love don't always overlap. They can, and it's lovely when they do, but we're human. Imperfect. We have needs, and it's possible for one to be met while the other isn't."

"Then I shouldn't feel guilty? Cuz I do. I mean, I've been trying not to think about it, but it was a fun night, a good night and I felt comfortable with him."

She says nothing.

"And I didn't have one of those nightmares."

"Can you take it as a positive experience and move on? Leave the door open if things with Nick don't work out?"

"Why wouldn't things work out with Nick? That's ridiculous."

"Katy..."

"What the hell? Are you suggesting I don't love him?"

"What's happening right now?" she asks. "You're getting amped up."

"No, I'm not." I grab my backpack and hug it close to my chest. "I'm not amped in any direction. You're the one acting like I'm being indignant or something."

"I'm sorry," she says. "I've upset you."

"Well," I sputter. "I'm not indignant."

She sits motionless in her chair, looking all patient and unaffected and calm.

I pet the backpack, which is now doubling as a therapy dog. "Okay, I might be slightly indignant."

"Why?" she asks, swinging one bony leg over the other.

I push the therapy-doggy-bag off my lap. "How should I know?"

"I get the sense you're feeling defensive about spending time with Quinn."

My cheeks get hot. "Is spending time a euphemism for a shit-ton of sex?"

She smiles but doesn't respond.

"Maybe I am defensive. For cheating on Nick."

"Because you and he are exclusive?"

"No. We don't talk about dating."

"Hm." She clears her throat. "Can I tell you what this sounds like to me?"

"Sure," I say, feeling my face contort into what is probably an unattractive, smart-ass expression.

"It sounds like you're experiencing guilt based on both your past relationship with Nick, which if I remember correctly, wasn't a committed one, and a future relationship which hasn't been defined or even discussed yet."

My shoulders sag. "Those are very reasonable points."

She wipes her nose again.

I wiggle mine; a subconscious reflex if I were to guess. "We've been talking about all sorts of things, but getting together hasn't come up."

"Sounds similar to the way you described your friendship with him in college."

"What does that mean?" I ask.

"Last year, you described the relationship as friends with benefits. There was no discussion of a commitment." She pulls her glasses off and squints at me. "Do you remember what you said? You thought pressuring him would make him run."

I nod. "Yeah."

"Are you still afraid?"

"I dunno."

"It's okay to want something good for yourself. It's okay to ask for it."

"Uh-huh," I say, and wonder how quickly I can get a toast with a bunch of butter and apricot jam into my mouth. "You're telling me to just come out and say date me? Be my person?"

"It's exactly what I'm saying. If you truly want him to be your person. Do you?"

"Yes, obviously." Or a toasty bagel. I'm so hungry.

She puts the iPad on the coffee table and leans toward me. "Then give yourself permission to go get it."

CHAPTER 29
I'VE GOT THIS PUDGE

On the drive to The Point, I give myself permission to stop at Panera and purchase a toasted whole wheat bagel loaded with cream cheese. By the time I walk into work, I have what my dad used to call "happy-belly".

I'm still licking crumbs off my fingers when I see Mom and Russ talking in the kitchen. She studies my bag from Panera, not with total disdain, but maybe forty-nine percent. The remaining fifty-one percent, if I were to guess, is some internal dialogue about where she went wrong raising me, or if my hands have seen soap in the last few days. Possibly even why I'd eat out when we own a restaurant.

"Hi Mom. You're here bright and early."

"Did you wash your hands before putting them into your mouth?"

"Of course," I tell her. This is a lie. I take an extra cream cheese bagel from the bag and toss it to Russ.

He catches it. "That's my girl."

Mom smirks at him. "Why do you eat food from another restaurant? We have so much here."

Bingo.

"How did you sleep last night, Mom? Is everything okay at the house?"

"Very well, dear. Now I am ready for the meeting about the future."

"Future?" I ask, washing my hands. Better late than never.

She gives me a paper towel. "I am happy how Russell is moved up in his responsibilities."

"This is happening now?" I lean against the counter.

Her eyebrows furrow. "Why not?"

I glance at the digital clock above the sink. It's 9:48 a.m. We open at noon. "Okay. Let's do it."

Russ wipes crumbs from his lips. "Do you want me here for this?"

"Yes, Russell, of course," Mom says. "I am grateful for the help you are giving to Katy. I think you are her right man."

"Right-*hand* man," I say quietly.

Russ winks at me. "You wish, darlin'."

"No, *you* wish," I say, sticking my tongue out at him.

Mom tells us we're behaving like children and presses on. "I have decided to only be working a few days during the week."

"You only want to be here part time?" I ask.

"Yes, dear."

"Why? What else do you have to do?"

Russ drops his head, stares at the ground. I'd do the same, but my eyeballs are caught in the hellfire of Mom's death-glare.

"I am going to write."

"Write what?" I pull a bright green scrunchy from my pocket and begin gathering my hair into a ponytail.

"A book. It is already started."

"What kind of book?"

"I am not prepared to discuss this yet. I have joined the Dufferin Beach Writers Club, and they will be helping me."

"Helping you how? When did this happen? You've only been home twelve hours."

"I emailed with them while I was in Paris, and I will meet with them this Saturday."

"You're going to write some book when you're not at the restaurant?"

"Yes," she says. "I think also you should be closing the restaurant one more day of the week. Sunday is not enough, and you are both working too much. I know this now…life is too short."

A shadow passes over her face. The shadow of her life with Dad. All the hard work, saving the reward for later. She's right about taking another day off, but I'm genetically predisposed to argue.

"We can't close on the weekends," I tell her. "We make a ton of money Friday and Saturday nights."

"Then take Monday," she says.

I shrug and nod at Russ.

"I dig it," he says. "I could use an extra day off."

Mom smiles at him. "I hear also that you examined the menu?"

"We started taking a more detailed inventory." He steps closer to me, probably for cover. "To see what sells more."

"And what sells less." I finish his sentence. "It's been enlightening, and we'll save money when we stop buying and prepping things nobody orders."

"I am in agreement," she says.

"You are?" I ask.

She takes her apron from a wall hanger, ties a perfect knot behind her back, then opens a plastic container of flour. "Do not look like the stunned rabbit. You can show me these informations later. But now the meeting is over. It is time for working."

• • • • •

And we do work. Straight through a busier-than-usual lunch rush, probably because the fine citizens of Dufferin Beach have learned that Mom is back in town. I move from cooking to waiting tables with Melissa. Heads swivel toward me each time I walk out the kitchen door, but I'm not the one they're looking for.

After powdering her nose and reapplying lipstick, the Widow Kiss makes her entrance into the dining room at two-thirty. I watch old friends surround her before retreating into the back. It makes me smile, makes me happy. Thirty years of living in one town should get her something, and that something is the support she'll need to lean on from this day forward.

A few hours later, Russ and I show her our Excel file in the office.

"Liverwurst sandwich." I point at the computer monitor. "It's gotta go."

"Your father's favorite." Mom takes a deep breath. "But yes, I am agreeing to this."

Russ pulls his blond curls loose from a tight ponytail. "Katy made mac and cheese a couple of weeks ago. We have to add it. It's crazy good."

"Mi az?" Mom asks what he's talking about.

"Sonkas tészta," I tell her, then translate for Russ. "Ham and pasta." Everyone nods. We're on the same page. Magical Ham & Cheese is going on the menu.

I hear the back door open and close. Oh joy. My maternal unit is about to meet Cricket.

Russ hears it too and immediately finds a reason to run errands before we begin prepping for dinner. He slides past the fashionable Cricket, checking out her hot pink pants on the way. They lock eyes for a split second, and it reminds me of how infatuated I was with him as a teenager. Every girl was, but thankfully, he never had time for a kid three years younger than him. Had he made time, we wouldn't be friends today.

"Hi Cricket. This is my mom, Andrea Kiss. You probably met at your mother's salon."

Cricket grins and drops her pack with a thump at our feet. "Hello Madam Kiss. I believe we met way back when I was younger, and you were, too."

Mom's pretty brown eyes darken a few shades.

"You may not remember since it's been a long time, but I'm Cricket Calliope Punch."

"Of course I do, Crick-ette. How is your mother?"

"She's very well. I suppose then she told you about how I was meant to come out a boy baby, but I came out a girl baby instead, so she got all discombobulatory and named me after her dead great-granny, who was a no-good, man-stealing drunk."

"That is so not a word," I mumble.

Mom glances at me, then looks back at *Crick-ette*. "No dear, she did not tell me this."

"Well, she usually tells everyone." She rubs her eyebrow. "Anyways, she'll be happy to know you're home from the broad."

"Abroad," I mumble a bit louder. Why is it always my job to correct everyone's grammar?

"I will call her soon, dear. Katy tells me you are in high school?"

"Yes, ma'am. It's very enjoyable except for P.E., which is physical education in case you don't know. I had to tell your daughter what it was, too." She keeps speaking, hands awkwardly dangling at her sides. "But I like my other classes pretty well, and at lunch I help the front office walk passes and notes to the classrooms. Mother purchased me a step-tracker because she said I have to exercise more because I've got this pudge." She lifts her shirt and shows us *the pudge*. "See it?"

Mom leans away, her mouth partially agape.

"Anyways, I'll start working now. Is that okay?"

I smile, impressed with her power to render my mother speechless. "Yup, go for it. The tables need a quick wipe-down. Get started there."

"You okay?" I ask after Cricket leaves the office. "She's a handful."

"I am feeling the damages. Is this how you say it?"

I giggle. "Yeah. You feel damaged. She has the same effect on everyone. Did you see how fast Russ blew out of here?"

She stands up, blinking. "He is right to blow away from here. After this strange girl, I have had enough of this day, too."

CHAPTER 30
BLAH BLAH BLAH

Mom continues to have "enough of this day" on Tuesday when steam from the espresso maker burns her thumb. On Wednesday, she has enough before having any, and never makes it into work. Thursday's *enough* consists of helping prep, then heading home as the lunch rush begins. Jetlag, she says, is finally kicking in.

Her mood, which I'd describe as the murky yellow glow before the storm, infects us all. Russ snaps at Cricket, Melissa threatens to quit after graduating from the university in a few weeks, and I've stopped sleeping again, in fear of another nightmare.

Quinn calls, texts, then drops flowers and a four-pack of fuzzy kitten toys on my doorstep early Friday morning. I text him to say thanks, but this is pissing me off more. I used him. He used me. We're even, though in a remote corner of my brain, a light is blinking with the memory of the sweet smile on his face when I woke up next to him. Dylan would occasionally smile at me early in the morning, but it wasn't a show of affection turning his lips up at the corners. It was him wanting sex, and it always made me cringe before turning me into a liar, because let's face it, women tend not to have their periods eight times in one month.

Friday afternoon the kitchen is a free-for-all. Melissa's off to Nashville for her best friend's bachelorette party and Cricket is out with strep throat. Russ brings in his younger cousin to wash dishes, and Mom steps up like a trooper. We slog through the day with masks on, hoping strep won't make the rounds with us or our customers. By eight p.m. we collectively decide to call it, and I update our social media feeds. *Blah blah blah, someone is sick. Be assured we took every precaution while preparing your meals. Out of an abundance of caution, the restaurant is closed until Tuesday.*

CHAPTER 31
MY TEMPERATURE IS 160,000!

Tuesday comes and goes. Russ catches Cricket's strep, and I get the flu from my mom, who probably caught it on the flight home from France. The doctor diagnoses our severe sore throat, high fever, and nausea as Flu A. We get drugs and a lecture on hydration. I spend days in bed, trying to swallow orange juice and downing way too much prescribed cough syrup. Cough syrup that alters my nightmares into fantastical dreams where I'm followed around by a sparkly German Shepherd the size of a horse while rollerblading down a highway made of typewriter keys. I know it makes no sense, but I can barely control the situation when I'm awake. Why would I do better in a medicated sleep state?

I send random texts to those closest to me.

Jessseee. I love you!
Go to sleep, Katy. I'll stop by later and check on you.
But my temperature is 150.
Stop drunk texting me.

It's drug texting. not the same.

Hi Russ. Are you alive?
Improving Katy-Bell. Go to sleep.

Nickety! When you gonna be here.
...

Hi Quinn. I'm dying. Did you hear?
I heard. I'll bring some soup by. Do you need me to take you to the doc?
Nooooo. He doesn't care. Penney hates me.
She doesn't hate you. Did you see the flowers I left out front?
...

Mommmmmmie. My temperature is 160,000!
That's nice, dear. Take more medicine.

• • • • •

By the next Friday, my temperature normalizes. My behavior as well, and I cringe, scrolling through the messages on my phone. Someone should have taken it away from me.

With the restaurant still closed, I take Friday afternoon to breathe outside air at the beach. The sun, warm on my skin, has never felt so good. But for the occasional cough, I manage a two-mile hike up and down the shoreline without passing out or saying inappropriate things to the few people stretched out on the sand. The sound of the seagulls calms me, not because I enjoy shrill shrieking noises, but because this is the soundtrack to my life. Water sloshing, birds squawking, and the muffled chatter of beachgoers. I feel the same about football on a Sunday afternoon. In small pieces, it's nothing but the crowds cheering, players ramming into each other, coaches barking instructions. Sew them together and it becomes soothing. The sound of things that should occur when all is as it should be.

CHAPTER 32
OLD KATY

Penney is waiting for me by the front door when I get home from the beach. This is the longest my kitten and I have been separated in the last week. She demonstrates her dismay by biting my feet. I open a can of kitty food. She forgives me.

"It's Friday night, Penney. Should we celebrate?"

She turns in a circle, hunches over and pukes up undigested beige paste.

"Not exactly what I meant." I clean the mess, then toss a fuzzy mouse in her direction. She plays hockey with it. Inserts her baby claws into it. "That's from Quinn, by the way. What do you think about the tulips he brought me?" I pour fresh water into the vase filled with tiny pink buds. "Guess I'll take a shower."

Forty minutes later, I'm feeling clean, bored, and lonely, with no plans until tomorrow when my mother, Jesse and I are scheduled to meet for lunch.

I stare at my phone. Nick's been radio silent since the last incoherent message I sent him. Screw it. I'm sending another one.

Where the fuck are you, Nick?

Nothing. I count to thirty. It's the middle of the night in Europe. If that's where he still is.

My phone buzzes. *Love it when you talk dirty.*

I tap on the screen. *Is that what it takes?*

Perhaps. Do some more.

I look around the room, clench my jaw and draw the line right here. Self-respecting women shouldn't have to send dirty texts unless they want to. I've never done it before. Why would I start now?

Not my thing, Nick. Watch some porn.

Come on. Just a little.

Nope

Old Katy would have.

I laugh out loud. Old Katy was a pushover who disappeared the day Dylan grabbed her by the arms and called her a cunt. I drop the phone onto the counter and walk away. His turn to wait.

CHAPTER 33
CHICKEN, PICKLES, POUT, TALK

Jesse and I offer to take Mom to Birdies for lunch on Saturday, but she insists it's not the kind of place an ancient, widowed woman should be seen. We're invited to her house instead, because she's been out of the country for a long time, and she'd like to stay close to home.

She's not there when we arrive. Fifteen minutes later she strolls in, and I decide my mother is ironic, and always a step ahead of me.

She gives Jesse a European-style peck on both cheeks. "It has been quite the long time since we have seen each other."

"You look great Mrs. Kiss. Guess Katy's flu was worse than yours." She gawks at me, then turns back to my mother. "I'm really sorry about Mr. K."

"Please dear, call me Andrea. And yes, of course, we are all very sorry." She looks me over. "Katika, you have just now gotten out of bed?"

"No." I smash my hair into place. "Where were you just now?"

Jesse swats at my head. "You know, I don't think I've ever seen you brush your hair."

"Shut up, Jess. Where were you, Mom?"

She drops a folder on the dining room table. "I am telling you this already. I have been at my first meeting of the Dufferin Beach Writers Club."

I motion to the folder. "Is this the stuff you're writing? Can I see it?"

"No."

"Why not?"

"Because I have said so." Her jaw sets in a stubborn frown.

"I don't get it. Why can't I see it? And since when do you write?"

"You are making me exasperated, dear. What can I tell you? I am writing about a town which is in the southwest of Florida. On the beach."

"Sounds like this town."

Jesse moves past me to the kitchen and fills the teapot. "She doesn't want to tell you, Kiss. Leave her alone."

"Thank you, Jessica," Mom says. "And yes, it is this town, but the name will be something else."

"You're writing about Dufferin Beach?" I ask.

"It is not called the same name."

"You can't do that," I insist. "Duff Beach is real. You can't make up a town that's exactly right here and call it something else."

"Why not?"

"Because." I try to look sure of myself. "It's not a thing."

"But I have already done it."

"Well, stop it. Write about some other place."

She stares at me. "Why?"

"I dunno. It's creepy. You can't just replace Chicago or New York and give them different names."

Jesse shoves a chunk of French bread into her mouth. "Ever heard of Gotham?"

"Yes, what's your point?" I watch her chew. "Okay, I get your point, but so what?" I turn back to my mother. "It's a free country, I guess. Do you want me to make some food?"

"I have already made the rizses csirke."

Jesse looks at me.

"The chicken and rice stuff you like," I tell her. "Let's set the table."

Mom nods and pulls a casserole dish from the fridge.

I open a jar of dill pickles. It's a Hungarian law. Meals must be accompanied by bits of something sour or sweet, like beets, pickles, pepper rings. "What's the story about, Mom?" Okay, not law, but tradition, expected, civilized.

"When I am ready to show it to you, then you will see it."

"Fine," I mumble.

"Fine," she says.

• • • • •

Twenty-five minutes later, Jesse makes sex sounds while shoving forkfuls of chicken into her mouth. "Mrs. K., you missed a lot while you were out of town."

Mom gingerly wipes her mouth with a cloth napkin. "Yes. Thank you for helping my daughter with the divorce. It is not what I wanted, of course, but it seems Dylan was not a good man."

I pierce a slice of pickle. "Total dick, actually."

"Fuj," Mom objects. "Please do not speak this way. You come from the good Hungarian family."

"Uh-huh. Sorry."

"Well," Jesse continues. "She did great in court. You would have been proud of her. Did you hear she even went on a date recently?"

My parental unit blinks. "Nicholas has come to Dufferin Beach?"

"No," I sputter. "I told you we're only talking on the phone."

"What does this mean? You have gone on a date with somebody else?" She places her utensils slowly down next to her plate and inhales enough air to fill a balloon. "Is it Russell?" she asks, exhaling. "Are you having the sex with this boy?"

"He's not a boy. He's three years older than me. And no, I would never do anything with him." I give my bestest friend the evil eye.

"Deal with it," Jesse says. "You're a grown woman and Quinn's a great guy. Spending the night with him is not a bad way to pass the time."

"Quinn?" Mom looks from Jesse to me. "Are you speaking of Dylan's friend? The tall boy with the brown hair?"

"That's him, Mrs. K., but he hasn't been friends with Dylan for a few years."

"I do not understand, Katy. Why would you go to bed with somebody like this?"

A veil of shame descends on me. Getting to the bed was only the beginning. What we did there…

"Like what, Mom? You don't know anything about him. Also, in France you were down my throat for being single. And by down my throat, I mean standing there while I passed right the fuck out in front of you."

Her cheeks flush dark pink, her posture becomes rigid. The knives have come out. "You fainted, dear. You did not die." She twists the napkin between her fingers. "I looked."

"How reassuring. What did you do? Check for a pulse? Poke me in the ear or something?"

"Not the ear," she says with a smirk.

"Beautiful. Your kid wipes out on the floor and then what, you check for vitals before ducking out long enough for me to leave the country?"

"You guys," Jesse says, "I didn't mean to start a fight."

"Too late," I say, keeping my eyes on my mother. "I thought you'd be pleased that I was getting around. Isn't it what you wanted?"

She doesn't move or speak, but her cheeks have graduated from pink to atomic red.

"And who should I be going out with? Someone more like us? More like our family?"

"What does this mean?" she asks. "What do you even know of this man?"

I pick up my dish and stomp to the sink. "I know he's nice, and he brings cat toys for Penney."

Her eyes get wide. "You have a cat?"

"Yes. Oh my God. I told you all about her on the way home from the airport."

She pulls Jesse's plate away from her, which leaves Jesse dismayed, as she hasn't yet licked it clean. "I do not remember. Does this Quinn work? Does he have money?"

"How is that relevant?" I ask as the doorbell rings.

"I'll get it." Jesse jumps up from the table, leaving mother and daughter to stare each other down in the narrow galley kitchen. In a new world without the intervention that's kept us from murdering each other for the last twenty-six years. I swallow hard and try to remember Dr. Jonas' advice. Being mean won't help. Yelling, accusations, blame. None of it will do any good.

"How about we try to talk about this like adults, Mom?"

She pushes her short bangs off her forehead.

"Are you pouting?" I ask.

Her cheeks, puffed out in frustration, make her look fifteen-years-old, and it occurs to me, possibly for the first time, that my mother is a person. Pre-Katy, someone who had a life before marriage, parenthood...being widowed.

"Mom?"

She looks at the ceiling, trying to blink away tears. "Yes?"

"I'm sorry." I glance at the front door, but it's closed, and Jesse is nowhere to be found. "Want to sit out by the pool?" I ask before sending a text.

Where you at, Tanner? Who was at the door?

She responds quickly. *Pizza delivered to the wrong house. I sent them away, then I sent myself away. Seems like you all need to work some shit out. Tell Mom-Unit thanks for the delish food.*

I text back. *Seriously?*

She doesn't respond, and I'm left to wonder how my family is messed up enough to chase off the most combative person I've ever met.

Mom is two steps ahead of me, out through the Florida room to the backyard. The breeze stirs tiny baby waves in the pool. They crash with tiny baby slaps into the bright blue glass tiles edging the rim.

"We scared Jess off," I say, pulling a lawn chair close to her. "She says thanks for lunch."

"She does not like the subject of this Quinn either."

"She's the one who brought him up." I watch her for a reaction. Nothing. I move on. "Let's chat about some other stuff."

"Chat?" She emphasizes the word sarcastically.

"Why are you making this so hard?"

She leans into the sun as I gather my thoughts. Two pelicans dive into the canal. The seagulls sing. Mr. Lizard chases Mrs. Lizard across the deck. I have to focus.

"Let's not talk about Quinn," I say. "You don't really know him, so there's no use."

"This is fine with me, dear."

"But there is another thing I need to ask you about."

"Yes?" Her tone is clipped.

"I found some papers in the house when you and Dad were gone."

"This house?"

"Uh-huh."

She crosses her hands in her lap.

I continue. "In your bedroom."

"What are you doing in our room?"

I hesitate. "I don't remember. Checking on something, probably."

"And what papers did you find?"

"*The* papers," I say. "You know what I'm talking about, right?"

She glances at me, then looks away.

"The briefcase? The one you hid in your closet. The story about Bela getting taken away by the Nazis."

"Please do not be so loud." A trickle of sweat rolls down her forehead. "We do not need the neighbors to hear."

I look behind me, beside me, over the fence. "Are you kidding? You're afraid of the neighbors?"

"You know nothing of this." An acerbic scowl spreads across her face. "This is why you are angry? How does it matter? This is the ancient history."

"For you, maybe."

"Look, we come to this country to find a better life. Why would we want to drag the old life with us?"

"You don't believe I deserve to know?"

"Deserve?" Her eyes narrow. "You think you are owed something?"

"Ethan and I read the letters about Dad's family. His parents survived the Holocaust. We talked to Grandma about it. We asked her about Bela and all those men getting taken by the SS."

"And?"

My face twists into a grimace. "And? What about your family? Did they go through the same thing? Why did you guys hide something so huge from me?"

"You do not understand anything about this time. And the secret is not only kept from you."

I lean toward her. "What do you mean?"

She squashes her lips together before loosening them. "Miklos, your grandfather, was never told what happened that day."

"He wasn't told how his dad was shot along with those other two old guys?"

"No, Katika. And those were not just *old guys*, as you say. They were his father-in-law and uncle."

I sit back. "Oh, God."

She nods. "Yes. But the family did not feel it was correct to tell Miklos. You see, the secrets in the family, they are not only for you."

"How did Dad find out about it?"

"He found the letters after Miklos died. Just like you, going to places where you are not invited."

"That's your opinion. What did Dad do when he found them?"

"He read them and understood why the family would allow his father to write these letters."

"And why is that?" I ask.

"Because it gave the boy hope of his father coming home one day."

"Hm." I wipe sweat off the back of my neck. "That's why the letters exist? Because the son didn't know his dad had been killed? Incredible. And after the war? Why not tell him then?"

"I do not know. Ask your grandmother." She takes another look around to make sure we're not being spied on. "And still, this is nothing except the history lesson for you. What is it good for? Now you are feeling something. Anger. Disgust?"

"Outrage?" I offer.

"Fine. This is a very colorful word. You learn we are Jews and now you will fix it? Suddenly the people will like us instead of always hating us?"

"I dunno, Mom. Isn't it better to talk about it?"

She snorts. "Everybody is already talking about this. How one race does something terrible to the other. What does it help, Katy? People will not be acting better, they will only get more angry how you are telling them they have done something bad. We do not need anybody to be sad for us. We are fine."

"Do you think it could happen again?"

"Again?" She scoots her chair a few inches into the shade of the pool umbrella. "It has never stopped. Look at the history. Learn from it. And I do not mean on the little bubbles and pictures on your telephone."

"I wasn't planning on getting my education from social media, Mom. But your way to deal is pretending it didn't happen to your family at all. Put it away, literally into the closet, and never talk about it again?"

"Yes. Exactly."

"Wow, Mother."

"Vow you," she spits the words at me.

"What about the stuff your family went through?"

Her feet tap on the white concrete. At the same time, up, down...tap, tap, tap. "What were you doing inside of our closet?"

"Hanging up the clothes you left in the dryer."

"Why did you looking into our dryer?"

"Stayed here for a while before we served Dylan with papers. I was trying to avoid him."

She nods; feet tap, tap, tap. "What is it you will like to know?"

"You're going to answer my questions?" I ask. "Just like that?"

"No. I am only curious."

"Oh," I mumble, chewing on the skin around my index finger. "For a second, I thought you were going to make it easy."

CHAPTER 34
WAR STORY

Being easy will have to wait for another day. I'm shooed out of Mom's house so she can focus on writing the next chapter of *not* Dufferin Beach. In the late afternoon sun, I walk home, deliberately stepping on the cracks of the sidewalk. Dr. Jonas has forbidden me from being surly with my one remaining parent, but I need to vent, and this passive aggressive behavior is my only method of objecting to twenty-six years of lies about the past, my half-brother, and God knows what else. She didn't even flinch when I busted her out about the briefcase, and her words still ring in my ear. *Why drag the old life with us?*

I duck under a cloud of gnats. The old life is my past too, isn't it? Or is my history relegated to Dufferin Beach and this street where I grew up; an unchanging landscape except for the grass growing, palm trees getting taller, and the homes getting brightly colored facelifts.

No, I'm not buying-in. Whatever created me comes from outside the Sunshine State. It's baked into those dominoes Dr. Jonas and I spoke about last year, and filled with questions, anxiety, and behavior people around me have always questioned. Dylan, more than anyone else, mocked my choices, my work at the restaurant, my entire life. Now I know it's because my origin story has more to it than this place, and my family's past is the missing link to filling it in.

• • • • •

Once again, Penney meows upon my arrival, then prances to the fridge.

"Promise you won't puke it up this time?" I spoon tuna slop into her bowl and tickle her cheek as my phone beeps with an incoming audio message. "It's from Nori," I announce. Animals are excellent cover for talking to yourself.

She rubs her face on my hand before pushing me out of the way, then dives into her meal. I slump onto the couch, hit play, and listen to my grandmother and Nori chat.

Nori: Hi guys. Grandma thought it would be good to record these stories one at a time. She was going to write them down, but her hands are shaking a lot lately. And Katy, she's not ignoring your emails. She's thinking about it. Okay, Grandma. You ready?

Grandma: Do I speaking now? Hello Katy and Ee-ten?

Nori: We're recording Grandma. It's not a normal two-way call. They're not on the line.

Grandma: Ahh. Yes. I talking now?

Nori: Yes, right here, into my phone. Also, Grandma wants to practice her English because she mostly speaks French and Hungarian here. Right Grandma?

Grandma: Oui!

I hear them both giggle, then some shuffling, muffling noises. My grandmother coughs and begins speaking in English.

Grandma: Dear Katika and Ee-ten. I hope you are both very wells. Katika, I still thinking of this question you asking last time. Why nobody telling you nothing? Még mindig nem tudom. She slips into Hungarian for a moment. *She still doesn't know.*

Now here is story. The Nazi don't coming into Hungary until very late. Already 1944. Before this, our men taken away by Magyar army and the Germans. This mean my father is sent to munka szolgat.

Nori: *That means prison camp, right?*

Grandma: *Yes. So now in the house only my mother, my sister, Eva, and me. After short time, the military sending other young men to us. Jewish boys who are prisoners. They taken from their family too, just like my father.*

Nori: *Wait. A bunch of men stayed in the house with you guys?*

Grandma: *Igen.*

Nori: *You weren't allowed to say no?*

Grandma: *This is not choice, Nori. The boys maybe eighteen years old, and during day, off they going to working. Cleaning bombing damages in city. At night, they staying with us. We are making the foods for them. In the morning and night when they coming back.*

Nori: *Wasn't it uncomfortable? It seems inappropriate for a bunch of young men to be living with two young women.*

Grandma: *Et alors? You thinking anybody asking if this okay? No. This how war is.*

I giggle. My grandmother is doing her thing. Speaking English, French, and Hungarian all at the same time. No wonder I jump from thought to thought. My youth was spent in the company of people who spoke multiple languages in singular sentences.

Nori: *I guess not. So, your father's sent away to a work camp, and you guys are basically housing war prisoners. Did the boys...you know, behave themselves?*

Grandma: *Very polite. Very frightened. At these times, Mother is having...how you say? Having the head in the book? Every book, every paper she finding. Her head always down, reading. I think this her way to keeping brain safe, you know?*

And Eva, she cleaning everything. Clean and clean, and then playing piano. This her way too, of not thinking bad things.

Nori: *What did you do, Grandma?*

Grandma: *I am only ten years old. What do I care? I run and play like always.*

Nori: *Didn't you think it was weird that your dad was gone, and a bunch of strangers were living in your house?*

Grandma: *Nem tudom. I do not know. Maybe I am too young to understanding. Then planes coming over our heads, and the sirens beginning. Then I am very...um. Féltem. You understanding?*

Nori: *You were afraid?*

Grandma: *Igen. When siren happening, mother scream for us to going to bombing shelter. I hearing this terrible noises, even now, in my head. The planes sounding like this fütyülő. You know this?*

Nori: *Whistling?*

Grandma: *Igen. Whistling and the motor so loud, and they flying in shape like the V, you know?*

Nori: *Were they dropping bombs?*

Grandma: *Yes, in some of the place. I do not know if this German plane, or Russian or American. But there is Eva, sitting and playing musics on piano. We have the grand piano, the Bösendorfer. She keeping to playing even with mother screaming and screaming. So stupid, these two sound in the same time. It is enough to making someone crazy.*

She stops talking for a moment, blowing her nose before continuing.

Grandma: *But she not listening, so mother taking only me to shelter. There is no more time.*

Nori: *You left your sister playing the piano while the planes were flying over your heads?*

Grandma: *What is there to do?*

Nori: *Oh my God, guys. Are you hearing this?*

"Yeah," I whisper into the empty room, imagining a young girl bent over a keyboard while the air raid sirens blare overhead. I shiver, wondering if I would have been brave, or would I have curled up into a ball?

Nori: *What happened then?*

Grandma: Nothing. *The siren stopping. We live, thanks to God. But I never forgetting these sounds. I never forgetting every time we running and leave Eva alone. How terribles this was.*

Nori: *Did you guys ever talk about it? Did you ask Eva why she wouldn't come with you to the bomb shelter?*

Grandma: *No. We never talk about it.*

Nori: *Why not?*

Grandma: *We live, so we don't asking the questions. We saying thank you to God, and...what this saying, to keeping the face low?*

Nori: *Keeping your head down?*

Grandma: *Igen. This my first story, childrens. This enough for me now. I tell another soon.*

Nori: *She's wiped out, guys. I'll do another audio message when she's ready. Love you!*

I replay the message again and again, each time getting chills thinking of my great-aunt sitting at a piano; head down, literally the way my grandmother just said, fingers moving along the ivory keys, creating sound she could control in order to drown out the sound she couldn't. What a horrible melody that would be, the piano playing alongside the sirens, the bombs falling, people screaming.

"Why do people suck?" I lift Penney onto my knees. She stuffs a paw into her ear, shakes her head, then folds herself into a tiny purring donut on my lap. After twenty minutes of feline therapy, I text Quinn. It's early, and I don't want to spend another night alone. He responds immediately, and it occurs to me, in a way I wouldn't like to say out loud, that he could teach Nick a thing or two about manners. But I'm not being fair.

Nick's in another country, in another time zone. I'm sure his phone coverage isn't as good as Quinn's, who suggests dinner downtown, or in St. Armand's Circle in Sarasota.

This would mean getting dressed in something other than jeans and a tank top. So exhausting.

I return his text. *Would it be wrong to eat ice cream for dinner?*

Ice cream is never wrong. Want me to bring it over?

Yes! Sounds perfect. Give me thirty minutes.

He sends a dessert emoji, and I set to work ridding the house of Flu A paraphernalia. I clean the kitty litter and the bathroom. My plan to leave it dirty last time backfired on me, and Quinn was subjected to my slovenliness. Not that we're sleeping together this time.

We are not. Doing that. At all.

He rings the doorbell. We're not doing that.

We do *that* before the ice cream makes it into the freezer. And once again after.

Two hours later, he constructs a sundae for two in an oversized coffee cup, adding caramel syrup and a mountain of whipped cream on top. I watch him work and realize how familiar I'm becoming with him. With his body. The spattering of freckles on his cheeks, the tiny chip on his left front tooth, the curve of his neck.

He pushes the cup toward me. "Try it. Tell me if you recognize the flavor."

"Of the ice cream?" I ask.

"Uh-huh." His eyes get big as I take a bite.

"Is this Choco-Toffee-Yum & Crunch?"

He grins. "Thought I could switch out a bad memory for a good one."

It's a calculated move to offer the same flavor I was eating at the ice cream parlor last year when he told me to screw off.

"I was done eating when you showed up. It was in my stomach, not my dish."

"True," he says.

"Should I be creeped out? How did you know what I ordered?"

"I asked at the counter when I was leaving."

"Why?"

He takes a deep breath as his expression morphs into shame. "I knew I'd done something shitty. I was coming up with ways to fix it."

"Wow." I put the spoon on the counter. "Talk about thinking ahead."

"I guess," he nods. "Shaky outcome either way. I go with the lie or tell you the truth right there and then. Come out and say Jesse wants me to do this thing, and we're going to pretend I did."

I lick caramel off my thumb. "Would have been easier at that moment, but I don't have much game, Quinn. No poker face, not a good keeper of secrets. Jesse had it right. I would have blown it and who knows what would have happened."

"Still," he insists. "I don't like being a pawn. There should've been some other way." He motions to the sundae, asking if I want more, but we've both lost our appetite.

"Want to hear something semi-interesting?" I ask, needing to turn the subject away from one of the most humiliating days I've ever experienced.

We sit on the couch, and he pulls my feet across his lap. "More than anything."

"Okay," I say cautiously. "There are some things you don't know about me."

He smiles. "Hit me."

I puff out my cheeks, contemplating if I should share this part of my life. He cocks his head to the right, sort of like Dr. Jonas does sometimes. He's prettier, though. No disrespect to my angular shrink.

"Okay," I say.

"Okay." He grabs my right hand and kisses my fingers. "So far, so good."

"I haven't said anything yet."

"But your fingers are cute and little and sweet like Toffee Choco Crunch."

I wiggle my nose. He's kind of adorable. "I found out some information about my family last year. I told you about Ethan, right?"

"The brother, yeah. The pilot who lives in Denver."

"There's more. Like stuff other families might not have."

"Every family has more," he says, studying my thumb. "Everyone has wrinkles. Some people are just better at smoothing them out."

"How deep." I stop for a few seconds, wondering if I should send him away. Call it a night and count myself properly sexed-up for the weekend. His honey brown eyes twinkle, which is weird, because the sun's set, and there's no light shining in his direction. Obviously, they're lit up from the inside. This is stupid...my endorphins must still be at full throttle. I take a deep breath. "I'm Jewish. My family lived through the Holocaust. Well, most of them. And I didn't know until last December. Nobody ever told me anything."

He stares at me with an intensity I'm uncomfortable with. Once again, the same thought occurs to me as it did last year in therapy. I'd prefer to participate in my life from a darkened room, with a bag over my head, away from the judgment. Mostly my own. I avert my eyes. Stare at my lap.

He squeezes my fingers. "Not the most shocking thing I've ever heard," he says as a pensive expression moves across his face. "Don't you celebrate Christmas?"

"We do."

"I thought so. Your parents are too young to have lived through it. You must be talking about grandparents and great-grandparents."

"Yeah. I found a briefcase in Dad's closet late last year filled with letters. And some other stuff."

"Stuff?" he asks, still holding my hand.

"Uh-huh. And he left me his own letter, coughing up all the secrets. It was part of his will."

"It couldn't have been easy to read. How does that..." He grins, winks, and lowers his voice an octave. "Make you feel?"

"Very funny, Dr. Phil. How would you feel if you found out your entire family was lying about your history?"

He looks away from me, then back. "Did I ever tell you about my mom?"

"No. All I know is that your parents live in Miami."

"Yeah, they live in Coral Gables. Mom is Spanish, raised Catholic. But her great-grandmother was half Jewish. I think on the dad's side. So, I'm like one-tenth or something. My dad's English. His family is from London. Well, outside of London."

"How did I never know any of this about you? You and Dylan hung out for years."

He lets go of my hand and shrugs. "Did we seem like two people who would have a serious conversation about religion or culture?"

"Not so much. Did your mom know she was part Jewish? I mean, when she was a kid?"

He stands up, walks to the window, and glances at the street. "I think so. We've talked about it a couple times, and I've seen some old pictures of...what would she be? My great-great-grandmother? They always stuck in my mind because she seemed so tiny, but her hair was big and wild. My sister and I got scared every time we saw those photos because her hair stood up like this silver halo around her head. It was like she'd been plugged into a light socket."

I giggle, picturing the Bride of Frankenstein hairstyle.

"Now you and I have something in common. At least a sliver of something." He leans forward toward the glass. "Think Jesse just drove by. She's got the silver Prius, right?"

"Yeah," I say, as Penney strolls onto my lap. "She's probably checking on me."

He turns around. "Is that a thing with you two?"

"It is lately. She's just making sure I'm okay."

"Hm," he mumbles and returns to the couch. "Looks like she had a passenger."

"It is Saturday night. She's probably on the prowl for her Sunday, day of sex."

"Day of what?" His eyebrows move up. "Never mind. I don't want to hear the details." He lifts the cat off of me and runs his fingers across my stomach. The conversation about my secret Jewish history officially comes to an end.

CHAPTER 35
MUSIC BOX

I thought a big, strong man sleeping next to me would stave off the nightmares.

No such luck. Quinn can't keep me from this pit in the earth. My nostrils fill with the pungent odor of mold and decay. Glowing, powdery soot floats not down, but sideways, which seems normal, because gravity isn't a thing in dreams. An air raid siren blares. I drop to my knees and cover my ears.

"Stop it!" I yell into the darkness.

"Such a baby." It's the Elevator Man, and he's close by.

The siren winds down like a music box—lingering, coming to the end of its tune, one faltering note at a time. I crawl backwards, brace myself against an earthen wall and pull my knees to my chest.

"How many times will we do this?" he asks. "Why can't you learn, Katy?"

There isn't enough light for my eyes to adjust. "Get the fuck away!" My arms flail out, batting the air.

"You have to pee, don't you?" he asks.

I move again, squirming across the dirt, trying to create distance from the sound of his voice. "Leave me alone!"

"You do, don't you? You need to pee. Oh well. Tough break, Little One."

"What the hell do you want from me?"

Elevator Man chuckles.

"Let me out," I whimper and rub hot tears off my cheeks. "I need to go."

"Hold it, Katy."

"What if I can't?"

"There is no can't."

"I'll try," I promise.

"Try isn't good enough. You know what happened to try." This isn't a question. It's a statement. He grabs my foot, and I scream.

CHAPTER 36
PTSD

My right hand makes contact with Quinn's face before I'm fully awake. He jolts upward, his brow furrows in confusion.

"What the hell, Katy?"

I cover my mouth. "Oh my God, did I slap you?"

He rubs the angry pink skin on his cheek. "Hell of a way to say good morning."

"I'm so sorry." I reach out. He leans away.

"You were whimpering and kicking. Look at your fingers. They're balled into a fist. I was trying to wake you up."

My nails dig into the soft flesh of my palms. "It was one of those dreams. It's not you."

"What dreams?" he asks. "What are you talking about?"

I nod, move the covers off and furtively touch the sheet underneath me, paranoid I've wet the bed. Dry, thank God. "Hold on," I say, smiling, trying with all my might to act casual. "I gotta pee."

• • • • •

Twenty minutes later I've taken a shower, put on fresh clothes and applied a touch of makeup in an effort to look "dewy" or whatever those reels on Instagram go on about. I creep out of the bathroom because Quinn's fallen asleep again, his face partially buried under the pillow.

I tiptoe to him, check his cheek, and see the pink has faded. At least I didn't leave a mark.

In the kitchen, I double the beans for espresso and slide a bowl of whipped cream from the fridge. Penney puts her front paws on the bottom shelf and sniffs the butter dish.

I pat her head. "Smells good, doesn't it?"

She purrs while I ponder if a big fat breakfast of eggs, bacon, and pancakes will be apology enough for smacking the person in my bed. I don't understand what's happening to me. I had bad dreams when I was a kid, but the last time was from *Nightmare on Elm Street 2,* where Freddy Krueger makes the track marks on Taryn's arms come to life. It took months to wipe the image away, but it's back again, turning my stomach while I scramble the viscous egg whites into the yolks, and drop pancake batter into a cast iron pan. I shiver, and when Quinn lays his hand on my shoulder, I let out a blood-curdling shriek and jump a foot off the ground.

"Holy shit, Katy! All I did was put my hand on your arm."

I swear to myself, turn away from the stove, spatula in hand, and apologize for the second time in one morning. "I'm sorry! I was thinking about Freddy Krueger." I watch the irritation grow on his face. "Did I hurt you?"

"No," he answers curtly. "Do I remind you of him?"

I turn the heat down on the stove. "No, of course not. It's not that."

"But?"

"But now I'm having these crazy nightmares, and I have no idea what's going on."

He sighs, and I imagine all the irritable thoughts streaming through his head right now. Regret for spending the night, for spending any energy on me at all.

"What the hell are they about? Because your reaction, jumping out of your skin when all I did was barely touch your shoulder. It's weird."

"They're stupid. I don't even know where to begin." I stare at the floor, ashamed.

"Stupid or scaring the shit out of you? Look, I'm not saying this in a mean way." He smiles. It's forced, uneasy. "Something is obviously going on."

"Maybe."

"Do you know what it is?"

I chew on the inside of my cheek. "Nope."

"How long have you been having the dreams? Do you think it's PTSD from Dylan?" He gently pushes my bangs out of my face. "Katy, did he ever hit you?"

"No. I mean, there was the one time he grabbed me. But I hit him back."

His eyes narrow. "That was at the end already, when he told me you beat the crap out of him."

"Whatever, he's a man baby."

"Are you telling me the truth?" he asks.

"Yes."

"Did someone else hit you? Did someone hurt you?"

"No, Quinn. Nobody's ever done anything to me. I've been wrapped and swaddled and protected like fine china my entire life."

"Then why do you have nightmares and freak out when someone touches you?"

I watch Penney pry open a cabinet door and slither inside. "I have no idea."

"Should you check into it?"

"Probably," I answer. "I made breakfast."

The look on his face. He wants to leave. I can feel it from the tippy top of my head down to my freezing cold toes.

"You don't have to stay, Quinn."

"It's not that," he says.

"Then what is it?"

"I have a flight to catch at one-forty out of Sarasota." He shuffles his feet. "Business trip."

I nod. "Business, huh? Some medical thing, right?"

He crosses his arms. Body language is such a drag. "I sell practice management software."

"Right. I don't really know what that means."

"We've talked about it before. I'm the closer. The guy who convinces hospital boards that our product can save time and maximize profits." He stops short. "You get the idea."

"Right. Sales. Didn't I call you slimy a couple of years ago?"

He smiles. This time it's more genuine. "You did. And it was hurtful."

"That's fair. You gotta go sell slimy things."

He bites his lower lip. "I'm going to hug you now, and you're not going to freak out or try to kill me with your plastic spatula. And then I'm going to fly to Seattle, then Austin, then home."

I nod.

He continues. "I'll text you while I'm away, and you're going to text me back."

I try to look cheery, but my face isn't working. My cheeks feel hollow, my lips are numb.

He wraps his arms around me, but the motion seems empty. More duty than desire.

"Will you talk to someone about the dreams?" he asks, pulling away. "You said you were seeing a therapist."

"Sure."

"Good." He grabs a slice of bacon and walks out the door.

"See ya," I mumble to a now empty house. "But probably not."

CHAPTER 37
MY PERSON

Pancakes are stacked high on a dish. Bacon, eggs, all cooked up and ready to serve. A twinge in my gut reminds me of what might have been the last night I ever spend with Quinn, from the sex to the way he folds his hand around mine when he sleeps. I shake it off because attachment, for me, leads to breaking, and breaking leads to hurting. This is how it works. I'm into someone. I ruin it. So predictable, my fucked-up fairytale.

I pour espresso into a coffee cup, top it off with whipped cream, and contemplate my day. Another one of those Sundays where I'll read a paper, clean, and gaze into the void that is my life. Perhaps I should preemptively smell the non-existent tomato soup.

Penney licks her chops, stretches, then darts into the bedroom. She's perpetually playful, hungry, or sleepy. Why can't I be more like her? Why can't we all? I replay my grandmother's audio message and wonder why she never spoke to her sister about sitting in front of the piano while the world went to hell around her. Was it fear, shock, avoidance, or a stubborn young woman unwilling to let a world war alter her afternoon plans?

A car pulls into the driveway as I forward Nori's audio clip to Ethan.

"Quinn?" Did he change his mind? Miss his flight?

I open the door and watch Jesse emerge from the driver's seat.

She puts her hands on her waist. "Hey Kiss, remember last Christmas when I brought you a gift?"

"Yeah," I say. Who could forget that day? It's when she showed up with Ethan.

Her shoulders rise and fall. Her expression, seldom seen, is tension. "I got another one for you."

"Another gif…" I begin, but the end of the word sputters out. "Oh no."

• • • • •

In college, he told everyone he was 6´3. In my eyes, he was lean, clumsy. The boy who'd grown a foot taller over summer break and hadn't yet found his center of gravity. His pale, baby-face and pretty blue eyes gave him cover for the many hazards he posed.

Nickety-Nick. He swings the passenger door closed and smiles. The baby-face is gone, and the boy is a man.

I press my lips together and stare at Jesse for help. She returns my stare with an, *I don't know what to tell you,* shrug.

He hugs me, rests his chin on my head, and the last five years dissolve. This feels exactly the way I remember. The safe space close to his chest, the scent of him, and those words he's said a thousand times before. "What's going on, Sweet Katy?"

It's an out-of-body experience. He asks questions. In a haze, I respond. Jesse says something about driving by the night before. I stare at her stupidly.

"Nice place." He squeezes my arm and walks into the house.

"Uh-huh," is my stellar response.

While he uses the bathroom, Jesse tells me he was the person who showed up at Mom's house Saturday while we were having lunch.

"Why didn't you tell me?"

"You were having it out with your mother. The doorbell rang. That was Nick. He didn't know where you lived, but he remembered your parents' place."

"You said it was a pizza delivery person."

Her eyes bulge. "Obviously, it wasn't, and then we drove by last night, but Quinn's car was still here. I played it off and told him it was your mom's car."

"Oh, shit."

"Jesus, woman. You look like someone punched you in the gonads. Get your act together."

"I don't have any…" I trail off. If anyone could convince me that I do, in fact, have gonads, it would be Jessica Tanner.

"You know all your sheets are on the floor?" Nick asks, returning to the kitchen. He grins. "Must have had a busy night."

Jesse snorts while he pops a room temperature strip of bacon into his mouth. "Sorry about not giving you a better heads-up about coming to town. Business is booming. Gotta go with the flow."

I smile. "Go with the flow. Uh-huh."

He says more words. Jesse does too. Is this a dream? I slide my finger across the counter, hold my hand over the burner, still warm, and one more test, poke a hole into a pancake. They all seem real.

I smile again, the way I did in my stoner days in high school. My face over here, on the front of my head, and my lips, mouth, and tongue, detached from my physical body, floating in the ether, making grunting noises I hoped would convince others of my coherence. I hear Jesse's voice. They're arguing.

"It's a crap idea," she says.

"What?" I ask. "What are we talking about?"

Nick grabs my hands and pulls me toward the front door. "It's a great idea. Let's do it, Katy. Let's take the boat out."

CHAPTER 38
BOAT WHISPERER

My brain recalibrates over the next hour while we gather supplies. Sunscreen, towels, drinks, snacks, a baseball cap for Nick. At my parent's house—Mom's house, we pull into the driveway and unload our boating gear. It's April. The weather is perfect, eighty-four degrees according to my phone, breezy, sunny with white billowy clouds moving slowly to the east. A lovely day to take *Happily* out for the first time since the day. The bad day.

Mom's car is gone, which is strange only because it's different. Most Sundays, she'd be home with Dad, or we'd all be out on the water. Now, she's widowed and acting like an entirely different mother than the one I grew up with. I stop for a moment and glance at my dad's old Volvo. My throat tightens as I wish for an hour of our old life back. One hour to run inside and see them both sitting at the table, having ham and green pepper sandwiches with iced coffee. Funny how the mundane scenes tie themselves around my neck. Normal days when nothing unusual happened are the most comforting. And the most suffocating.

"Kiss!" Jesse interrupts my sad-sack reverie. "Let's hit it. The sooner we get this over with, the better."

Nick, familiar with the house, walks past her into the backyard. "Still don't like sailing, huh?"

"Not a fan," she says, trailing behind him. "Where's your mom, Katy?"

"I have no clue. She must be out having her new life."

On the canal, I pull the boat close to the dock and help Jesse onboard. She calls me a water monkey and drops down on the bench seat. Nick follows and I hop on last.

"Does the toilet work on this thing?" Jesse asks as I slide open the cabin door.

"It works, but then I'd have to clean it. Go use the one in the house."

"I'll pee in the ocean." She winks at me and pops open a beer. "You don't need me to do anything, do you?"

"Like you ever do," Nick says, bringing the last of our bags onto the boat. "How's the motor?"

I unwrap the bindings from the mast and mainsail. "Engine's good. Had it serviced a couple weeks ago. Think we're ready. Want to start her up?" I step onto the dock, pull the ropes away from the bumpers and pilings, then give the nose a push. *Happily* rotates, and I jump back onboard.

"Have you ever fallen in?" Jesse asks me.

"You've asked me that a hundred times."

"I don't recall," she mumbles.

I grab the throttle and adjust the speed to putter down the long canal, then make two turns to the right, dodging the boaters who can't follow directions. "You ready?" I glance at Nick and kill the engine.

"Always." He grabs the rudder.

"Cool beans." I climb up to the deck, unbind the sail, tell Jesse to watch her head, and begin pulling.

"Why can't I just sit here?" she sasses me. "What the hell am I watching for?"

"The boom cracking your skull open."

Nick rotates the outboard motor up out of the water and cranks the winch to tighten the lines. "You always ask the exact same questions: What's the deal with the boom? Has Katy ever fallen in?" He looks at me. "I think it's some mantra she thinks will keep her safe."

Jesse raises her eyebrows, annoyed, but doesn't deny what Nick is suggesting.

The boat sits dead in the drink. Wind teases the sail. It flutters and plays hard-to-get until an insistent gust has its way with it. It puffs out, waves slap the bow, and we're in business. I remain standing for a few minutes, staring into the deep blue of the horizon, again thinking of Dad. I'm not going to cry. I'm not going to...but I'm still so pissed he went away.

One more time, Jesse's voice pulls me back to reality. "Beer?" she asks as I sit down and take the rudder from Nick.

"No thanks. Just water. I don't drink and drive."

Nick laughs and touches my knee. "Lightweight."

I try not to react. Did he touch me on purpose? Has he touched Jesse's knee? I look at his silly crooked grin. So innocent. I think it might kill me.

Jesse tugs on her ball cap. "Has Nick told you about his big job?"

"Kind of." I wave to a woman skimming past us on a windsurfer. "Something about banks?"

Nick leans forward and turns his pale face to the sun. "Not going to lie. I'm kind of a big shot."

Jesse pulls open a bag of barbecue chips. "In your own head."

"If only. I'm the money man. The mover and shaker."

"Of Monopoly money?" She licks her fingers.

"Yeah, sure," he says, rolling his eyes at me.

They begin again with the good-natured ribbing. Sort of good-natured. I focus on the bubbling sound of the whitecaps rushing by and pull the line tighter. *Happily* acknowledges my instructions, leans to the port side and speeds up.

The quiet settles in. Not the silent type of quiet, because motorboats pulling wakeboarders are blasting by, and the sound of their passengers carry along the wind. But the other type of quiet. The type that calms the mind, the nerves. Nick and Jesse stop arguing. Maybe they sense it too. We slice through the water, moving down the coast. Salty sea spray cools our skin, and my ears fill with delicious bubbling white noise.

Jesse, sitting on the opposite bench, stares over my shoulder. Or at me. I can't tell what's going on behind those oversized sunglasses. Her right foot taps. Her fingers fidget with her beer bottle, and her facial expression is parked in neutral. No expression, lawyer mode. What the hell is she thinking?

Nick has his back to me, studying whatever is ahead of us. His left hand is out over the water, catching the tops of the waves as they glide by.

I sneeze. He turns around, winks, says, "gesundheit!" Oh, dear God. What am I doing? What about Quinn? I am not that girl. I don't "do" people the way Jesse does. I don't bounce from bed to bed. This is so confusing.

"How do you turn this tub around?" Jesse asks.

"You want to go home already?"

She slams her hand over her mouth, jumps up, and leans over the railing. A stream of undigested food pours out of her, lands in the water, and floats away. Not fast enough.

"Holy shit!" Nick covers his eyes. "I did not need to see that."

I swallow hard. I didn't either. My stomach turns over as I check the surrounding traffic. "Time to go home. I'm going to slow down. Watch your head because the boom's coming over."

"Again?" She wipes her hand across her lips and slides down on the seat.

"Lines?" Nick asks.

"Yup." I say as he brushes past me and puts his hand on the small of my back. Just like old times. Subtle signals, unspoken, a tremor.

We turn into the wind. *Happily* slows and bobs in the water. The boom swings over our heads. "Come on, baby," I whisper. "Let's dance." The sail flutters, rebuffing the breeze. Nick again cranks the winch, and I hold my breath. "Come on," I coax. She hears me, because we've got it like that, and after a few seconds, we begin moving forward.

Jesse sucks on ice cubes. "Boats stink. If we belonged in the ocean, God would have given us gills."

I hold the rudder tight and turn toward the shore. A yacht blows by us. *Happily* pitches from side to side in its wake. The movement doesn't help, and now I'm green around those gills God didn't give us. We head home while Nick regales us with a sermon about the banking system and mansplains the meaning of a democratic republic and the U.S. Monetary Fund. Jesse looks a lot like she wants to toss him into the ocean and feed him to the fishes. Before dropping the sail, it occurs to me the strongest feeling I'm having right now isn't excitement about Nickety-Nick being back in town. What I'm experiencing right now is guilt, and a very real need to puke.

CHAPTER 39
LITTLE PLACES

It's funny how greasy food is the best antidote for a sour stomach. After a lunch of burgers and fries, our outlook is much improved. We secure a ten-by-ten space at the beach, with the cooler, bags of snacks, and bottles of sunscreen placed strategically to hold the four corners of our oversized beach towels down. Jesse slathers herself with lotion and falls asleep with a beer in her right hand, and her discarded shirt covering her face.

"What should we do, Sweet Katy?" Nick gingerly pokes Jesse's arm. She doesn't move, though it would be no surprise if she were to pop up like a Jack-in-the-box and slam his head into the ground.

"About what?" I ask.

"About things," he says. "You and me."

I slurp orange juice. *You and me.* Nick and me. I've dreamed of this moment, and fully expect fat pink hearts to float out of my eyeballs.

He jumps to his feet. "Gonna take a dip. Don't go anywhere."

"Okay," I tell him, shielding my face from the sunshine. I sigh and wonder if I've been overcomplicating my life for no reason. What if fate is real? Could all the organic gibberish Dr. Jonas talked about be true? Was it my destiny to live through a horrible marriage in order to recognize a good one? I hum "Stay with Me", by Sam Smith, grab a bottle of sunscreen and drizzle it on my arms.

"Stop it, Kiss. You're tone deaf."

I look down at Jesse. "I thought you were asleep. Did you hear what he said?"

She pulls the shirt off her cheeks. "Indeed, I did."

"What do you think?"

"You know how I feel. And what about the guy you spent last night with?"

"You're such a buzzkill, Jessica. Quinn got pissed at me this morning and left. I'll probably never hear from him again."

She sits up. "Pissed about what?"

"Nothing. It's stupid."

"You're stupid. Tell me why he got angry."

"He said I was thrashing around in bed, so he tried to wake me up."

"And?"

"And I might have hit him in the face by accident."

"Holy shit. What's going on with you? First you get scared of me and now you're hitting people?"

"It's those dreams I've been having."

"You told me you dreamed about Russ and Cricket. There's more?"

"Yeah, they've gotten worse. Quinn said I should get help. I probably freaked him out." I pick my cell phone up. "Doesn't matter, he won't be calling me again." I look at the screen and let out a sigh.

"What?" she asks.

I turn it toward her. Two texts from Quinn and three from Cricket, who's confused about the restaurant's new hours. Each of her texts begins with, "Mrs. Katy."

"So much for never hearing from him," Jesse says.

"Hear from who?" Nick asks, dripping on our towels. "Let's put some music on. Katy, go through your playlist and pick the song you think I'd like the best."

"Self-involved much?" Jesse asks, lying back down. "Why can't Katy pick out something she wants to listen to?"

He lets out an uncomfortable snort. "Still a bitch, after all this time."

She smiles and holds up both hands, both middle fingers.

"You guys are idiots," I say, standing up. "Let's go for a walk."

• • • • •

Nick and I head down the beach, our feet sinking into the slurping wet sand as the tide rolls in. The seagulls fly over our heads. They fight over popcorn and remnants of sandwiches.

"Sometimes I miss it here." He adjusts his sunglasses. "It's been a long time."

"Not much has changed in town."

He glances at me. "Doesn't seem like you have either."

I move away from him and let a group of older women power walk between us. I'm not in the mood to recite my resume of growth. A marriage, a divorce, the death of a parent. I'm an open book. Okay, I'm the opposite of an open book. Why would I divulge the evolution of my personal journey?

"What are you thinking, Katy?"

"Nothing. Have you changed?"

"Absolutely," he says. "I was unserious in college. Wasteful of my time. Bumping into the next thing without purpose. Now I have a mission. A clear plan."

"Which is what?"

"That's where it gets complicated." He stops, bends over, and picks up a small pearlescent shell. "I already have some of it.

The career is going well." He hands me the shell. "I'm upwardly mobile, as my dad says."

"Are you now?" I rub the jagged edges and drop it discreetly back on the sand. Upward and mobile? Unlike me, locked into my family's business. Living the life of no rock star ever.

"Yeah," he continues. "I hate to say it, but I'm pretty much loaded."

I glance at him. "Don't think you hate saying that. And you've always been loaded, Nick. Your parents are doctors."

He leans toward me. "I need more. My own money and influence. To be the puller of the strings."

I stop in my tracks. "Where do the complications come into play? You want money and power? Seems like you're on your way."

He continues walking and talking. His voice grows fainter the further he moves ahead of me. He's twenty feet away before he notices I'm not next to him.

"What are you doing there?" He stretches his arm out to me.

I shake my head and catch up to him. "Life is more than that."

"Is it?" He wraps his hand around mine. His skin is sweaty. Grains of sand rub against my palm. "Because I don't think so. Big things flow from the top. Make it there and all the rest falls into place."

"Hm," I mutter.

We continue our stroll, quietly now, both lost in our thoughts. In college, Nick was often in debate mode. He and Jesse sparred about all the usual things and then some. Why do we exist? Should future employment depend on past drug usage? Should men raise babies? Should women put up with men? I would chime in occasionally when I didn't feel outwitted. Mostly, I tried to keep the peace, or rather, keep Nick from getting angry and going away. I step over a clump of seaweed and wonder how much I gave up by giving in. By not arguing or being afraid to make waves.

He swings me around, and we head back. "What do you want from life?" he asks.

"What do I want?" I repeat the question, needing time to find an appropriate response. Isn't the thing I want, the thing I've dreamt of—a wedding ring from Nickety-Nick? Babies, everlasting devotion, straight hair, a lifetime supply of chocolate.

"I'd like to be happy," I say instead.

"Happily, like your grandma said?" He squeezes my hand. "What'll it take?"

We circle around a toddler digging in the sand. He's slathered in sunscreen, sweat, and the determined expression of a child fully immersed in his adventure.

"Not sure, exactly." I smile at the little boy. "But I'm working on it."

"Working on it in Duff Beach?"

"Yeah, of course. I love this town. I've been here my whole life."

"You think you can do anything worthwhile in a place like this?" He drops my hand. "Seriously?"

I wiggle my fingers, so abruptly abandoned. Did I do something wrong? He quickens his pace. I hurry to keep up.

Jesse is standing on the towels when we return. "How was the walk, kids?"

"Excellent." He pulls a beer out of the cooler. "If you believe great things come from little places."

CHAPTER 40
BUCKET

Sunday night ends quietly, awkwardly. Nick insists on staying at Jesse's for the evening. He has business calls to make, he's jetlagged, and has a touch of sunstroke. Evidently, the sun still shines at full power in tiny, irrelevant Dufferin Beach.

Penney is in a mood, hiding, and tearing up the furniture. Quinn texts again, but I find no relief in his messages. I hope, in a way I can't fully admit, much less say out loud, that I'd like his words to be spectacular, full of color and promise and emotion. A reason to be dragged over to his side. Team Quinn. But all I get is: *Landed - cold here. Getting fish from the place where they throw them. Toss Me! lol.*

I reply. *Stay warm.*

Mom texts at ten. She tells me she's had a good day with her friends. By the way, was I at the house? The neighbor, Mrs. Nosy-as-Fuck, (Dad coined this name) reported on me taking the boat out with strangers. Additionally, Mrs. NAF asked where Dylan was these days, and who was this other young man joining her harlot of a daughter on the boat.

I switch my phone to silent mode. Shut up, Mrs. Nosy-as-Fuck. Stay out of my life. I climb into bed with a pad of paper and do the homework Dr. Jonas assigned, jotting down as much as I can remember about the dreams. I need to be ready in the morning for my appointment. Maybe writing the words out will help, because I would very much like to be rid of the Elevator Man.

But he doesn't want to be rid of me. He's back, all night, in flashes, moving in and out of the shadows. He asks if I'm cold, juggles an assortment of headless, squirming fish and shrieks at me to catch them, which of course I can't. A new fish appears magically every time I miss, silvery scales glimmering inexplicably in the darkness.

"Hold it!" he yells.

I shake violently. "I'm trying!"

"There is no try!" his voice booms. "Try fell, Katy. It fell in a bucket."

"What?" I ask before jolting myself awake.

CHAPTER 41
A POOL IS A KIDNEY

Monday morning, Dr. Jonas settles into her chair of judgment and studies my face. "You look tired. Are you okay?"

"Not so much. I'm exhausted." My body hurts, and my head feels like a bag of rocks. I offer her the paper filled with scribbles about my nightmares. "Can you read any of it?"

She turns it upside down. "Um."

"You had it right the first time."

She rotates it again, bringing it closer to her face. "You have them numbered. Good." Her lips move as she silently reads.

"Would it be bad if I took a nap while you do that?" I slide down on the couch. "Is that wrong?"

She looks up, brows furrowed. "Well…no, it's not wrong. Go ahead while I get through the rest of these."

"Okay," I say, trying to keep my eyes open. Nonsensical thoughts flutter through my mind. Who sleeps in their shrink's office? The couch is scratchy and stupid. This is all ridiculous. Circles should always be round, like bowls, or hula hoops and pools. But a pool is a kidney. No, a pool is a pool, shaped like a kidney, like the one Eudora Jonas is about to steal from me.

But she's not. Instead, she stands up, pulls a key from her pocket, and locks the file cabinet. That's all I remember.

• • • • •

"Katy?"

I blink. "Huh?"

"It's okay," my shrink lady whispers. "You fell asleep for a few hours."

"Hours?" I ask, pushing myself upright. "What time is it?" I grab my phone. Ten after two. "Four hours? What about your other clients? Oh, God. I'm really sorry."

"We have extra office space." She smiles. "I made use of it."

I rub my face. "I'm sorry. I don't know what's going on."

"Well." She holds up my crinkled papers. "Something is, so let's talk about it."

"Now?" I glance at my phone again. One missed call, and several texts from Jesse and Russ. Another one from Cricket. *Dear Mrs. Katy...*

"Is there someplace you need to be?" she asks.

"I guess not. The Point is closed today, but I've been here for hours."

"It's a first, I'll admit. But..." She again looks at my list of psycho dreams. "I'm concerned."

"Why?"

"Because what you wrote here is frightening enough to keep you from sleeping at night."

"No, it's not."

She gives me the death stare. "You passed out in your therapist's office."

I take a swig from my water bottle. "That's fair."

"Are you alert enough to talk about it?"

I push my bangs away from my face. "Uh-huh."

"Great. Let's go chronologically. The first dream."

"The one when I was at work." I try to remember the day, sending Russ home to check on Penney. "He wasn't in it yet. The elevator dude. I wasn't asleep for more than ten minutes."

"What stands out the most?"

"Just what it says there. I felt cold and scared and alone. Not alone in the room, but like, nothingness alone—cosmically alone. That sounds crazy, right?"

"It sounds like a bad dream. And nothingness," she repeats, making notes on her iPad.

"Yeah. I mean, nothing around me. No walls or floors or ceiling and I got scared it wasn't temporary, but forever. Deeply forever. Does that make any sense?"

"It does. Do you have a tendency toward nightmares? I recall you had some unpleasant dreams when your father passed."

My jaw clenches. I hate this gently avoidant terminology. He passed alright, right out of existence. "Those were sad, or like I was grieving. They weren't frightening."

She studies the paper, then looks at me. "I'm trying to figure out if something could be triggering them. You had the argument with your mom in Paris, then the panic attack. It's something we should consider, though I wonder what else is going on. Is anything bothering you that we haven't spoken about?"

"Everything bothers me," I tell her. "The world, shitty drivers. I get pissed-off if someone doesn't use their turn signal. And the fight with my mom wasn't great. I mean it was ugly, but we've fought before. This is different."

"Talk about that," she prompts.

"Um, I guess these feel threatening. Can that be right? Could I be afraid of something?"

She nods. "Let's backtrack. Did anything else happen in Paris? You said you walked around a lot. Were you alone? Did anyone frighten you?"

"I was around people, tourists. I know the places to avoid. Other than the argument with Mom, nothing kept me up at night. My Aunt's situation is sad, you know, her dementia, but I'd be lying if I said I spent all day thinking about it."

"Have you ever lived alone before?"

"Nope. I went from my parents' house to college, back to Mom and Dad's, and then Dylan."

"Does being alone in the house bother you?"

"I didn't think so. I mean, I lock all the doors and windows at night, and I put the alarm on, but let's face it, Duff Beach isn't exactly a war zone."

"Okay." She checks her watch. "Actually, I've got something in Naples at four. Do you have time for another appointment this Wednesday?"

"You want me to have two appointments in one week?" I shove my phone into my bag. "Isn't that kind of thing reserved for serious stuff?"

"Yes," she says. Her posture softens. Her back curves, as if she's making herself smaller, apologizing for the bad news.

"For real?"

"Yes," she insists. "There's something here, and sleep deprivation can be dangerous. I don't need you cutting a digit off before you begin taking it seriously."

CHAPTER 42
THIS IS WHAT I WAS WAITING FOR?

Never have I ever had a conversation where the term digit was used in a non-sarcastic way. This thought consumes me until it crashes into another. I haven't been to work for over a week, and all the time off feels bad. Feels idle. If I had a husband or a family, let's face it, if I had a life, the break would be coveted.

A third thought intrudes. Will I see Nick today?

Penney is waiting by the door when I return from Dr. Jonas' office. She rolls on the ground, and I swear, peeks to see if I'm watching.

"Are you apologizing for tearing the carpet to shreds?"

She squeaks.

"I'm going to the shrink again on Wednesday. Guess I'm bat-shit crazy."

This gets no response. The cat is not interested in my mental health. The phone rings, my stomach grumbles. I push the speaker button and begin assembling a Katy-Sandwich.

"Hi sweet girl. Should we take two?"

"Hi Nick." I smile and pop a slice of rye bread into the toaster. "What does *take two* mean?"

"You know, have a second convo. I was tired last night. The sun got to me."

I wrestle open a package of bologna and unwrap a block of cream cheese. "Convo?" I check myself. This is the man I've pined for. I swallow a mouthful of sarcasm. "What are you up to?"

"Nothing," he says. "Got all evening. I'm all yours."

"Where's Jess?"

"Working late."

"Oh," I say. "We could go to Jimmy's."

"I'm in," he says. "What's all the noise?"

"Vacuum sealed meat product and assorted utensils."

"What are you making? Would I like it?"

"I'm making a Katy-Sandwich. You had them when we were in school."

"Did I? I don't recall. Come get me. I'm ready now."

I cram a slice of bologna into my mouth and promise to pick him up as soon as possible.

• • • • •

As soon as possible turns into forty-five minutes. Ten of those go to answering texts. Ethan asking about our grandmother's audio message, Quinn asking how I'd slept, and Nori telling me she's recorded another session and would be sending it by the end of the day. And Cricket, oh Cricket.

Mrs. Katy, is the reason we're not working again today due to a financial concern? Mom says maybe the restaurant is in dire straits. I asked her to explain where the dire straits are, but she said to ask you. That's all for now. This is Cricket Calliope Punch, in case you didn't know.

I spend another fifteen minutes staring at my reflection in the mirror, applying makeup, wiping it off, and being confused about what to put on first, moisturizer or primer. What is primer, anyway? Isn't it something you spray on a car before you paint it? Cosmetics are not for people like me, who look the same in the before and after picture.

It's almost five-thirty when Nick and I roll into the gravel parking lot of Birdies by The Beach. A bar run by three generations of the Dalton family. Generations of men resembling Popeye, with heavily muscled upper bodies, and skinny long legs miraculously holding them upright. I feel a sense of déjà vu dropping my sandals by the front steps and walking past the *indoor people* who crowd around the bar and pool table. We head out to the deck facing the Gulf of Mexico. How many times did the two of us do this in college? Walking out here together when we were still fresh and new and stupid.

"This must be what he renovated." I say, taking in the refurbished wood planks under our feet, and the new furniture. White rattan chairs with colorful cushions, low teakwood tables, and a fresh coat of paint on the thick columns and wooden overhang. "It's great, but it doesn't feel like the same old beat-up beach bar."

"I was here the other day with Jesse," Nick says.

"Saturday? How was it?"

He grins. "She's interesting company."

"She's a bit more than that."

He waves down a server. "Yeah, of course. She's Jesse, full of spit and hell fire."

"I guess," I say, gazing at the outgoing tide. The movement of the water leaves ripples in the sand, miniature mountain ranges littered with shells and seaweed. I inhale the briny air. "She saved my life pretty much."

"Heard all about it."

We order drinks. A Greyhound for me, a beer for Nick. We're offered the choice of fried sweet potatoes, fried pickles, or fried calamari. He orders calamari on my behalf, then taps my foot with his and smiles, a little crooked, with a twinkle in his eye that lights me up. I am, in this moment in time, hovering happily, a moth to his flame. The center of his universe. My eyes sting with emotion. Is this man my future? My middle age, old age, my end? Father of my fat Hungarian children? The tiniest knot forms in my stomach.

"Why did you marry that loser, Dylan?" he asks after several minutes of soaking up sunshine.

The light dims, the moth implodes. "I dunno. It's complicated."

His eyebrows rise then lower as he stares at me…studies me. A seagull lands on the deck railing, wings outstretched, searching for a meal.

"I've got time," he says, swatting at the bird.

I grit my teeth, trying to summon a tactful response. "I needed to get away from my parents. You remember how controlling they were? Always breathing down my neck."

He waits to answer while our order is delivered. "I didn't see them that way."

"Because they weren't your parents."

He picks up his beer and wipes the condensation off the side. "You got married to get your parents off your ass? That's it?"

The Greyhound calls to me. Freshly squeezed grapefruit juice, ice, vodka. I take one sip, then another. "I was lonely."

He helps himself to the calamari, then offers it to me.

"No thanks. I don't eat tentacles."

"Since when?"

"Since ever," I say. He knows this about me, or I thought he did.

He shrugs. I drink a little more. The seagull watches us. Its white feathers flutter in the breeze.

"Okay," he continues. "Loneliness and parents. Guess the pickings are limited in a place like this."

"You didn't mind Duff Beach when you lived here. I chose the wrong guy. It didn't work out."

Jimmy seats a group of college kids near us. He turns to me, drops his head and smiles before heading inside.

"That dude is weird as ever," Nick says, watching the commotion.

"Jimmy? He's not weird. He's sweet."

"He's dumb as hell."

"No, he isn't," I say, taking another swig of pulp and juice and vodka.

"No? Why don't you marry him next?"

"What the hell, Nick?"

"You look shocked," he says, looking sort of shocked himself. "It's a fair question, and I mean, where are your standards if you hook up with a dude like Dylan and think Jimmy is a genius?"

I search for an answer at the bottom of my glass. Wish I would have finished making my Katy-Sandwich instead of downing a mouthful of flat pink lunch meat.

"Sorry." He stands up. "I'll grab some more drinks."

I force a smile as he walks away. The alcohol is lowering the guard rails in my brain, and the intrusive thoughts begin to spill over. I do not have low standards. I was too nice, and too nice people get trampled on. It's human nature...lie flat on the ground, someone will surely walk over you.

"Deep in thought?" he asks, putting a second drink in front of me.

"Thanks," I tell him, fishing an ice cube from the glass.

He sets his beer down. "What did you learn from marriage?"

"Back off, dude. What's it to you?"

He looks aghast. There is no other word. "Katy, I..."

"What?" I interrupt. "Stop playing twenty questions with me. I made a bad decision and knew enough to remove myself from the situation. Those are my standards. I don't hang out when things go to hell."

He opens and closes his mouth.

"Furthermore, I obviously wouldn't have married Dylan if I'd known what a jerk he'd turn out to be. He was nice while we were dating, you know, normal. It's not like I was on a mission to find the most fucked-up person in southwest Florida."

"Okay," he says, holding his hands up in defeat. "I get it."

"Good, I'm glad." I take an extra-large gulp of my delicious drink. "I hope I've satisfied your curiosity."

"I'm digging the fight in you, girl."

"Great," I respond, partially relieved to have said something he approves of. To pass a Nick-test. Another part of me wants to walk out. To cement the lessons I've learned in therapy about feeling worthy. I am a whole human with a mind and feelings and opinions. I am not less than.

He continues. "You were a pushover in college." He dips a twisted piece of calamari into red sauce. "I probably took advantage of it."

I grip my glass, empty half the contents, and crush ice between my teeth. "In what way?" I ask, though I know all the ways. His ups and downs were driven by pot or beer. He was my angel and devil packaged together, and now I wonder which one I was most attracted to.

"I made promises I couldn't deliver, and you..." he stops talking, chews. Fried batter crumbs stick to his lips. "You were receptive. Bright-eyed and bushy-tailed."

"Yup," I say under my breath, remembering those days all too well. Days of mood swings controlled by someone else. By Nick. And here I am again.

"Those promises weren't empty," he adds. "They were premature."

My heart thumps while my emotions duck my intellect—all the wisdom Dr. Jonas has imbued upon me. His words float in the humid air, time distorts.

He moves closer and grabs my hands. "I have a plan, and you're part of it."

• • • • •

Time returned to its proper speed when he kissed me. But I hadn't eaten all day, except for the pink slice of bologna and one point five cocktails. And his breath smelled like marinara sauce, garlic, beer, and a deep fryer. So yeah, I threw up on his sandals, his pale legs, toes, ankles. Even his cargo shorts got splattered.

CHAPTER 43
IF NOT FOR

By seven-thirty Monday night I'm home, alone, and tucked into my bed answering Jesse's texts.

Would have paid to see you puke on Nick.
Not funny, Jess. Definitely my bad.
He's still in the shower.
That's probably good. Gotta go. Ethan's calling me.

I take a breath to wallow in the shame of the most romantic moment of my life turning into juicy Duff Beach gossip. Katy Kiss vomiting on some dude at Birdies.

"Hey Ethan."

"Hey kiddo. Nori sent another audio file. Want to listen together?"

"She did?" I sit up and move my plate to the nightstand. I'm on my first toast topped with butter and apricot jam.

"About an hour ago, but I just got into the hotel."

"Where are you?" I ask, scrolling through my phone.

"Teterboro."

"Where's that?"

"New Jersey, right outside Manhattan."

"Never heard of it." I open Nori's email and click on the audio file.

Ethan pulls the tab off something, a beer or a pop. "Better than flying into Newark or JFK or LaGuardia. You ready?"

"Yup," I say, and we listen together to our grandmother's second installation of horrible, terrifying war stories.

Nori: *Hey guys, it's me. Here we go. Okay, Grandma, we're ready.*

I take another bite of burned toast, and sip watered-down apple juice, which I usually drink straight, but tonight felt overly sweet on my tongue.

Grandma: *I talking now?*

Nori: *Into my phone.*

Grandma: *Okay. Hello Ee-ten and Katika. Today, I like to speaking of when we leave the ghetto. You remembering how my father is in the working camp. In 1944, when Nazi come to Hungary, they also taking our things. Taking...stealing. The furnitures, the painting...the piano, jewelry, monies. Very disgusting. They having no shame. They take all, and then moving us to ghetto like we nothing. Like we not humans.*

Nori: *God, Grandma, I can't even imagine. How old were you?*

Grandma: Tizenkettő.

Nori: *Twelve.*

I text Ethan an eye-rolling emoji about her need to translate for us.

Grandma: *But we together. My mother, grandmother and grandfather, my sister Eva, of course. After some time, they tell us now time to leave ghetto too, so we walk, all the Jewish prisoners. We walk in the streets, across the bridge. We don't know where we go next. I remembering so much of how the other peoples watching us. The free peoples.*

Nori: *You mean the people who weren't Jewish watched you march through the streets?*

Grandma: *Yes. Some of them looking very sad. Others...not so sad. This I see in my minds still and it make me angry now even. They smiling, you know, not nice smiling, but the bad. The smile that meaning hate. They looking at us like we...what the word? Mintha megérdemeltük volna.*

Nori: *Like you deserved it?*

Grandma: *Igen. Like this. I remembering how ashaming I feeling. Is this right word? For the older peoples to looking at us, even the young childrens this way. I can never forgiving this, even for now.*

Nori: *Fucking jerks. How long did you walk?*

Grandma: *Nori, not for you to using this languages.*

Nori: *Sorry Grandma.*

Grandma: *Okay. I know maybe this...I say in French, difficile, to hearing. We walk for many of the hours.*

Nori: *Where did you walk to?*

Grandma: *To brick factory.*

Nori: *Why a brick factory? Why did they take you there? I mean, where did you sleep?*

Grandma: *We sleeping on floor. They letting us childrens play outside. We are there only for two of the weeks. Then one of the mornings, they telling us train is coming. We have to pack. To getting ready.*

Nori: *What does that mean? Ready for what?*

I gulp apple juice. Ethan is silent, processing the information in a hotel room a thousand miles north of me.

Grandma: *I remembering mother packing my suitcase. The soldiers telling us how I going with my grandparents on early train. You know, at this time, we not understanding what this meaning. But I remembering the Rabbi's son has...how you say, he liking my sister Eva very much.*

Nori: *He had a crush on her?*

Grandma: *Yes. The son, oh so in love with her. He come to mother and is saying do not letting anyones getting on this early trains. Not anyones! Waiting until the end of the day and going to the last train together only.*

Nori: *Hold on. The soldiers were trying to send you and your grandparents on a separate train from your mom and sister?*
Grandma: *Yes.*
Nori: *Why would they do that?*

The audio is silent for almost thirty seconds. Long enough for me to stare at the phone and make sure it didn't get cut off.

Grandma: *The old and very young, you know, they go to Auschwitz. This where they trying to sending us. But Mother does not allowing this, she keeping us quiet and out of way. We stay together until the last train coming.*
Nori: *Are you kidding? Oh my God!*

"Oh my God," I repeat, just like Nori. My head swims. I close my eyes and pull my knees to my chest. Breathe in, breathe out. This is it? This is how much control we have? A pretty girl catches the eye of one person and poof, their entire future is changed? If not for my aunt's beauty…what if she'd been plain, or not his type? "Shit," I mumble. Then none of us would exist today.

Grandma: *We are lucky. So many are not.*
Nori: *I guess, but you still got taken somewhere, right?*
Grandma: *We taking last train that evening to Austria. But this story for other time. You seeing now? We all live. Katika, please to calling me when you not busy. We talk about these questions you asking before. About why nobody telling you the things. And Ee-ten, please asking your Mami to calling me. Bye-bye for now.*
Nori: *Okay guys. I'm sorry, I feel kind of sick. I don't know how she's so strong. Come up here and we can all talk about it together. Love you Ethan, ha, I get to say that now. Love you Katy-Baba.*

The audio stops.

"You still there?" Ethan asks.

"I am."

"Gonna Facetime you."

"Yup," I say, finishing off the apple juice. It settles in my stomach like Lake Michigan. "Give me a second. I need to use the bathroom."

• • • • •

"Your hair's short!" I look at my brother on the screen.

"Yeah." He runs his fingers through his abbreviated curls, cut down in their prime. "It was getting too long and the powers that be weren't happy."

"Can you tell the powers to jam it?"

"Only if I'm willing to give up flying." He smiles. "That was intense. I've heard a few stories here and there, but nothing firsthand."

"Changes the perspective, doesn't it? Have you seen those documentaries showing the concentration camps filled with people in those goddamn striped jumpsuits, staring like skeletons? Jesus, Ethan, they could have been our family."

"But it wasn't, Katy."

"I know, but still, doesn't it freak you out to hear how easily it could have happened? Who the hell has the right to pick who exists and who doesn't?"

He smiles. "That's a really big question. I'd need about five drinks to go down that road." He takes a bite from a sub sandwich. "I wonder where they ended up in Austria."

"I don't know," I grumble. "To some place where she lived. Where she survived."

He takes another bite. "Sorry for chewing, I haven't had food since breakfast. How are you doing? How's it going with your mom?"

"Pretty good. I think she may be over-adjusting. Staying a bit too busy. She joined a writing group."

"Better than doing nothing. I didn't know she was into writing."

"She's not. Who knows what's going to come out of her."

He cracks up. Shredded lettuce falls from the sandwich as he lifts it to his mouth. "What else is going on?"

"Stuff," I say, pulling the blanket over my legs. "How are you doing? How's Denver?"

"All good. Flying a lot. Probably drinking too much. Noah and I went hiking last weekend."

"Fun," I say, tugging on Penney's tail. "Does hiking happen at the same time as drinking?"

"Sometimes. We're bad influences on each other. It's always a race to see who gets shit-faced first."

"Aren't you a little old for that?"

"Pilot," he says, as if this explains everything. "So, what's the stuff?"

"Stuff?" I repeat, trying to look mystified.

"You said stuff is going on. Then you got that expression on your face where you think I didn't notice."

I pull Penney close. "Oh, it's nothing. I got a cat."

"I know about the cat. You send me twenty pictures a day."

"Twenty? Really? Sorry."

"What's the stuff, Katy?"

I swallow. "I'm having nightmares, which makes me not want to sleep, which makes me really damn tired. I fell asleep at my shrink's office this morning."

"You mean you nodded off?"

"No. I was out for hours."

He frowns. "Are you kidding? She didn't wake you up? Is it kosher to crash on your therapist's couch?"

"I don't know, but she said she had other empty offices and seemed okay with it."

"Is that professional?"

I lean toward my nightstand and grab another piece of bread. "It's Duff Beach. The usual rules don't apply."

He nods. "Yeah, seems weird as hell. What are the nightmares about?"

"They're stupid. I'm always stuck in some small dark place, like an elevator, and this man's in there with me."

"Creepy. What kind of man? Do you know who it is?"

"I can only hear his voice. I can't see his face."

"Sounds a little messed up."

"Tell me about it. He says mean shit to me. Like he's gaslighting me. I call him the Elevator Man, by the way. He keeps telling me I'm a baby."

He shifts in his chair. "Why Elevator Man?"

"It's a long story. Dr. Jonas seems kind of worried about it. I think it's why she let me sleep."

"What else happens in the dreams?"

I take a bite of toast, sink my teeth into a layer of sweet butter and tart apricot preserves. "Do I have to tell you?"

He pops a second can open. I see now it's Dr. Pepper. "Yes, you have to tell me."

I finish chewing and swallow. "He says I have to pee."

"What?"

"I know. It's gross, and when I wake up, I run to the bathroom."

"Like he's suggesting it? What would be the point?"

"How the hell would I know, Ethan? He asks if I have to go, then tells me to hold it."

"Katy," he moves his face closer to the phone. The dark pupils in his green eyes grow. "What the hell?"

"No clue. Then I tell him I'm trying, you know, to hold it, and he gets angry and kind of threatening." I stop for a few seconds. "Not kind of, but very. Like it's creepy."

His face twists in concentration. "Do you have a bladder infection or something?"

I burst out laughing. "For the last three weeks? I think my kidneys would have shut down by now."

He grins. "It was just a thought. Does he say anything else?"

"He did last time." I wipe crumbs off the bed. "But I can't remember. Something about trying or falling maybe?"

"You're falling in the dream?"

"No. I told you. I can't remember. Something about trying is falling somewhere, but it's kind of jumbled in my brain."

He clears his throat and moves the phone away from his face.

"What's wrong?" I ask.

"Nothing. Sorry, my flight coordinator's texting me." His face comes back into view. "Passengers are changing their plans again. Can I get with you later in the week?"

"Sure. Passengers are important."

"A hundred percent, kiddo," he says, grinning. "Try to get some sleep and we'll talk in a few days."

CHAPTER 44
FALLING DOWN

There are no bad dreams on Monday night. My alarm fails to alarm me, so I don't roll out of bed until 10:45 in the morning.

I feel refreshed, starving, and late for work. Penney steals the cap from the milk bottle and plays soccer with it as I inhale a bowl of Cap'n Crunch and check my text messages. One from Quinn, asking how I slept, another from Nick, saying he's headed north for a couple of days on business. Business, my ass. He's bailing on those big plans he was about to spill. Or pop...the question. Can I blame him, though? Who'd want to make a life with someone who pukes on you?

I crouch on the kitchen floor. "Bring me the lid, biddy kitty."

She sweeps it under the couch, lies flat on her belly with her tail swishing behind her.

"Or not." I push the lidless milk back into the fridge and run out the front door.

Mom's already at The Point, dusting the butcher block with flour. She acknowledges my arrival with the smallest of nods, then returns her attention to a vat of butter and a rolling pin.

Russ winks at me and holds the door open for the delivery man, who is hauling in crates of meat and fresh veggies.

We exchange pleasantries with him, as we've done for the last two years. I think his name is Brandon. Or Brendon, or Brayden. I'd ask, but too much time has gone by, and there isn't a tactful way not to look like a jerk.

"Brendon?" I ask after he leaves.

"The young man's name is Brian," Mom says.

"It is not."

She claps her hands once. Flour shoots off like fireworks. "Yes dear, it is."

Russ drops an armful of potatoes into the sink. Melissa trudges about, shoulders sagging, looking tired and hung over. We ask her about Nashville and the bachelorette party. She says she'd prefer not to discuss it for at least another day. Or ever.

We prep for lunch, and over the next few hours, get slammed by a mob of diners complaining about the restaurant being closed for an entire week.

At three, we catch our first break. Forty minutes of calm before Cricket strolls in, looking fresh, rested, locked and loaded.

"Hello Madam Kiss." She bows to my mother, then turns to me. "I'm fully healed from the strep throat. Do you need a note from my doctor?"

"Nope," I tell her. "All good."

"Excellent," she says. "I didn't go out very often while I was ill, but I did see you and Mr. Jesse and another man at the beach Sunday at four-thirty-eight p.m."

Mom pats Cricket on her shoulder. "I believe she has brought this same man to my home."

"Quinn?" Russ leans into the conversation. The smell of his breath wafts under my nose. Coffee, garlic, mint gum.

I recoil from the stench. My hackles rise. Why must I be subjected to this trifecta of inquiring minds?

Mom moves closer, stares me down. "I do not approve of this Quinn."

"The man was holding her hand, Madam Kiss," Cricket announces. "It seemed romantic. But it wasn't Quinn. I would have recognized him because his hair and eyes are both brown."

Mom gives me the evil eye. "I see."

"Also," Cricket continues. "This other man was not as muscular. He was extremely blond, and though I couldn't make out his eye color, it felt very much like they'd be a lighter shade due to his pasty white skin. I personally did not find him to be as attractive as Quinn."

They all stare at me. Six eyeballs. The unease builds. Steam in a tea kettle. My beach day is not their business.

"So?" Mom prods, her eyes in the barely discernible squint I recognize from years of doing, saying, and hiding stupid things. Things she found distasteful or "unfortunate."

"It's not a big deal," I say, backing away from the gaggle.

They follow me, taking short steps and bumping into each other.

"Who's the dude, Katy?"

"There's no dude, Russ." I squirm. Cold dampness prickles the back of my neck. Oh no, I can't have another panic attack. I close my eyes and inhale. Why couldn't I have picked a smellier soup? Black bean, corn...

"Why is your face red, Mrs. Katy?"

I touch my cheeks, burning hot. My fingers tingle.

"Are you having the sex with all of these men?" Mom asks. "And what about poor Nicholas? What will he think when he hears there are many others? He will not want to marry a woman like this."

"Back off, Mom! You took my head off in Paris for being too single. Now I'm too," I stammer. "I can't think of the word."

"Slutty?" Cricket offers. "Like Great-Granny."

My mother wipes her palm across her forehead, leaving a trail of unbleached white flour embedded in her frown lines. Her face blurs as she reaches toward me. I duck, step backwards, and trip over a crate filled with eggs. Someone screeches my name as I tumble onto the floor. It happens in slow motion. No pain, just a flash of bright white light, the crunching sound of eggshells, their contents, cold, runny, covering my arms, and the pungent scent of bleach from the mop bucket near my shoulder.

• • • • •

Coming to from a head injury isn't the same as waking up from a dream. It's my first thought, since I keep blacking out in a nonconsensual way. Guess it's what I do now as a divorced woman who is having "the sex" with a bunch of men. My second thought, the sensation of cold. An ice pack pushing against my skull. Third, my mother's gaping expression. Round eyes, worried with a tinge of irritation.

"Do you hear me?" she asks. "Can you see me?"

"I'm fine." I flinch. "The ice pack is dripping into my ear."

"I'll get a towel, Madam Kiss."

I focus on Russ, next to me, his arm protectively around my shoulders while mom grieves the eggs.

"So many good eggs wasted," she murmurs.

Russ grabs my waist and lifts me onto an old wooden stool. "What the hell, girl?" He crouches with his hands on my knees. "I've seen you bleed, puke, light shit on fire, but I ain't never seen that look on your face, baby."

I turn from him to my mom. "What's wrong with my face?"

She bites her lip, takes the towel from Cricket, and wipes my cheeks. "You were looking afraid. Like the deer in the crossfires."

"Head lights," I correct. "And I'm not sleeping with two men."

She nods. "If you are saying so."

Cricket snorts. We tell her to find something useful to do in the dining room.

Mom suggests I go to the ER. I insist on staying at work. We compromise. I'm getting sent home early with someone to watch over me. That someone being my parental unit, which makes me wonder if the hospital might be the better choice.

CHAPTER 45
VAKE UP!

Cleanliness is subjective, and not a priority for a single person living with a kitten. Mom disagrees. I can tell from the way her nose wrinkles as she walks through my house. She's taking it all in. Her daughter's disinterest in a tidy home, the slight odor coming from the litter box, and the brightly colored cat toys strewn across the floor. She gathers them in her arms, a rainbow poof ball stuffed with catnip and four toy mice in varying shades of purple.

"Do cats see color?" she asks, scooping up the last fuzzy mouse. "Where is this animal?"

I lie down on the couch and tuck my right hand under my head for support. "She's checking you out. Give her a minute."

"It smells a bit, dear."

I close my eyes, wonder why I agreed to this, and drift off.

"Katika. Vake up!" Mom yells, wrapping a throw-blanket around me.

"I'm not asleep."

"If you have the collusion, you cannot go to sleep."

"Concussion."

"Yes, this is what I have said. Please keep your eyes open."

"Okay." I rub my toes together under the covers. She's been bundling me into blankets as long as I can remember. Always the same way, first tucking it under my legs so tight I can't move, feet last, wrapped up like a burrito. Then the squeeze, perhaps reassurance I'm still in there, and the same short story about doing this since the day I was born.

"Is it too tight?" she asks. "I did this on your first day in the hospital. You were the beautiful pink baby. And so much hair you had. The nurses put the red bow on and said you have the most hair they have ever seen."

"I know," I tell her and happily wiggle my toes. I'm an adult, right? I'll be twenty-seven in a few weeks. I doze off again.

"Katy! Vake up!"

"Still not sleeping, Mom." I flinch as Penney pounces on me, strolling from my midsection to my face for a sniff to make sure I'm the same human who left here a few hours ago. Then she backtracks to check out the new person.

"What is her name?" she asks, holding her fingers out for the cat to inspect.

"Penney."

"Nagyon édes."

"She is very sweet. And I'm not having sex with a bunch of guys. I promise."

She stares at me, then nods.

"Tell me a story, Mom."

"I cannot think of a story under demands."

"On demand."

She rolls her eyes. "Look at this." She pulls her cell phone out. "I have made the Spotifying account. I read to you my songs."

"Great, let's hear your playlist."

"These are not plays." She shakes her head. "These are musics."

"It's Spotify. Not...whatever you just said."

"Igen. Okay. Here we are going. Abba. Have you heard of this? 'The Dancing Queen'"?

"Of course. They're great."

"The Rolling Stones. 'Angie'"?

"Very groovy, Mother."

She snorts. "Von Morrison and his "Moondance". Bobby Die-lawn. I like him very much."

"Who is that? Let me see your phone."

"Why?" she asks.

"Because I've never heard of anyone named Bobby Die-lawn."

"Fine." She tosses the phone to me.

I catch it and begin scrolling through the songs. "Bob Dylan."

She smirks. "This is what I said. Bobby Die-lawn."

"If you insist. And It's Van Morrison, not Von. I remember you and Dad playing "Moondance" at the restaurant."

"Yes. Sometimes."

I keep reading. "Abba, Fleetwood Mac, Billy Joel." I grin at her. "Wasn't Dad more into classical music?"

"Yes. It was his favorite. He did not like these songs very much."

"Why not?"

She rubs Penney's ears. "He was a bit older than me. We did not always have the same taste."

"Guess five years can make a big difference." I continue scrolling. "Eagles. 'Brandy'. I remember Dad singing that one."

"This was our song," she says quietly.

"I didn't know you guys had a song. Should we play it?"

"No." Her facial expression shifts through a range of emotions a stranger wouldn't notice. But I do. Sadness, frustration, stoicism. The last one, holding it all together. Toughing it out. It's what she does best.

"You didn't get to listen to the music you liked while you were married?"

"I was not with him every minute of every day. I am having my own life."

"It never occurred to me. You seemed like a unit."

"What do you think? We are the two-headed monster?"

"There's a hell-of-an image. But it seemed like you guys were on the same page, or in the same brain."

"Really? You think we agreed on all the things?"

"Kind of. It's how I remember it. Is that bad? You liked him though, didn't you? I mean, you loved him, right?"

She nods. "Of course. But marriage is complicate. Someday good, someday bad." She tilts her head to the right. "Are you ill, dear? You are pale and sweating on your face."

I touch my forehead. Clammy. "I don't feel great."

Her wide brown eyes flicker. "We go to the emergency?"

"No, Mom, I'm nauseous because I didn't have lunch."

She's quiet, contemplating her next words. "You are not pregnant, are you?"

So predictable. The word nausea has been an automatic prompt for her, starting when I was young enough to notice boys. "No, I'm not pregnant. I got my period this morning."

"Thanks the Gods. Why do you need to be having the sex with two men?"

"I told you, I'm not."

She frowns at me, tight-lipped. "Do not lie to your mother."

I blink. "Sleeping with one man. Spending time with two."

"Who is the two?"

I grind my molars together before answering. "Nick."

The corners of her mouth turn up. This information pleases her. "Nicholas?"

"Uh-huh."

"He is here in Dufferin Beach?" she asks. "When did this happen? Is he asking you to marry?"

I swallow hard. My stomach contracts, begging for food or perhaps relief from her questions. "Why do you jump to getting married so fast? I've only been talking to him since the beginning of the year."

She smiles now, a full-bodied, toothy grin. "I have always liked this boy."

"Me too. Jesse thinks he's a piece of shit, though. You know he wasn't great to me in school. I mean, sometimes he was. He's changed though."

"Fuj, Katy. You are from a good Hungarian family. You do not speak with these words. And any of the ways, how does this matter?" She swipes the cat off her lap. "You are both young then. This is to be expected."

"You're saying women should expect guys to be crappy when they're young?"

"Men are stupid in this time." She stands up and straightens her blouse. "Men are stupid when they are old, too. Like your father."

"Is there an in between age?" I ask. "When they're functional?"

"It depends on the man, dear. I think Nick is in this stage now, where he is smart enough to know when you need the husband."

"I don't need a husband. I won't die without one."

"We do not know this. Maybe you will. How terrible you look right now. Green like the sick frog."

I shrug. My phone lights up with a text from Jesse.

WTF? Russ said you hit your head. U okay?

I'm fine. At the house with Mom. Please save me.

"Who is sending you the texting message?" Mom asks. "Is it Nick? Please tell him he is to have dinner with us on Sunday."

I glance at her. "It's Jesse, and okay, I'll tell him."

"You bring him to me. I will fix it for you. It will be good to have a man back in the family. Now I make you the toast."

"You really like Nick?" I ask her.

"Yes, he is the nice boy. A little too thin, if I remember, but of course, a good woman will plumb him up."

"Plump, Mom."

"Igen," she says, heading to the kitchen. "Why are you wasting time with the other boy? I hope you are not telling Nick about this."

"They don't know about each other, and I do like Nick. I think we're sort of different now, or whatever, have gone different ways, but he's still my person. I feel it. I can tell." I stop for a moment, debating the benefit of the next sentence. "Quinn has been really sweet, though. It's a little confusing."

She slams a bottle of apricot jam on the counter. "It is not confusing. He is not the right one."

"Have you ever had a conversation with Quinn? Ever actually spoken to him?"

"I do not need to do this."

"What if I'm more into Quinn than Nick? I mean, I'm not. But what if I were? In theory?"

More food is abused by my mother. Two slices of bread are aggressively inserted into the toaster, and the butter is vivisected by a dull dinner knife. She huffs. Her exasperation is louder than the A/C kicking on.

"This is ridiculous, Katika. Nick is from the good background. His mother and father are both doctors. He will take care of you. He is the right man for this family."

I watch her massacre toast, butter, and jam. Breadcrumbs soar through the air. Even Penney is alarmed, ears perked, tail fully fluffed-out from the cacophony of meal prep in the kitchen. It all makes me want to argue more. Cooperate less.

"The family?" I ask. "Seriously?"

"Yes." She stalks toward me with two flattened toasts. "Eat. How are you expecting to get the man when you looking like the sad frog with the head collusion?"

I sit up as she lays the plate on my lap. "Concussion."

"Yes, dear."

"Thanks for feeding me."

She pats my cheek and sits down by my feet. "The bread makes every troubles go away."

"Even my collusion?"

"Yes," she winks at me. "Even this."

• • • • •

The guard changes. Mom leaves, and Jesse takes the second shift to make sure my collusion isn't terminal. I'm on the phone with Russ when they make the switch.

"Who are you talking to?" Jesse asks, sitting down on the coffee table in front of me.

"Russ," I whisper before ending the call. "The ice machine is on the fritz."

"Bummer. What did you do to your pretty little head?"

"Tripped over some eggs."

"More details." She stands and heads to the kitchen. "I need to eat. What do you got?"

"Toast. Froot Loops. And there are no details. I put my foot in the wrong place and wiped out."

"Wiped out, huh? Toast isn't real food. What else is there?"

"Leftover paprikas from work. It's in the round glass dish with the nokedli."

"Just say dumplings, Kiss."

"Dumplings." I roll onto my side. "Is Nick still out of town?"

She places the dish into the microwave, hits start. "Yeah. He's in Jacksonville."

"When's he coming home?" I ask, wondering why my *men* keep leaving town. Quinn hasn't texted all day, which is fine. Perfectly fine. I'm a modern woman, and he's my sex guy. Or he was. Now that Nick is back, those nights with Quinn are off the table. And the couch. And the bed. My face warms.

"Not sure when he's getting back. Think he said the weekend."

"Why didn't he tell me he was leaving?"

"Probably because you threw up on him."

"Not great, right?"

She pulls the container from the microwave with a blue and green striped kitchen towel and returns to the living room. "He's your person. I'm sure he's cool with it."

I wiggle my feet inside the blanket. "He was about to say something to me when it happened. Something big."

She bites into a chicken leg. Talks with her mouth open. "Indeed."

"Did he say what it was?"

She nods and sucks meat off the bone.

"What, Jessica?"

"I'm sworn to secrecy. You don't want me to piss off your dream-man, do you?"

"Come on!"

"Fine. He does have a plan. A question to propose." She stops talking long enough to lick the sauce off her fork. "But it's not what you think."

• • • • •

Jesse remains tight-lipped. By twelve-thirty a.m., I know as much as I did three hours ago. We try staying up by arguing about politics, social media, and if Johnny Depp is hotter as a pirate or unhinged author.

Pirate, by the way. Any fucking day of the week.

By one a.m., we're both losing the will to keep me awake, and by extension, alive. We'd rather sleep. She slouches over on my legs, and I'm stuck, wrapped in my burrito, topped with a layer of Jessica Tanner.

"Don't sleep, Kiss."

"Uh-huh."

"It'll be my fault if you die." She yawns before drifting off.

I pat her head, then grab my phone and text Nickety-Nick. *Are you awake?*

The "read" receipt appears. I wait. My eyelids droop.

I try again. *Sorry I got sick. Hope your sandals survived.*

Another "read" receipt. I shake my head. Blink once. Twice.

Elevator Man is near. "Hold it, Katy. Use the pink one. The pink crayon."

"No!" My muffled outburst is silent, caged inside the vacuum of a dream. Still, it's enough to wake me up. The phone says two-seventeen a.m. No response from Nick.

What the hell? He could answer in less than ten seconds. My eyes adjust to the darkened room as I reposition the blanket to cover Jesse's shoulders. She groans and grinds her teeth.

Penney leaps onto me with a squeak, pushes her paws into my t-shirt and settles in the crook of my neck. I sneeze, wipe cat hair away, and stare at the screen. Not going back to sleep. There's no way I'm letting the elevator dude near me. But I'm so tired. And what does any of this have to do with a crayon?

I rub my eyes, consider the options, and do the only thing I can think of to stay awake.

Hey Quinn. What's going on?

A minute goes by. A text bubble pops up, three dots.

Hi beautiful. Why are you awake?

I feel a flutter. Definitely, positively a flutter. Not of love, but gratitude. Someone has said something nice to me, and my low self-esteem is temporarily soothed.

Can't sleep. Where are you?

Austin. Why can't you sleep?

Long story. Are you having fun on your big business trip?

Fun? No. Should we use the PHONE feature of our phones?

I grin and tap on the keyboard. *No. Jesse's here babysitting me. I don't want to bother her.*

Why's she there? What's wrong? Is it the dreams?

I hesitate in my response. Only Dr. Jonas and Ethan know how bad the nightmares are getting.

No. Smacked my head at work. She was supposed to keep me up.

WTH? Are you okay? What happened?

Tripped on a shit-ton of eggs. I'm fine. Mom was here earlier, now Jess.

Sure you're okay?

I stare at his words. How dare he be nice?

Yeah. Sure.

K. I miss you.

Fuckety-fuck. I chew on my nails. Stubs, really, with faded black polish. Nobody's ever missed me. People are amused by me, curious, often irritated. But miss me? No, that's not a thing. My fingers hover over the screen.

He texts again. *Can't stop thinking about our ice cream night.*

There it is. He doesn't miss me. He misses getting laid. Asshole.

Oh, I text back.

It was really great.

Nice, Quinn. Gonna catch some sleep. Hope Texas gets better.

Jerk. I put the phone on silent and toss it onto the table, grumbling and squeezing my eyes shut. Just a quick nap. I doze off in mid thought. Relationships are hard.

They're complicated.

Men stink.

Love is a black hole.

Maybe I'll get another cat.

CHAPTER 46
TRY FELL WHERE?

"It's you and me, kid." Elevator Man's voice rumbles toward me. Thunder cracks the darkness open. The sound rolls over me. Through me.

"Where's my mom and dad?"

"They're gone. Draw a picture. It's gonna be a long while."

"Liar," I screech, but what comes out of me is more hot air than words or argument. I look down. An open carton of crayons sits upright on a desk. They're new, arranged perfectly. Slender soldiers with sharpened waxy tips and colorful uniforms of green, blue, yellow, and red.

"I'm cold. I want to go home."

"I'm cold and I want to go home." He mimics me.

"Stop it!"

"Stop it," he repeats, but his voice isn't like mine, filled with fear. He's mocking me. He's angry.

"Where am…" I squint into the darkness and sense him more than see him until he comes into view. His head is unnaturally narrow, his body two-dimensional, like pulled taffy. "Why the long face?" I ask, immediately regretting these words, but my frustration is growing. It's pouring out of me in the usual way— my big mouth, always ten steps ahead of my brain.

"That's a mistake." His deep voice vibrates in my ears. I shake my head from side to side, trying to clear the sensation. Panic. Heat prickles my arms. I search the room that isn't a room and find nothing but this distorted cartoon version of a man. No walls, no ceiling. I rub my palms together the way I do after spending too much time in the walk-in fridge at work.

"Where am I?" I ask, cupping my hands to my cheeks.

"Where am I?" he repeats.

"Fuck you!"

"Fuck you," he says calmly. "What a pretty picture."

"What?" I ask, but I'm no longer standing. I'm sitting at a children's desk. A white sheet of paper hovers an inch above the wooden surface like a quivering magic carpet. A pink crayon appears, clutched in my hand.

I try dropping it, but it's glued to my fingers. "I don't want this! Get it off me!"

"You made such a pretty picture, kid."

I look at the paper again. Someone's drawn a crude stick figure body topped by a pink daisy head. Not someone. Me.

"This isn't happening," I whisper, trying unsuccessfully to squeeze out of the desk.

"This isn't happening," he echoes.

My stomach lurches. My bladder is hot and full.

"I have to pee," I tell the Elevator Man.

"I have to pee," he echoes.

"Please. I need to go."

"Hold it."

"I can't," I plead, and fling the crayon away. It shoots forward, then free-falls, tumbling in slow motion, past the place where the ground should be. I fixate on it, gracefully floating beneath my feet.

"What did I teach you, kid?"

I blink. The room rocks to the left and right.

His voice becomes more insistent. "What did I teach you?"

"I remember now," I whisper apologetically. The answer is clear, bubbling to the surface of my lost memories. The correct response. The only one he'll accept. I sit up straight and carefully repeat the words that have been lying dormant in my mind. "We don't try."

"Why don't we?" he asks, laying a warm, floppy hand on my head.

"Don't touch me!" The words fall out of my mouth. Fall to the floor that isn't here. His fingers snake through my hair. The damp heat from his skin travels through me.

"Say it!" His delivery makes the command non-negotiable. Fear rains down on me, soaking my shirt, my pants, my legs.

"There is no try." I recite mechanically, just as he taught me. "Try fell. Try fell into a bucket and drowned."

CHAPTER 47
WEE KATY

If Jesse's expression reflects mine at this moment, then I've turned into that deer in the crossfire Mom was talking about yesterday.

"What, Jess? Why are you staring at me?"

"Smell anything funky?" She pulls the blanket away from me.

I wiggle my nose and feel the wetness between my thighs. And the odor, acrid, ammonia. Urine.

"What the hell?" I squeal and spring off the couch. "What's happening to me?"

• • • • •

Ten minutes of steam cleaning the cushions and thirty minutes in the shower erase the evidence, but not the shame. Jesse's waiting for me in the kitchen, sipping apple juice.

"Feeling better, wee Katy?"

"Shut up," I say, stepping past her to the fridge.

"You need to talk to Dr. Jonas. You were having a nightmare. Full on, writhing around, saying weird shit about a bucket. Something's going on with you, and it's getting worse."

I stop in my tracks. "I'm aware."

"Do you remember anything about your dream?"

I nod and pour milk into a coffee cup. The words are etched into my brain—like they've always been there. "I do," I say with the same mechanical rhythm from the nightmare. "Try fell. It fell into a goddamn bucket and drowned."

CHAPTER 48
IM-BOO-SEEL

It's hump-day at The Point; historically, the slowest day of the week. We work like a well-oiled machine, prepping, cooking, plating, but without the oil. Mom's distracted, talking into a miniature tape recorder. Dictation, she says, for her next chapter. Russ slices his finger open cutting celery. Melissa, having completed her final college exam ever, would rather be at a graduation party. I'm in full on bitch-mode, scowling as heavy cream churns into pillowy white mountains in the stand mixer. Mom bumps into me with a plastic tub of soup stock, some of which sloshes onto the floor. Russ slips on the spilled stock, and Melissa trips over him. She catches herself but drops a tray of salt and pepper shakers without the tops twisted on.

Outbursts follow. Melissa yells at Russ. Russ yells at me while my mother tells us we're a funny little collection of "im-boo-sils", and I do absolutely everything in my power not to scream or cry or insert my head into the mixer so I can die a slow, painful death via cream-covered wire beater.

Upon completion of our communal tantrum, the tension dissipates. Russ is bandaged up, and somehow we pull off a successful lunch service. At three, I excuse myself and head to the second appointment this week with Dr. Jonas.

• • • • •

"I promise not to fall asleep this time," I say after collapsing on her boring beige couch.

She sniffs the air. A puzzled expression clouds her angular face.

"Onions, probably peppers," I tell her. "Definitely some chicken soup. I came straight from the restaurant."

"You smell like dinner," she says. "Now I'm hungry."

"Sorry." I tug on my ponytail, wondering how to respond to her comment. Avoidance seems easiest, so I change the subject. "I've never had two therapy sessions in one week."

"It's not uncommon. Things come up and we need a little extra work."

"Come up?" I ask.

"Yes. Let's get straight to it, shall we?"

I nod. "Guess you read the rest of my notes?"

"Yes. You did a great job. You have excellent recall of your dreams."

"They're nightmares. But thanks."

"You're very welcome. The Elevator Man. Tell me about him."

"What do you want to know?" I ask. "He wasn't there at the beginning."

Dr. Jonas tilts her head to the right. "Looks like it began with a nap, and then something scared you." She skims my handwritten documents. "Who's Cricket?"

"Cricket works at The Point part time. And yeah, the dumpling dream. I can't remember if he was there yet."

She studies the paper again. "You wrote about being called a baby. Someone was in the dream with you by that time. A disembodied voice?"

"Yeah." I rub my hands together. "It's kind of creepy when you say it out loud."

"Agreed," she says. "It's disturbing."

"I sort of remember. I'm always in this dark place, with no walls or floors, and it's never been light in any of them. Or warm."

"Sounds really unpleasant. Why is this person named the Elevator Man? Is that information he gave you?"

"No. I named him. It was when Mom came home." I roll my eyes. "This is stupid, but I was picking her up at the airport, and there was this couple making out in the elevator. I mean, aggressively making out. I had a nightmare about them that night, and for some reason, the guy in the elevator started representing the bad guy in my dreams, so I call him the Elevator Man now."

"Did you have any contact with the couple at the airport?"

"Are you asking if they spoke to me? The real people? I don't think so."

"Uh-huh," she answers quickly.

"Honestly, I can't remember."

"But they obviously made an impression on you. Did you feel threatened?"

I giggle. "No, I was embarrassed. Not sure they even noticed I was in there with them, so no, I'm pretty sure they never said anything to me."

"You describe this Elevator Man as very tall."

"Yeah. He was super tall. Both the real guy and the dream guy. And the woman too, now that I think about it. Did I write that down?"

"You did. Both the man and woman in the dream spoke to you. How would you describe your overall feeling about the event?"

I sit back on the couch. "Fear, probably. Being alone. And they kept telling me I had to go to the bathroom."

"Hm. They were both saying those words?"

"Uh-huh."

"Okay. Let's move on to the next one." She brings the paper close to her face and adjusts the glasses on her wicked sharp nose. "Air raid sirens."

"That was after my grandma was telling us a story about the war in Hungary."

"A fairly straight line," she says. "You wrote again that the Elevator Man said you needed to pee."

"Right. That's in every one of them, lately. He says I need to pee, then says I have to hold it."

She frowns. "Like he's setting you up?"

"I guess, but to do what?" I ask, uneasy about admitting what happened earlier today. I'm almost twenty-seven, and this might be the first time I've wet the bed...or a couch.

"Setting you up to fail possibly? To frighten you. Can you describe how it feels in your body when you wake up from these dreams?"

"Fail how?" I ask. "And what do you mean, in my body?"

She focuses on the ceiling for a few seconds, then looks back at me. "Where do you sense the fear or the tension?"

I stare at the ceiling too, though I'm not sure why. "In my chest, I guess. I get short of breath, and my heart beats real fast."

"But this doesn't feel like the panic attack you had in Paris?"

"No. One is panic. The other is straight up fear."

"Anything else?" she asks.

"Yeah. Well, this is another strange part of it. I super need to go when I wake up."

"Is that unusual?"

"I mean, no, but it's more...um, more urgent, I guess?"

"Okay."

"Okay what? What does it mean?"

"I'm not sure yet, Katy. Let's keep going."

"Something else happened when I woke up this morning."

"What was that?" she asks.

I puff my cheeks out. My stomach grumbles, and suddenly all I can think about is sleeping. I glance at the couch and wonder if she spreads powdered valium on the cushions in between clients. I shake my head, trying to clear my exhaustion.

"Katy?"

"Sorry, I lost my train of thought. I just got super tired."

She grins. "I see it on your face. Can you handle a few more minutes? You said something happened this morning?"

"Yeah. I had another dream about him, with the whole needing to pee and having to hold it, thing."

She blinks twice in rapid succession.

"It's really embarrassing."

She remains quiet. Her empathy is well practiced, but it can't smooth over my humiliation.

"He said the same stuff about going and holding it. I said I'd try to, and then I said something strange."

She shifts in her chair, leans forward.

"You're not going to tell anyone about this, are you?" I ask. "About the weird shit I say?"

"Absolutely not." Her jaw clenches, then releases. "I take confidentiality very seriously. Why are you asking?"

"Dunno," I tell her. "It's not important."

"What's the strange thing you said in the dream, Katy?"

I summon my will inside this room filled with spider plants and textbooks about personality disorders and broken people. "Okay." I clear my throat.

She smiles in a way that's maybe sixty-eight percent patient and waits for me to speak.

"I peed on myself," I confess because what the hell, how can this get any worse? "And I figured out what he wants me to say."

She raises her hands in front of her, stopping my confession. "Your cheeks are getting so red, Katy. Please don't ever be embarrassed in this room. You're safe here, okay?"

"Uh-huh. Thanks."

She continues, "I appreciate you sharing something so difficult with me. Do you have any history of bed wetting?"

My face heats up to match my red cheeks. "No. Not that I know of."

"It's probably something you'd remember." She crosses her legs, and her right shoe, an ugly brown flat with thin tan laces, falls off her foot. "What did he want you to say?"

I fixate on the shoe. Does she know it's not on her foot anymore? Should I tell her? Would that be wrong?

"Katy?"

"Uh-huh." I stammer. "With all the other dreams, he kept going on about the word *try*. Try did this or try did that. Which is nuts, right?"

"It's an odd way to combine those words."

"I thought so too, and it didn't make sense. Then this morning, when I was dreaming, all of a sudden I got it. I knew the entire sentence like it had always been there."

Her head turns slightly to the right, and it reminds me of how I sometimes close one eye to focus better. "What's always been there?" she asks.

"The thing he wants me to say. Like it's been locked away in my brain."

Her head turns a little more, as if she's tuning into the erratic sounds of my brain waves. Waves that sound like a high school orchestra on acid, with some skinny kid pushing his tongue between the strings of a used violin and a short kid putting his head between the cymbals and then smacking them as hard as he can. And all the other kids, convinced they're making beautiful music. But no. They're tripping. Because of the acid.

That's my brain. It's why my shrink lady has to work so hard to understand the messed up things I tell her.

"What was I saying?" I ask. I have to work hard too.

"Something was locked away in your brain. What does that mean, Katy?"

"Oh yeah." I swallow because these words are twisted. Sour. "The sentence was locked away," I say, sitting up straight, repeating the phrase that's familiar and unfamiliar at the same time. "Try fell into a bucket and drowned."

Her expression becomes pensive.

"What does it mean?" I ask. "How could I possibly know something like that?"

She looks at her iPad, taps her pen on the screen three times.

"What's wrong with me?"

"Have you ever heard someone say those words?" she asks. "A relative or a friend?"

"I don't think so, and I feel like I'd remember because it's so damn off."

Two more taps, a pause, then two additional taps before she speaks. "Do you remember last year, when you talked about your parents being very controlling with you? You told me your mom was so protective that a mosquito couldn't have gotten close to you."

"Yeah, of course I remember."

She sits erect and folds her hands into her lap. "I don't think it was a mosquito they were protecting you from."

She continues speaking, but I've stopped listening. All I can do for the rest of the session is nod politely and respond in one-syllable grunts. And ask myself: Why would they have to protect me? Why would someone want to hurt me?

CHAPTER 49
STORM

Dr. Jonas' words consume the rest of my day. I struggle with the urge to confront my mother. But where would I even begin? *Hey Mom, I urinated on myself today, and there's this nasty elevator dude in my dreams with crayons and darkness and btw—anything else hiding out in the back of your closet?*

It's drizzling on my short drive home. Russ mentioned a tropical storm forming in the gulf earlier, but I had bigger things to worry about. And a tropical storm? No, this is Florida. We're already in the tropics, which is why we just call it a storm here.

In the driveway, the drizzle becomes more insistent. I swing the car door shut and pause outside. The palm trees sway in the dim light of the moon. The plants rustle. I inhale the smell of the ocean, the rain, and all the green things releasing their scent into the night.

Inside, Penney is tense, sitting on the windowsill, watching water fall from the sky.

"It's all good," I tell her, sweeping my hand over her little munchkin head.

After a shower, I text Nick and ask how the weather is in Jacksonville. It's a legitimate question, also a cringy conversation starter because weather related discussions seem superficial to me. Words we say in passing to a neighbor. Idle chitchat about the UV index or pollen count because saying nothing while we pull our garbage can to the curb would be rude. After five minutes of internal rationalization about my lackluster conversational skills, I text Jesse.

Hi. I'm crazy now in case you were wondering about this morning.

Did you figure it out? What's Dr. J's opinion? Want me to bring you a diaper?

Nope. She thinks something happened to me.

Happened when? And what? Something bad?

Unsure. We think my mom might know.

Did you ask her?

Not yet.

You okay? Need me to come over and hold your bladder?

Screw u. No.

Hear about the storm?

It's only rain, Jessica.

Might get bad. Batten down the hatches.

Sure thing. Thanks for caring.

Anytime, my wee-freaky girl.

I smile, grateful to have someone in my life to keep me tethered to reality. I pick up around the house while replaying my past. Wouldn't I remember something traumatic happening to me? I recall only an uneventful childhood, always in close proximity to my parents. They didn't even let me go to summer camp because I'd be out of their line of vision. Work was under their noses at The Point. School—normal, other than trouble with math, and the pressure of my teacher demanding I instantly add 568 and 913 in my head.

Vacations, never alone. I was always with my parents or in Montreal, where I'd be cocooned inside the Hungarian mob. Okay, not the mob, but *the* family and *the* friends, every single one of them connected inside the gigantic spider web to Magyarország. To Hungary.

My phone rings in my pocket as I scrub the bathtub. Might as well have things clean if I'm losing my shit. The house ought to be tidy when they come to collect me.

"Hey kiddo. How goes it?"

"Hi Captain Ethan. Where are you tonight?"

"Home."

"A quick trip," I say, trying not to slip on the wet porcelain.

"But successful. Passengers said they'd be requesting me from now on."

"Congratulations! That's actually done?"

"Private aviation. You pay, you get." He sneezes, then continues. "Which means Palm Springs on the weekend."

I dry my feet on a towel. "Bless you. Is it pretty there?"

"Thanks. Yeah, if you're into the desert."

"I'm into Florida. What's going on? Did you get an email from Nori?"

"No, I wanted to find out more about the dreams you were having."

My shoulders slouch. It's been almost twenty minutes since I thought about the Elevator Man. "I'm fine. It'll pass."

"You think?"

"Not really." I drop the sponge into the sink. "It got bad last night…this morning. Whatever."

"What happened?" he asks.

"It's embarrassing. Don't tell anyone, Ethan. Not even your mom."

"She's on a river cruise on the Rhine with her friends."

"Sounds lovely."

"If you're into that kind of thing. She sent me an email saying the passengers are so old, they're calling it the prune barge."

"Young people eat prunes."

"When's the last time you had a prune, Katy? And stop dodging the question. Tell me about the nightmares."

"Fine." I shut off the bathroom light, sit down on my bed, and regurgitate the same story I told Dr. Jonas, stopping short before the end.

"You drew a picture of a flower with a pink crayon? Why does that sound familiar to me?"

"I have no clue. How familiar?" I ask.

"Not sure," he says. "It's like *déjà vu* or something. What happened after?"

"The dude tells me I have to pee again. Just like he did in the other dreams. I told you this last time. He says I have to go, then tells me to hold it."

A clap of thunder shakes the windows. The lights go out.

"What the hell was that?" he asks.

"That was thunder and the power going out," I say.

"That sucks. You okay?"

"Yeah, just a storm." I squint, trying to adjust to the darkened room. "Anyway, I'm not sure how, but I knew what he wanted to hear. It sounds nuts, but it popped into my head, like when you can't remember a name or something, but as soon as you stop thinking about it, the word is there right where it's supposed to be."

"Yeah," he answers. "It happens to me all the time. What's the thing? What did he want to hear?"

"It's a phrase." I say, then notice that my hands are shaking. "Try fell into a bucket and drowned."

He doesn't respond right away. The line is quiet. Outside, the wind sounds like spinning helicopter blades, buffeting the side of the house. Then finally, almost inaudibly, he says, "There's no fucking way."

"What, Ethan? Tell me!"

"Are you absolutely sure those were the words?"

"Yes. Trust me, I don't get it either. *Try* doesn't, you know, do stuff. That's not how that word is supposed to fit into a sentence."

"Fuck," he whispers.

I swallow what feels like needles, trying to recall the exercises Dr. Jonas showed me about staying calm. They elude me now, because who can concentrate when they're freaking out? In fact, doesn't the act of freaking out negate the ability to think? To find the happy place on the beach filled with colorful umbrellas, bottles of sunscreen, baking humans...flies.

"This is insane, Katy."

"You're weirding me out, Ethan. Do you know what it means?"

Lightning flashes outside. Penney darts into the room and slides under the dresser like she's stealing second base.

"I haven't heard it in years," he says. "Not since I was a kid."

"Are you kidding me?"

"I wish I was."

Thunder rumbles.

"Who says that?" I ask.

"This is nuts." The connection falters. The line fills with static.

"Ethan!" I yell, then inhale through my nose. *Smell the soup.* Tomatoes, basil...

"I'm here," he says. "I didn't want to think about him ever again. He was such a dick."

"Who are you talking about?"

"He'd only say it when he was really angry. He'd set me up, make me do something I couldn't handle, then out it came."

The rain comes down harder. Hail pelts the roof. Duff Beach is going through the carwash from hell. "Who is *he*, Ethan?" I ask, though it's not necessary anymore. He doesn't need to say it out loud.

He does anyway. "My stepdad."

My screen lights up. He switches the call to video.

"I don't understand," I say, covering one ear. The thick vines of the bougainvillea outside the living room window thrash in the wind. Their thorns claw at the glass.

"That's not just a storm." He brings the phone close to his face. Day old stubble on a familiar jawline. Dad's.

"We have these here all the time, Ethan. It's Florida. Clouds get dark, the rain, you know… rains."

"Not sure what weather you're looking at, but I checked a satellite image, and it's showing a solid red line smack on top of Dufferin Beach. It's not an afternoon sprinkle."

"Fine, I'll be careful, but can we please get back to this crap about your dad?"

His green eyes narrow. "Stepdad."

"Hell, I'm sorry, but what does he have to do with me? I don't even remember meeting him, and it's not like I've seen him recently."

"No clue. He's been out of the picture for a long time." He squashes his lips together. "Your family was here when you were little. Remember the photo album in my basement?"

"Yeah, what about it?"

"Your parents and you in the snow?"

"Right. We were in Denver when I was about three, right? Do you think he yelled at me or something?"

He frowns. "Would you be having nightmares twenty-something years later if some guy yelled at you?"

Another bolt of lightning turns night into day. More thunder. My phone beeps, low battery. "Fuck," I say, looking around for the charger. "He was tall, wasn't he? Your stepdad."

"Yeah, and thin as hell. The guy looked two-dimensional."

My stomach turns over. The Elevator Man. "Did he have a low voice?"

"Real low," he says. "How could you possibly remember that?"

A wave of heat travels through my arms and settles over my shoulders, the small of my back, my face. I drop the phone, run to the bathroom, and throw up until there's nothing left but dry heaves, exhaustion, and confusion.

CHAPTER 50
COOK ME UP

Puking is bad enough. The power going out ups the ante. My phone dying is the cherry on top. In the dark, I fumble around my bedroom, sweeping my hands over the covers and bedside table, searching for the charger.

"Shit," I mumble to myself. "I left it at work."

Penney brushes her face on my ankles and trails me into the kitchen. As a Florida native, I'm fully prepared for these weather eventualities. There are two flashlights in the miscellaneous drawer, neither with working batteries, and some birthday candles in the pantry. Over the stove, I light one, silver with pink diagonal stripes, and push it into the unwrapped block of cream cheese to keep from burning my fingers.

"Good to go." I pull my laptop from my backpack. It's also dead, though I have the cord, but again, no electricity.

The streetlamps are out. Lightning illuminates the water whipping across the driveway and flooding the front yard. Flower petals, torn leaves, and broken twigs sail past the window. I close the blinds, but there's no silencing the howling coming off the gulf.

"It'll be over soon." I cradle Penney close to my chest and carry her into the bedroom. Her tiny ears are at full attention, her round eyes wide open. Poor baby, this must be her first storm.

I climb under the blanket and try not to think about Ethan's stepdad, my mom, or the boat, which I didn't have time to secure. I could make a run to her house. I could also get knocked out by flying debris.

Penney purrs, my stomach grumbles, the storm grows.

I fall asleep.

• • • • •

I wake with a start to someone banging on the front door. Jesse and Russ are outside, both in bright yellow rain slickers. Water streams down their faces. I move out of the way as they rush inside.

"Did you have to bring the monsoon into the house? You're getting the floor all wet."

Jesse pulls off her coat. "We've been calling you for hours. We thought you were dead. Okay, not dead, but injured or pinned under a tree, struck by lightning. Drowning in your driveway."

"Wow, Jess, you've put a lot of thought into my demise."

Russ shakes his head. Rain-soaked ringlets eject water. His golden retriever energy is on full throttle. He might as well be running through a sprinkler. "Your mom's flipping-out, girl, and The Point is about to flood. We gotta get sandbags."

I rub my cheeks, still warm from being in my cocoon. "My phone died. What time is it?"

"Four-ten," Jesse says. "Could you have emailed? Anything?"

"Laptop's also dead," I say, heading to the bathroom.

She follows me. "You're aware that if Armageddon comes, you will not survive more than three minutes."

"No kidding. Store me on ice and cook me up if you run out of food."

She winces. "You're disgusting."

I pull on jeans and a sweatshirt. "But practical."

Her eyebrows knit together. "No, you're one of the most irrational people I've ever met. Also, you don't have enough fat on you. You'd taste like dried out chicken."

"So what? The only useful talent I bring to the table at the end of days is knowing how to drive a stick-shift." I sit down on the bed and pull my socks on. "Throw me my sneakers. Use your flashlight. They should be right behind you."

She lobs them at me. "You can cook."

"This is true."

"Ready to rumble?" she asks.

I smile as she takes my hand and pulls me to my feet. "Yes, ma'am. Let's do it."

CHAPTER 51
SANDBAGS & CRAYONS & THUNDER, OH MY!

Having something bigger to worry about than my nightmares is a welcome reprieve. The strangeness of the past few days and nights retreats to the back of my mind while city employees and locals congregate at the beach to fill and hand out sandbags.

With the thunder and lightning subsiding, we work together in a steady downpour, under the glow of emergency lights and trucks with their high beams on. Because of the curve of the shoreline, my house and Mom's sit farther away from the water. But The Point is directly across from the beach, and the rising tide poses a serious threat. It's nothing we haven't done before, though last time, my dad was here with us. I remember worrying he might have a heart attack, barking orders and throwing sandbags into the beds of pickups. He didn't. Not that day.

I stare at the starless sky, wondering what he'd have to say about our lives now. My mom's new writing career, my divorce. The Elevator Man.

"Katy, we have enough. Let's get back." Russ tugs on my jacket and heads toward the street.

I follow him through the mushy, waterlogged sand, and check on friends who check on us. Small towns are like that. A common cause brings out the best in us, no matter how much we bitched or gossiped the day before or will the day after. We make a wide circle around a pickup truck dropping the bags of sand near the front door of The Point. Mom directs the driver but stops in mid-arm wave as soon as she sees me.

"Thanks the Gods, Katika. I am thinking you are dead."

"Jess texted you when we left the house, Mom."

"Before I did not know. Why are you not keeping your phone open?"

"My charger broke last week, and I keep forgetting to buy a new one. I've been charging it up when I'm at work."

Her eyes narrow.

"I know," I say apologetically. "I didn't bring it home."

Without direction, and because we've done this dozens of times, we layer sandbags in neat rows, four high, against the front of the restaurant. It's hard work, and slow going in the rain.

At six-thirty, the sun climbs above the cloud cover and colors everything in a muted orange glow. At the back door, we peel off our coats, shoes, and socks, and wrap ourselves in the towels Mom brought from home.

"I need coffee," Jesse says, pulling a sweater over her head.

"No power, and the generator conked out last month." I slump against the wall with a fuzzy peach towel wrapped around my shoulders. "So...not great timing."

"You think?" Jesse grumbles. "I assume we can't open the fridge?"

We nod. This is the program. Conserve energy. Hope for the electricity to be restored soon, count our losses later. Mom takes a thermos and a colorful tin from her bag. Hot chocolate and cookies. We eat, drink, listen to the steady drumbeat of rain on the roof, and wait for the storm to pass. In the next few hours, we'll see how much mayhem the tide will bring.

• • • • •

By noon, the rain reverts to a drizzle. The power is still out, but the sandbags have done their job. It's Thursday. Dufferin Beach will spend hours cleaning, repairing, and thanking the weather gods for keeping us off social media, or the news outlets in constant search of the biggest disaster occurring right now—in this twenty-four-hour news cycle.

Mom's gone home to change clothes, and Russ is with his family. Jesse and I are tasked with mopping up the small lake that's seeped under the front door.

"I found out something else about the nightmares," I tell her. "Actually, Ethan figured it out."

She tosses a wet towel into a metal garbage can. "Spill it."

And I do, once again, cough up the story, everything I can remember. The Elevator Man, the pink crayon, the connection to Ethan's dad, and the phrase about the bucket.

"What the hell? No wonder you've been acting crazy. But what's the connection? It's not like you've seen the guy in years." She picks up a fresh towel. "Have you?"

"No. Well, I caught a glimpse of him when Ethan tore up his picture in Denver. That's a face I'd remember."

"Do you both get how wacked-out the whole thing sounds? What does that sentence even mean?"

"I don't have any idea. It's weird as hell."

"You need to ask your mom."

"I will," I say, checking my phone. I used my car to charge it to two percent, and now it's lit up with messages from friends, our family, Nick, Quinn, and Ethan.

Nick texts. *What a shit-storm. Ruined my Balenciagas. At least you didn't puke on them.*

"Jessica, what's a Balenciaga?"

"Really expensive men's shoes. Why are you asking?"

"Nick," I say, and continue reading his text. *Assume you're all okay, or I'd have heard. Storm came out of nowhere. Back later today.*

Quinn has left multiple texts, beginning just after midnight.

What's happening?

Call me.

I'm calling Jesse.

I look at Jesse. "Did Quinn text you?"

"Oh hell, I totally forgot." She grins. "Katy, Quinn texted you. You should call him."

"Nice. Thank you. Did you write him back?"

"Of course I did. I told him we weren't swimming with the fishes yet."

I bat my eyes at her and send him a short text. What does he care about how we are, anyway? All he wants is to get laid.

Ethan's left a trail of cryptic texts, and three calls without voicemails.

Are you okay?

Call me!

Figured something out about the déjà vu thing.

Call me or I'm flying out there.

The drawing....

I show Jesse the messages. She nods. "What's he talking about? What drawing?"

I run my fingers along the bottom of the door. It's wet, the wood is warped, and it will most likely need to be replaced. "He's talking about the nightmares I keep having. In the last one, I was holding this pink crayon and a picture of this stick figure with a flower head."

"You hate crayons," she says, pushing her hair behind her ears.

"How do you know that?"

"Last year at the temp hearing, you were wasted on Xanax and asking for stuff to draw with. I offered you a crayon and your eyes got all big and you said you hated them."

"I did? And why do you carry crayons with you into court?"

"I don't. I was messing with you. But I remember it because of the expression on your face. At the time, I thought it was because you were drugged up, and everything you were doing was exaggerated. Now, I'm not so sure." She tilts her head to the left and narrows her eyes. "Why do you hate crayons?"

"I have no damn idea."

"You gotta talk to your mother. I bet she knows something."

"What do I know?" Mom asks, strolling into the dining room with a dripping umbrella.

"Huh?" Jesse and I respond in unison.

"What do I know?" she repeats. "And why are you both looking like the cat who is chasing the canary?"

CHAPTER 52
HE'S BACK

We lie about which cat is chasing which canary because this is neither the time nor the place for me to get into it with my mother. I'd lose anyway, or pass out again, and as demonstrated by my tumble over the eggs, the floor at work isn't nearly as forgiving as the polished wood in my uncle's French apartment.

With the Point secure, I head to my mother's house to check on the boat, with a stop at home to feed Penney and grab a change of clothes. The front yard is a mess. Flowers have been knocked off their stems, torn leaves cover the windowsills, and giant palm fronds hang, ripped and twisted, off the tops of the trees.

The National Weather Service is promising more rain, and city emergency services are warning everyone that the storm, now named Tropical Depression Bethany, isn't done with us yet.

Mom's house has the same type of damage as mine. The pool, usually pristine, with only the water snake visible slithering at the bottom, is now littered with a soupy mixture of shredded botanicals. I step carefully down the slope of wet grass to the canal and hope like hell that *Happily* hasn't been beat up.

I survey the scene. A few scratches in the light blue paint where the hull missed the bumpers and hit the dock. Some debris, fallen from the trees, but the mast is standing, the sail is secure, and the lines are taut. I climb on board and stare out at the canal. Our neighbor waves at me while he attempts to lasso his rogue motorboat.

"Hell of a storm!" he yells, fishing the line out of the water with a rake.

I nod and ask if he needs help.

"I got it, but the cushions are a goner." He points to them, floating away from us in the canal.

I wish him well and head inside, where Mom is lighting candles and speaking on the phone with my grandmother in Montreal.

"Yes, everybody is safe. And Katika is checking on the boat." She smiles at me. "Boat is okay?"

"A little messy, but all good. Say hi to Grandma and thank her for the stuff she and Nori sent."

She mouths, "What stuff?" then continues the conversation with her mother-in-law.

I fight the urge to pull the phone out of her hand, commandeer the call and ask them both about Ethan's stepdad. Instead, I search the cupboard for crackers, and listen to gossip about the family, the storm, and Nori, presently expecting a ring from her boyfriend who makes more money than God. Her life has always been ordered. School, university, job, man, wedding forthcoming. I'm happy for Nori, and sort of jealous. How can we be so different? Why isn't she overwhelmed and anxious and weird? Why is she so normal?

"We will speak again tomorrow." Mom finishes the call. "Now we hope the rain is going away soon."

"I had no idea it was coming in the first place," I say, leaning against the counter.

"You are having your head inside the clouds, dear."

"Uh-huh." I shove crackers into my mouth. "Hey, Mom, do you remember anything about us going to Denver when I was little?"

It's her turn to look like the canary. Her hands give her away, moving nervously, folding a kitchen towel. "We go for a long weekend to visit Ethan and his mother."

"How did it go? Was it fun?"

"It was very nice."

"Was it? No awkward moments? Dad never said, 'Hi there, I'm Robert Kiss and we're here to visit my biological son, and by the way, thanks for marrying the woman I knocked up.'"

Her eyes narrow with an expression I know well. Dismay, *why the hell can't Katy ever keep her mouth shut?* Tension seeps into the space between us.

I can't stop myself. "Nothing like that? It was all friendly and chummy and stuff?"

She drops the towel on the floor, retrieves it, and begins folding again. "Yes," she snaps. "His mother, Lena, was married, and your father wanted to see the boy."

"The boy? You mean his son?"

"Yes. His son."

"And everyone was polite to everyone else?"

"What kind of question is this?"

I shrug and put the crackers down. "I need some chocolate."

Her brows knit together. "You do not like the crackers?"

"Too salty." I scan the counter and find a paper plate covered with aluminum foil. "What's this?"

"Brownies," she answers. "Cricket brought them from her classroom. I think they had the end-of-year party, and these are left over and sent home."

"She brought them to work?" I ask, peeling off the foil. "Why didn't she take them to her house?"

"Do you remember this word she is saying?" She pats her stomach. "Her mother says she is too fat, so she cannot eat them."

"Oh yeah, the pudge. Her loss. Our gain. They smell yummy."

She comes closer, sniffs and nods. "Yes, very nice." After inspecting each brownie, she picks one from the middle and takes a bite.

"How are they?" I ask.

She chews, covers her mouth, and dips her head. "Finom," she says. Tasty. "But not as good as we make."

"Tell me more about the trip to Colorado. How old was..."

A knock at the door interrupts my sentence. Nickety-Nick is outside, wet, soggy, his blond hair is flattened against his head. My heart skips a beat.

"Get in here," I say, pulling him into the house. "You're soaked."

"Hey, Sweet Katy. Jess told me you were here. Thought I could wait out the weather with you guys." He hands over a small bouquet of blue carnations. "These are for your mom." He cringes. "Not a great selection at the gas station."

"Thanks. They're pretty. Mom, you remember Nick?" I hand her the flowers, which are indeed ugly.

Whatever displeasure my mother felt thirty seconds ago, dissipates with Nick's arrival. Finally... *a man in the house.* She accepts the flowers, hugs Nick, and leads him into the kitchen where she offers food, coffee, sherry, and first dibs on her divorced daughter. Nick eats up the attention, though no coffee can be made since the electricity is still out. They cluck at each other. Two people who've met fewer than ten times find things to chat about. Storm damage, traffic on the highway. Is it only a matter of minutes before they begin working out the details of making Katy Kiss an honorable woman? I wonder if he'll require a dowry?

I zone out, fidget, add words in the appropriate spots, and ignore a growing sense of discomfort. Being in the wrong place at the wrong time. If my mother thinks Nick is the best thing ever, is he the opposite? I push down the sensation. He's my soulmate, my person, and I know every single thing about him.

"Katy, do you hear the news? Nick will be returning to school for the MBA."

My lips part. I didn't know that.

"He is already accepted to a program in New York," she continues.

"NYU," he adds.

"Great! Congratulations." I smile because smiling is what a normal person would do at this moment. "How long will it take?"

"Two years," he says, eyeing the brownies. "Starting fall semester."

"Please, dear, have one." Mom thrusts the plate at him.

He thanks her, takes one, crusty on the sides, with peanut butter chips protruding from the top. I nod. Watching them chew makes my stomach roll.

He winks at me. "You know some milk would be fantastic with this."

"I can't open the fridge. Honestly, everything in there has probably gone bad by now."

He grimaces. "That's disappointing."

I apologize for the milk, like I personally caused it to curdle. But I didn't. It's the storm, the wind, and the rain, still coming down in short angry bursts.

"Mrs. Kiss, show me Katy's baby pictures."

"Why do you need to see those? I was a weird-looking kid. Not at all photogenic."

Mom finishes her second brownie and daintily wipes the sides of her mouth with a napkin. "This is ridiculous. You were very beautiful. So much hair, even from the beginning. I will show your friend," she says, hurrying out of the room.

"Now I did it." He squeezes my shoulder. "Moms love me."

"Congratulations. You have only yourself to blame."

"I can stop her anytime I want," he says as she returns with a stack of albums, sits on the couch, and pats the seat next to her.

"Here is the year she is born," she says, lighting two candles on the coffee table.

I can't watch them. Instead, I return to the kitchen in search of other chocolate, or some banana peppers. My phone dings. It's Quinn.

Can I come see you later?

I bite my lip. I might be engaged later. And my life will move forward as Nick and Katy, Katy and Nick. I text him back. *Maybe. Busy with storm stuff.*

Are you all okay? Use me. I can help.

I lean against the fridge. He sends another text.

Promised the animal shelter a couple of hours Saturday. The outdoor kennel flooded.

Mom squeals with laughter. Holy crap, she's really putting on a show.

I turn back to the screen. *That's sweet, Quinn. The dogs thank you.*

Got any extra towels to donate? Sheets. Pillows?

I shuffle my feet, glance over at Nick and my mother with their heads bent over hundreds of ridiculous pictures.

How are the dreams? Are you sleeping?

Mom calls out to me. "Do you remembering when we have the picnic in Switzerland?"

"Yeah, on the roadside by the cows?"

She wipes a tear from her eye. "Milyen szép volt"

"What does that mean?" Nick asks.

"It means it was really beautiful. Do you have any pepper rings, Mom?"

She snorts. "A hűtőben. Please do not opening it."

"Why's all the good stuff in the fridge?" I ask, turning on the flashlight from my phone to search the pantry.

A message comes in from Russ. He's at his sister's house cleaning up. For the next ten minutes, I munch on stale Goldfish and exchange texts with him about how to move forward at work. We'll need to restock food, fix the door, and see what other damage there is.

Remembered one more thing, Katy-Bell.

What?

Don't eat the brownies Cricket left at The Point.

I glance at my mom and Nick. *Why? Mom brought them home.*

A one word response. *Pot.*

Are you kidding me right now, Russ?

No, man. They filled to the rim with MJ.

Are you sure?

Bit into one, tasted it. Spit it out.

Oh no, Mom's had two!

A text bubble appears, disappears, reappears. *Woop woop, girl. Your mama gonna be high as a kite.*

CHAPTER 53
THE THING THAT ALMOST HAPPENED

I send Cricket a message next. *Hi Cricket. It's Katy.*

Greetings. I gather that all is well.

My teeth grind together. I should ask if she's okay before launching into the brownie discussion.

We're all fine. How are you and yours?

My what?

Your family, Cricket. Is everyone okay?

Oh yes. Indeed. We don't live close to the shore. My window got broke due to a tree falling, but it's not <u>catastrophonic</u> because it's a sapling. That's a young tree, in case you didn't know. And Dad's car has some scratches on it and stuff because he forgot to pull it into the carport.

I grab my jaw and make a conscious effort to stop chewing the inside of my cheek. She obviously pays no heed to spell check.

Cricket, you know the brownies you brought to work?

Yes, Mrs. Katy. Mom said I had to leave them due to my pudge. Did you try one? Madam Kiss said you should have some on account of your being too thin lately. She said it's because you don't have a man, but I told her you had two men and then her face twisted all up and she said she didn't want to talk about it.

I inhale, trying to conjure the calming beach Dr. Jonas taught me about last year. It doesn't even have to be a beach. I'll take anything at this point. A deserted mall, a swamp at dusk with a million mosquitoes and a shit ton of hungry alligators.

I focus and text her back. *Great. Did you bake them from scratch?*

No, ma'am. Stevie Hunt brought them. Have you met him?

I haven't. Is Stevie a nice guy?

I mean anywhere. Directly underneath a crop duster.

He doesn't talk to me much due to the fact about him not being in my friend group, and also he doesn't come to class too often.

Why doesn't he go to class?

We're not supposed to know, Mrs. Katy.

Know what?

You can't tell anyone.

I won't tell.

Seriously. Under a bridge with some dude named Stan who's offering me lumpy gray liquid from a used ramen noodle container.

Pinkie promise?

My fingers pound on the keyboard. *Yes, pinkie promise.*

She stops texting. The silence is filled with the sound of wild giggling coming from the living room.

Cricket? Why doesn't Stevie go to school?

Due to him being a stoner. That's someone who smokes pot in case you didn't know. He gets into lots of trouble and recently came home from rehab somewhere in Utah where he had to live off the land and…

I drop the phone on the counter and rub my temples. Has my mother ever been stoned? She was a teenager in the eighties, in

Hungary, which probably wouldn't have been like America during that time. I watch them flip through pages, point, and laugh hysterically.

Mom wipes tears from her cheeks and looks at me. "Now I see why you hate these. You are always looking confused, like you have never seen the camera before."

Nick doubles over laughing and bumps into her shoulder.

I shove another handful of Goldfish into my mouth and sit down across from them. "You both doing all right?"

"Why, yes, Sweet Katy." Nick's snorting mutates into more giggles. "Why do you look so serious? Why is your mouth so firm?" He slaps his hand to his lips. "Not what I meant. I mean, your mouth is..." He stops talking, his eyes roll around in their sockets. "Baby, you are one stoic chick."

"Am I?" I ask. "Mom, sure you're feeling okay?"

"Yes, I am feeling very wonderful." She opens a new photo album. "We have taken many beautiful trips."

Nick scratches his head. The result is wavy, blond bed-head.

"We were young then, your father and I. Now we are old. Well, your father is not old. He is dead." She blinks. "Nicholas, have you heard my Robi is dead? He is having the sex with a prostitute and his heart is a big explosion." She slams the album shut. "Just like this."

Nick grins, trying not to laugh. "Yes, Mrs. Kiss. I'm so sorry."

"Hey Mom, can we talk about the trip to Denver some more?"

"Oh yes," she says, staring at her fingers. "This was the disaster. But you were a little girl, so you will not remember."

I sit up straight. She's walking right into it, unlike Nick, who's melting into the cushions with his head tilted back.

"Why was it a disaster?"

"Such a terrible story. I put it away here." She points to her head. "So I never have to think of this again."

"Why would you have to do that?" I ask.

"Oh, Katy." She stands up and looks around the room. "I will make dinner now."

"There's still no electricity. And it's not dinner time."

She turns around and studies the couch and coffee table. "Did you change our furnitures when I was in Paris?"

"Are you asking if I rearranged the room?"

"Duh," Nick mutters. "But let's focus. We need to talk."

I swivel from my mother to him. "Right this second?"

"Yes, now." He scratches his scalp again. "Mrs. Kiss, don't you think Katy and I should talk?"

"Yes, of course." She stares at him like she's never seen him before, then brushes past me into the kitchen. "Why are you looking at me in this way, dear?"

"What way?" I ask. "Are you sure you feel okay?"

"Pfhhh." She waves me off with a flourish of her arms. "You are always looking at me with the big eyes pushing out of your head. And why are you changing the subjects? You do this even when you are a little girl. One of the minutes you are chasing after the butterfly in the yard, and the next thing, you are crying how you lose your zokni."

"What's that?" Nick asks.

"My sock," I tell him. People have complained about this for years. My teachers, friends, Jesse. Dylan would regularly complain about my erratic thoughts; sentences drifting together, then apart, with no logical segue. Today, though, it's Mom who's skipping all over the place.

"You are having the very strange brain, Katika. You get this from your father. Who is dead." She huffs, pulls a warm can of Coke from the pantry and pops it open. "We will order the pizza for dinner." She steps in front of the mirror in the hallway. "Te jó ishten. Look at my hair! Such a mess. We cannot order the pizza. It is terrible idea with this rain."

"Uh-huh." I mumble.

She studies her soda. "The emergency peoples will be ordering the food. When you are calling for the pizza, please tell them we do not need one."

"You want me to call and not order pizza?" I ask.

"Yes. How do you not understand this? Maybe we go to the restaurant and make the foods for the emergency."

"Sure," I agree. "Let's do it."

"Oh. You think this is a good idea?"

"No, Mom. I don't, actually."

"You see, there you going again. Say the first thing and then the other," she huffs. "Now I go to fix my hair."

"Great," I say, and move over to Nick on the couch.

"What was the thing she said in Hungarian?" he asks.

"Te jó ishten?"

"What does it mean?"

"It means oh my God," I tell him, and scrape the soft candle wax making a puddle on the coffee table. "Not exactly, but it's what she means."

He tries to repeat the phrase, but for a guy who's been traveling the globe, his enunciation remains flatly domestic. He is apple pie, no matter the show he puts on.

"Nick, you're aware that you're stoned as hell, right?"

"Yuppers."

"I don't think Mom knows she's wasted."

"Yuppers," he repeats and rolls his head sideways. "I want to talk now."

"To me?"

"Yes, to you."

"Is this a good time?"

He yawns. "It's not goddam rocket science."

I'm taken aback. Not a great way to butter me up. "What would you like to talk about?"

"You and me, girl." He slows the words down. "You. And. Me."

I pull my knees to my chin and prepare for my proposal. It's not the most romantic scene, but it'll be a funny memory we can tell our grandchildren. In the midst of Tropical Storm Bethany, Nickety-Nick got stoned as fuckety-fuck and proposed.

"Here's the deal." He grabs my hands. "Over the last few years, I've been learning. Learning and traveling. Traveling and learning." He snorts again. "I've been out and about; in case you're having trouble keeping up."

"No trouble yet. Out and about."

"Correct," he shrugs. "Around the world. Around women."

"How wonderful," I say.

"Shoosh." He puts his index finger on my lips. "I'm talking."

"Uh-huh. Okay."

"With all my women, I've often wondered which of you is the right one. Who would I be most sorry to..." He stops, I assume, to pick his words wisely. "Terminate the arrangement with."

"Terminate?" I repeat.

"Is it Katy Kiss? Is it Courtney or Elyse? She was hot. She was a damn spider monkey in bed."

My shoulders tense. "Excuse me?"

He winks at me. "Man, she knew how to crawl all over me. Got into all the nooks and crannies, if you catch my drift."

"Oh wow." I tug my hands away from his grip. "You paint quite the picture."

"Or Brit. Lowest of the low in the IQ department, but always looked great and game for anything. She was cavernous, though."

"What the hell, Nick?"

He grins, and it's not sweet or warm or inviting. It's the opposite. A snake sidling up to a mouse and promising to behave. "Cavernous, you know, down there."

"Goddamn," I mumble.

"Right?" He reaches for my shoulders. "Loosey-goosey. Could not feel a thing."

I scoot away from him. This conversation is lighting up old memories in my brain of the times he'd get wasted in school. Sometimes he'd be loving and sweet, but by senior year he became what I called, *ugly drunk*. Aggressive, confrontational, pushy. Jesse was right. I've done the thing again. Created a person in my brain who may not have existed in real life.

"Anyway," he says, "I decided it was you."

"How fun," I say, not trying to hide my sarcasm.

"Yeah," he continues without noticing my tone. "I have a pros and cons list on an Excel sheet, and you, babe, came out on top. Money, appearance, percentage of not being a pain in my ass, and if memory serves —" He clicks his tongue as if I'm his horse being called in from pasture. "Not at all cavernous."

My mouth goes dry, and not for the first time in my life, reality slides out from under me. A reality, in this case, that may have never existed. "I came out on top?"

"On top?" He mimics. "Don't be naïve. Let's get to the point. I want you to come to New York with me."

"That's the big thing you wanted to ask me? What would I do there?"

"Move in with me. I'll have school and you can work." His head bounces a little. His blue eyes are hidden behind heavy lids, the byproduct of marijuana. "You look so shocked. I'm saving you from this pedestrian hell-hole." He yawns again. "It'll be great."

"You've gotta be kidding. Also, what if I want to go back to school?"

He giggles. "Like that would happen. Anyway, if things go well, if you and I get along, then perhaps after a few years we'll have the talk."

"The talk?" I sneer. "The marriage talk?"

He throws his hands up defensively. "Ouch, lady, so pushy."

"It's my future, Nick. The terms seem a bit ambiguous."

"Aw, poor little Katy's confused?" He pats my head. "Don't worry about any of it. It'll be like old times. You let me lead the way."

"We're not in the old times, Nick. You're wasted." I push his hand off my head. "So, I'm trying real damn hard to give you some grace right now."

"Extremely wasted." He rubs his face.

I lean close to him. "But I'm beginning to remember some things."

He grins. "What do you remember, baby girl?"

I bite my thumbnail, trying to steady my emotions. "Back in school, the only time you'd let your guard down is when we were fucked-up. It's the only time you were honest."

He wraps his fingers in my hair. "Honesty is overrated."

"Christ," I say, pulling away. "Can you be any more cliche? Have you had one healthy relationship with a woman?"

"What the ever-loving-hell?" he asks, looking bored.

I turn away from him. "I need to think for a minute."

"Such dramatics, Miss Kiss. You're not on a reality show. Maybe take it down a notch."

I let out a snort, stand up and begin pacing the room. "Why don't you take the condescension down a notch."

"Well, shit," he says. "This is tiresome."

"Is it?" I ask, walking in small circles. "Do you get how insulting it is to assume I'd leave everything I know so I can make your food and clean your house and, God forbid, not be cavernous?"

"What's the problem? Grow up. Everyone does it. We find the best fit and go. Cogs in a wheel and all that shit."

"You sound like such an asshole right now," I tell him, feeling the last six months of daydreaming about *my person* evaporate. That first time we met, the look in his eyes. Was that moment real, or did I edit the memory to fit through the keyhole of happily ever after? What if he was taking stock and checking to see if I had proper birthing hips? The sensation is palpable, like a length of twine sliding out from between my intestines.

"But you love me." His eyelids flutter. "What about the bad old days and college and all that crap?"

I stare out the window. The trees look depressed, their limbs slump groundward as slim rivulets of rainwater flow off the leaves' torn edges. "College was crap to you, Nick? Because then what are we doing here? Shouldn't we want better than crap?" I straighten my back, trying to keep up with the words coming out of my mouth. "I deserve better." I put my hands on my hips. "There, I said it. I deserve better than you."

He nods. One eyebrow moves slowly upward. "Sure thing, buttercup. I promise. We can work on it."

"Buttercup?" I stammer. "And what do you mean, *we* can work on it? How did this turn into my problem? Even if it was a reasonable thing for you to ask of me, which it's not, I don't have the energy with all the other stuff going on."

"What other stuff? Your dad died. Get over it." He smiles at me. "I soooo need some chips. Or a *pub-sub* from Publix. I do miss those fucking things."

I clench my fists, then release, in fear of reaching out and hurting him. "I don't want to get over it. Nobody gets over a parent dying. Not completely."

"Fine," he says. "What other big disastrous things do you need to work out?"

I study his face. His expression has smoothed into a sleepy, pot-induced, *I don't give a shit about anything*, gaze.

"I'm having nightmares," I tell him.

"Fucking beauty, man. So what?"

"Something might have happened to me when I was young."

He rubs his cheeks. "We all have something in the closet. You think yours is special?"

The air goes out of me. Asking him to change is a waste of time. "Nope."

"Then what's the big deal? Life's hard. Like I said, get over it."

I nod. This is what it felt like fighting with Dylan. Being made small, unimportant, the lowest priority. But here it is, my choice to make, and I'm choosing not to jump into the Nick fire after barely making it out of the Dylan frying pan.

"You should go, Nick."

"Are you serious? You're turning down my offer?"

I pause, floating in my out-of-body experience, watching my life with him dissipate. All the fairy dust getting violently sucked back up into a sparkly rainbow sky. "Weird right, since I'm such a pushover."

"You're ridiculous." He brushes his blond hair away from his face.

I walk to the front door and pull it open. "Don't think I am. Might want to take another look at your Excel sheet and add a column named nanny. That's what you're really looking for."

He pushes himself off the couch in a series of ungraceful movements. "What about all the grace you were going to give?"

I watch my person, who was never my person, stumble outside. "You rolled over all the grace I had, Nick. You ripped it apart, blew it away, and now I'm plumb fucking out."

CHAPTER 54
LOSING KATY

No sooner do I close the door on my future with Nick, that the judgment, albeit flawed, begins from my mother. Having snuck into the kitchen for more brownies, she's witnessed the last few minutes of our conversation. With her sense of tact extinguished by chocolate edibles, she lets me have it.

"You do not want a new man in the family? You want to grow old alone?" She leans against the wall, steadies herself, then wobbles back to her bedroom with a third brownie in one hand and a flashlight in the other.

"I just don't want that man," I say, hurrying behind. "Please don't have any more of those."

She sets the flashlight on the nightstand, slides into bed, and pulls the blanket up to her nose. "I know they are having the marijuana in them. So what? I like it."

"You like being high?" I ask, sitting down with her. "Since when? Have you ever even smoked pot?"

"Does not matter. Why you stupid and make the husband go away?"

"Did you hear what he was saying? That was not a proposal of marriage."

She squints. "Katy, why are you having three heads? Why are you making this face and pushing your mouth together like this?"

"It's called tension, Mother. Now please hand me the brownie you're hiding under the blanket."

"No."

"Mom."

"I like them. Especially these funny dots." She pulls the brownie out to show me. "The drugs are in the funny dots."

"The pot's baked into the batter. The dots are peanut butter chips."

"I see," she says slowly, then takes another bite.

"Oh my God, don't eat the whole thing." I reach my hand toward her. "Begging you. Please hand it over."

"Why?"

I inch closer. "Because you've far exceeded the suggested serving size and neither one of us wants to spend any more time in a hospital than we did last year with Dad."

She groans and hands over the brownie. "Here. Take it. I am feeling very good now, even though my daughter will be a spinning-ster."

"Really, you're calling me a spinster at twenty-six? Remind me later to tell you how not nice you are when you're wasted." I put the brownie on the dresser. "Let's talk about Nick when you're not high."

She lies back down and stares at the fan. "What are these dreams you are telling the boy about?" Her head moves in a circular motion, as if the blades were rotating. She smiles, then begins giggling. "This fan is going the wrong way."

I look up. "It's not on. It's not moving."

"No?" She wiggles her fingers in the air. "Why is the ceiling up? Why is it so far away?"

"It's the house growing," I tell her. "It'll shrink down to normal size when the pot's out of your system."

"Really? How wonderful." She rolls over on her side. "Tell me about the dream, dear."

"Now's not the time."

"Yes," she demands. "Tell me. My ears are very open. I hear everything."

I move over to Dad's side of the bed. "You might not want to hear this." I take his pillow and hold it close to my chest.

"Tell me, Katika. What can be so bad?"

• • • • •

Ten minutes later, she's rendered silent. I've told her about the dreams, the Elevator Man, the pink crayon, the phrase about the bucket, and the possible connection to Ethan's stepdad. She listens as intently as her drug-addled mind allows.

"What does this mean?" she finally asks. "This falling into the bucket?"

I squash the pillow closer. "Ethan says his stepdad used to say it."

She mumbles several Hungarian swear words, the most vicious of which translates into English as "dog's ear."

"What, Mom? What is it?" I ask as my phone lights with a text from Ethan.

Call me ASAP. We need to talk.

"Who is this calling you? Is it Nick?" She rubs the bridge of her nose. "I like this boy, but he is too thin, like the starving rat." She stops talking for a moment and pats my hand. "Your father was never too thin. He liked the good foods."

"I remember that about him. But he hated peanut butter."

She nods, fluffs the blanket, then drops her arms heavily back down. "Look at my feet. They are stupid. Why do animals have four and the people only having two?"

"Um, I'm not sure I can give you a good answer for that. Can we focus on the dream, though?"

"Oh yes, of course." She rolls onto her back. Her eyes glaze over, her expression is dazed, peaceful. "Now I see why people are taking the drugs. I do not care about any of the things from all of my life." She looks at me. "Not any of them, so I tell you this terrible story, because I do not care."

"Great, Mom. Hopefully I won't care either."

She whispers. "You will care because it was a very bad day. The worst day."

• • • • •

And so begins the story.

"Your father, Robi. You know your father's name is Robi, yes?"

"Uh-huh."

"He says we go to Colorado to see the boy. You are tiny then, three years old. I do not want to go because it is cold, but he says, yes, we go. So fine, we fly to this place and there is Lena and the boy." She narrows her eyes. "Ethan. You remember him? We meet him in Bangkok when your father has the sex with prostitute."

I clamp my hands together to keep them from shaking.

"Katika, what is your favorite movie?"

"What?"

Her head lolls to the side. "My favorite movie is the *LA Story* with Steve Martins."

"Never heard of it. Can we get back to our trip to Denver?"

"Such a wonderful movie. It is like magic." She picks up the remote and begins clicking. "We watch it now."

"Power's still out, Mom."

"Mm. During the week, then. We make the movie night date because you are the old spinning-ster."

I bite my lower lip. If she doesn't put the remote down, I'm going to fling it across the room. "Denver?"

"Yes. Okay. We are having a nice time. So much snow outside, it reminds me of home, you know. Of Szeged and Budapest. Beautiful in the winter."

"Uh-huh." My phone buzzes again with another text from Ethan.

CALL ME

"You and the boy are playing with the toy cars. I remember they are painted with all the bright colors. The little fire engine..." She trails off for a moment, smiling. "And we all are having a nice lunch. I think this is the second day we are there. The man, the husband, he seems angry. I tell Robi it is because we are speaking Hungarian, his mother and Robi and I. So, of course, I understand this is not the good manners, and we begin speaking in English, and what do you know?" She stops talking, her eyes flutter.

"Mom?"

"Yes? What was I saying?"

I move closer. "You began speaking English instead of Hungarian to pacify his dad."

"Igen. Yes, okay, but this crazy man is still angry."

"How could you tell? Did he say something?"

"You can see in his eyes. So dark, I remembering thinking how sad this is for Lena to marry him."

"It was totally unfair."

"Igen. Borzasto."

"It was awful. What happened then?"

"Ethan is yelling and jumping like the beans, 'Mommy, Mommy, can I go to park?' I never forget, he is very excited because of the snow. The husband says he will take you and the boy." She stops talking, sits up and plumps her pillow, then lies back down before continuing. "I look at Robi and I am thinking in my head this is not good. I feeling it, but Robi says it is fine. What can happen?"

"Why didn't you put your foot down if you thought it was a bad idea? Why would you let him take us?"

She props herself up on her arms again and looks around the room like she'd just arrived. "Have you really not seen this movie, the *LA Story*?"

"Not ever. Can we get back to the dude taking us to the park?"

She bursts out laughing while I watch, helpless, trapped in the middle of a memory I have no power to retrieve on my own.

"Katy." She sucks in air and tries to stifle her giggles. "Your face..." She uses her fingers to push her eyebrows together on her forehead. "This is how you are looking. So much worry like you carrying the world in your shoulders."

"On my shoulders." I get off the bed and begin pacing. "Can you focus, please? This is important."

She shakes her head. "I should not have had this last bite."

"No kidding."

"Have you heard of this sentence the Americans use, to sleeping it off?" She sticks her tongue out. Her head dips down, her eyes cross, trying to catch a glimpse of it. "My mouth, is it still here?"

I stop pacing. "Is your mouth still where, Mom? On your face?"

"Yes. Do you see it?"

"Of course. How would you be talking without it?"

"And my nose?" She taps her face. "Has it moved?"

I sigh. "It hasn't moved anywhere. It's also in the right place."

She nods. "I think now is time for sleeping. Please put the alarm on when you leave."

"Power's still off. Tell me the rest of the story."

She lies back down. Her eyes close. "Yes dear, of course."

"Mom?"

"Such a bad day," she says sluggishly.

"Mom!"

"We all promised."

"Who did? What did you promise?"

"We promise," she whispers. "We will never talk about it. Never."

"What does that mean? Talk about what?"

Pink splotches spread on her cheeks. She shivers, and her eyes, still closed, fill with tears. Her breathing slows, becomes rhythmic, and I lose hope of her saying anything else.

But she does, quietly.

"The day we lose our Katy."

CHAPTER 55
TEAM QUINN

I cover my ears and squeeze my eyes shut. Not for any good reason, other than the sound of my heart thumping like a drum. They didn't lose me. I'm right here. I've always been right here.

I inhale imaginary tomato soup, hold it, and try my hardest to blow the steam away from the bowl. Again, then once again. It works, except for the head rush.

"Wake up!" I poke her arm and gently tug on the blanket. She's out cold, smiling again, drifting in her loaded brownie slumber.

"Damnit," I whisper. Is there a second briefcase in this house, under a bed, in another closet, hidden like the one we found last year, but filled with a horror story about my childhood? How many secrets did my parents keep, and why is each one worse than the last?

I grab my raincoat and lock the carport door on my way out. A low curtain of clouds and mist distorts the sunset. The streets are wet, and I drive the three blocks home slowly, carefully. Not because of the weather, but because I'm distracted, wounded suddenly by some mysterious event.

I pull into my driveway, jog to the front door with my head down to avoid the drizzle, and slam into Quinn.

"Holy crap!" I step backwards. "You scared the living shit out of me."

He grabs my shoulders to steady me. "I needed to see you."

"Why? Quinn, oh my God, you're soaking wet." I look at the driveway. "Where's your car? When did you get here?"

He lets go of me and points to his car parked on the street, then moves out of my way so I can unlock the door.

"About an hour ago," he says, following me inside.

"I thought you weren't getting home until tomorrow."

He dries his face with his sleeve. "I was worried about you, so I caught an earlier flight into Sarasota and drove the rest of the way." He smiles. "Didn't love the landing in the storm. I'm surprised they didn't divert us."

"Why didn't you text me?" I ask.

"I did. You didn't answer."

I pull off my raincoat, then run my hands along the kitchen counter to find the birthday candle, which is now slumped over in the melted block of cream cheese.

"Sorry about not picking up. I've been a little preoccupied." I relight the candle. It does little to brighten the room. "Want some dry clothes?"

"Do you have anything?" he asks, scratching Penney's ears.

"Dylan left some pants behind."

He nods, and I creep into my bedroom and fumble around in the closet. A few of Dylan's jeans are in a donation pile in the corner. They'll be a few inches too short for Quinn's long legs, but that's the least of his worries because the biggest top I have is a light pink hoodie embroidered with "Daddy's Girl" on the front. I try not to stare as he strips off his dark slacks and button-down shirt. Then I try not to laugh because even in the dark, he looks ridiculous in his new outfit.

"Hot," I tell him, plundering the kitchen drawers for more candles.

"Pink is my color." He grins and sits on the couch. "Come and talk to me."

I find a single white candlestick. "About what? Do you need some food? Everything in the fridge has probably gone bad by now."

"I had a bag of chips in the car," he says, sliding over to make room for me. "Were you at The Point this whole time? I drove by but didn't see your car."

"No, I was at Mom's. She's stoned as hell."

I see the surprise on his face only because my phone lights up with another message from Ethan.

Please call me! I found out what happened.

I stare at the words. I did too...sort of, but like last year when my dad died, the information isn't processing. Mom's words, *the day we lost our Katy*, aren't sinking in. How could they have lost me when I'm right here?

"I have to call my brother back," I tell him. "But I have a question first."

"Shoot," he says.

"What would you say if I wanted to go back to school and get my MBA or something?"

"I'd say do it."

I try to read his face in the dark. "You would?"

He puts his hand on my knee. "Of course. It would be great for your career. You're smart as hell. If you want it, then go for it."

Now I'm grateful for the darkness, because I'm blushing. I can feel the heat on my face. I can feel the heat everywhere because his hands have magical powers. "That's so nice."

"I'll carry your books for you," he offers.

I lean close and kiss him. Jesse was right. About Nick and now about Quinn.

"Thanks. Not that I need your permission to go back." I add. "I was just curious."

"Now you know. You do anything you want." He pulls me close and kisses me again. "Except make me leave."

I don't know if I can blush any harder. I'm on overload. "I won't make you leave, but I do have to call my brother back."

His big brown eyes flicker in the glow of the screen as I make the call.

Ethan answers on the first ring. "Finally. Are you okay? I've been watching the weather."

"We're all good. There's some damage at the restaurant, but nothing we can't fix. And everyone is safe." I glance at Quinn. "Hey Ethan, my friend Quinn is here."

A pause. "Am I on speaker?" he asks.

"Yeah, if you don't mind. He knows about the dreams."

"All of them?"

Quinn speaks up. "Hi Ethan, I don't have to listen if it bothers you, but I want to be here for your sister. For whatever you all need." He lowers his voice. "For whatever you need. It's why I wanted to get back to you. I shouldn't have left in the first place."

A faint smile creeps across my face. The feeling of being in the wrong place, the wrong time, the tug in my gut I've so often felt, is acutely absent. "I'm okay with it, Ethan, if you are."

"It's your call, sister."

"Yeah, I'm good. And Mom's already spilled some of what happened."

Ethan's voice gets louder. "She did?"

Penney jumps onto the couch, lets out a tiny kitten yowl and gallops away. "Yeah," I tell him. "The beginning, at least. Some pot brownies got her talking, but then she passed out, so we didn't get far."

"What the hell?" he blurts out.

"She didn't know what she was eating. Well, not at first. She's out cold at the moment, but she started talking about us visiting you guys when I was little. She said your dad...stepdad, sorry, was pissed. I guess he felt left out because everyone was speaking Hungarian."

"Yeah, I got that from my mom, too," Ethan says. "He was angry from the second he heard you guys were coming out. What else did she tell you?"

"Nothing coherent. He offered to take you and me to some park."

Quinn scoots closer to me, squinting in concentration, trying to keep up with the flow of information.

"Right," Ethan says. "Mom told me I was making a fuss and wanted to go outside."

I lay the phone on the coffee table; nervous my hands will begin shaking again. "My mother said it was the day they lost me. What the hell does that mean?"

The silence swells in the cold, damp room. The words turn my stomach. Something happened to me. Something that sent me marching down a different road. An alternate future.

Ethan is the first to speak again. "Are you sure you want to know?"

"How bad can it be? I have no memory of anything. It's fine. Just tell me."

"It was my fault," he says. "I don't think any of it would have happened if I would have kept my mouth shut."

I roll my eyes. "That's crap. You were a kid. Don't even go there."

He sighs, long distance, and begins talking.

"Like I said, Mom told me he was extremely pissed off the second he found out you all were coming to Denver. He was a jealous bastard, and it didn't take much to set him off. It was tense from the get-go, and everyone was walking on eggshells. But that day, for some reason, he was acting a little better until everyone started with the Hungarian. And then the darkness came again." He hesitates. "The sadistic energy. It's like a thousand-pound weight."

I lean closer to Quinn, thankful for the warmth pouring out of him.

Ethan continues. "Mom thinks I was trying to appease him. We'd gotten good at it, you know? We had the signals worked out between the two of us and our methods to calm him down. Making him the good guy, and I say good guy with every fucking bit of irony that exists. He'd be the hero, and we'd be thankful. Dysfunction up the ass."

I search for words to soothe him, but nothing comes to me. I wait until he begins speaking again.

"Mom said I asked him to take us to the park so we could play in the snow."

Quinn interrupts. "Sorry, Ethan. Do you remember any of this?"

"No," he responds. "Nothing. I mean, bits and pieces of Katy and her family being here, and my dad always being angry. But nothing about that day."

"Sorry, man," Quinn says again. "Go on, I didn't mean to cut you off."

"No worries," he says. "He took us to the park. The one across from my house."

"The house you live in now? I don't remember seeing a park near your place."

He's quiet for a few beats. "Because it's gone. It's that big old lot with the dead tree."

"The lot we were talking about when we had hotdogs?" I ask, picturing the yellow grass, the decaying tree. "That used to be a park?"

"That's the funny thing, well, not really funny, but I've lived in this house before."

"What? Did I know that?"

"Nope. I didn't either until earlier today. Mom said we lived here for a couple of years after I was born. Then we moved out, and the old man started renovating it."

"So the house I visited just now has been in your family for years. The house with the creepy ass basement? You lived there as a baby?"

"Yep. I guess it's what he did. Buy old houses, fix them up. Sell them or rent them out. It happens all the time in this area."

Quinn moves closer to the phone. "You're saying there are two houses. One where you all were having the family reunion, and the one you live in right now, which is next to a park that isn't a park anymore?"

"Right," Ethan continues. "And it's where he brought us that day, to the park next to this house. At some point, he made me run home to get some gloves or something for you."

"Okay," I say, trying to put everything in the right place.

"Mom says I came into the house and asked for warmer clothes. She can't remember what it was either. Gloves, a scarf. It doesn't matter. She said she yelled at me for walking by myself."

"How old were you?" Quinn asks.

"Almost eight, I think. Old enough to know better."

I shake my head. "You were a little kid, Ethan."

"I was in elementary school." His voice breaks. "I left you alone with him."

"It's still not your fault. He was the adult. You were the child," I tell him, feeling the weight of his guilt.

"Wasn't it?" He clears his throat again. "Guess your folks got bent out of shape, and they brought me back to the park. When we all got there, you were gone, and my stepdad was acting all frantic about not being able to find you."

I shiver and look over at Quinn. He whispers, "You're okay," and folds my hands into his.

"What the hell? Where was I?"

"Mom said everyone freaked out. They called the cops and put people into groups looking for you. Like literally walking the streets, checking each yard, and knocking on doors."

I close my eyes, remembering the dreams, the dark void, the cold, the desk, the crayon. "How long did it take to find me?"

Ethan draws in breath, crying now, barely able to get the word out. "Hours."

Quinn pulls me closer, but it doesn't help. I'm shaking not because I'm cold, but because of this disgusting thing that happened to me.

"How many hours?"

"I'm sorry, Katy."

"It's not your fault. It was never your fault."

He sobs quietly. It's painful to listen to. How can he blame himself for someone else's actions? After a few minutes, he composes himself. "It took a long time. Mom said about six hours."

I pull away from Quinn and drop my head into my hands. "Oh my God," I mutter, not wanting to think about what my parents went through.

"Where was she?" Quinn asks.

I look up at him. "I know exactly where I was."

He wipes the tears off my cheeks. "What do you mean?"

"She knows because it's what started the nightmares," Ethan says, his voice still shaky. "She was in this house, and when I forced her to go down into the basement, she blacked out. It's what started everything."

"The little desk," I mumble. "The stick figure pictures on the wall, the ones I made fun of you for drawing."

"It was you." Ethan finishes my thought. "You drew them."

"You blacked out when you were in Denver?" Quinn asks, trying to catch up.

"I thought it was the air. The altitude getting to me. But it was trauma, I guess. A trigger. Who found me?"

"Do you even have to ask?" he says. "Everyone split into groups looking for you. Nobody saw my stepdad the whole time they were searching."

I cross my arms protectively across my chest. Of course it would be him. He was with me, hiding me in that tiny room.

"Mom said he carried you back, running to the command center they'd set up. So damn proud of himself for finding the missing little girl."

"What the fuck? Was he insane? Where did he say he found me?"

"In the house, hiding in a closet."

My teeth grind together. "Bullshit. That's a lie. Why didn't he find me right away then? I was right across the street from the park. Why wouldn't everyone have looked there first?"

"I don't know, Katy. Maybe everyone was panicking. Mom said that after they found you, the cops searched the house and found your coat and shoes down in the basement." He stops speaking for a moment. "And a rope hidden behind some trash in the corner of the room. She said it took a couple weeks, but they matched fibers from the scarf you were wearing."

"Rope?" A shudder travels through me. "Are you serious? He had me tied to something?" I ball my hands into a fist. "Did he do anything to me? No wait. Maybe don't tell me."

"They took you to the hospital," he says. "And, you know, checked."

"And?" Quinn asks, wrapping his hands around mine again.

"He didn't hurt you. Not physically. But there was no working bathroom in the house at the time."

"Right," I say. "You said he was renovating it."

"You were a toddler, Katy, with a toddler bladder."

The line is quiet, and once again, it doesn't take long to connect the dots in the nightmares. I have to pee, I have to hold it, try to hold it, try fell into a bucket... "That explains it. Wait, there was an actual bucket?"

Ethan's voice becomes lighter, despite the gravity of the conversation. "No. He said that to my mom and me, too. Try fell into a fucking bucket. It was his catch-phrase. His way of making you feel like shit about yourself."

"Well great. It worked. But why did he take me?"

"I don't know," he says. "Probably to cause pain. To convince himself he was in control."

"Nobody asked? Wasn't anyone curious? I know he was pissed, but that's the reason? That's why he'd kidnap a three-year-old?"

"I'm sure everyone asked, Katy. He was jealous. He was a piece of shit." He hesitates. "I'm so sorry. I wish he would have taken me."

I can't answer for a moment, stunned by his words. He lived with this man for years. That was abuse enough. "Don't do that, Ethan. This is on him, not you." I draw in a deep breath. It's not cleansing or calming. But now I know what happened, and while it's awful, it could have been much worse. "Do you remember last year when you told me your parents split up?"

"A euphemism," he answers. "Mom said it was the quickest divorce her lawyer ever worked on. She called it more of a protective order. A go-into-jail card."

"He went to prison?" I ask.

"Yeah, he did."

"Do you know where he is now?"

"No. I left Noah a voicemail. If anyone can find out, he can."

"Good. I hope he's dead," I say, picturing my mother sleeping off her high, crying, babbling about keeping this a secret.

"Your parents were completely freaked out."

"Do you blame them? What a goddamn psychotic thing to do. Wait, Ethan…did he ever hurt you?"

Another drawn-out silence. "Emotionally? He did some damage. Not physically. At least not that I remember."

Quinn pulls me close to his chest. I hear his heartbeat. Feel his warmth.

Ethan continues. "Mom said you guys blew out of here and things got chilly after that. It's why we didn't see each other again until last year."

"It explains everything, even what my mother said right before she fell asleep just now."

"What did she say?" he asks.

"She said they promised each other never to talk about it again." I run my hand along Quinn's cheek. Day old stubble tickles my fingertips. "And they never did."

CHAPTER 56
HAPPILY

Mom is ill-equipped to communicate the next morning. The pot hangover leaves her groggy, with dry eyes and a sour stomach. She doesn't react well to my news: The secret about Denver is out. I try letting her off the hook by saying it wasn't her fault, but she gets angrier. Using her calm and scary-as-shit indoor voice, she tells me I should have left all the wells enough alone.

I consider the options. She's stubborn to her core. Pushing her is the equivalent of ramming my head into a wall. A wall made of steel, with teeth…that are on fire. But I am her offspring, and obstinate as well, so we stare each other down for five minutes. Okay, not five minutes. Maybe fifteen seconds. She blinks first and admits that keeping the past from me hasn't gone according to plan. I win the smallest of battles—but will have to wait for the reward, because she's in no mood for chitchat or sunlight or the company of humans.

I accept this outcome and get ready to leave her house wondering why so much of my life is a lie, and how many more secrets are floating about in the Kiss Family ether.

Mom stops me before I head out the door and hands over a letter addressed to me from my grandmother. She mumbles an apology for the delay. It came in the mail a few days ago, but with the storm and the rain and power outage...well, she kept forgetting to give it to me.

• • • • •

I carry it with me on my way to work, where cleaning and continued assessment of the damage caused by Tropical Storm Bethany awaits. I make an executive decision to divert and soak up some cloudy skies at the beach before heading in. The weather is unusually cool, and the waves are still pissy, spitting and hissing as they run up on the shore. I test the water. Chilly for this time of year, but not enough to drive me away. I back up a few yards and sit down on the damp sand. The smell of the ocean is strong today. The seaweed and shells and saltwater have been churned up by an angry gulf. It reminds me of the earthy scent released from the herbs I chop and smash on the wooden cutting board at the restaurant.

I try to relax. Feel at one with the ocean. It works for approximately twenty seconds, my brain flowing in a straight line, with one thought beginning to end. Here's the thought: The strap on my flip-flop is about to break.

A tiny sand crab surfs onto the beach near my foot. Near my almost broken flip-flop. Should I read my grandmother's letter now? Should I call her instead? It would be like calling someone before listening to their voicemail, so they're forced to repeat the entire message one more time. The crab uses its little claws to burrow into the sand, underneath a bottle cap for cover. People shouldn't litter.

I decide to read it now. The envelope is big, the size of a greeting card, and the handwriting is hers, though sloppier than it once was. Nori mentioned last month that her hands are less steady these days.

The crab hides. A seagull does a fly by, taking a look.

I carefully tear the seal open, expecting a card inside. But Grandma isn't a greeting card type of girl, so what I find is heavy stock paper, beige, matching the envelope, filled with her words.

Édesem, Sweetheart,

This not easy to writing these days, but I wanting this just you and me. When you asking before why nobody telling you nothings, I thinking about this for many hours. Nori also showing computer mails where you asking what happening when we going to Austria.

I tell you now.

Austria: We living in the big horse barn. Sixty of peoples inside and three or four other barn on land of Austrian estate. I think owned by noble man, not sure how to saying this word. All the peoples, the prisoners, have job. The childrens taking bloody sock from soldier and cleaning, then giving what left to adult who making the new sock for other soldier. Big fun, yes?

When not working, the childrens running and play. Sometimes farmer on field giving us foods. Mother putting potato on stove to cooking. We have stove in the barn. She make very terrible soup with old vegetables. How I hating this soup.

Then also this. One day in spring, guard taking us to forest to picking this (How to say in English?) áfonya.

"Blueberry," I whisper, then check on Mr. Crab. He's still hiding. His little pinchers open and close, as if he's expecting someone to deposit a wondrous thing inside of them. I begin reading again.

This soldier, he is young man, and he take us because he liking Eva. Every boy falling in love with my sister! This day is so beautiful. The sky blue and I remembering how close he walk with her. This for me is like the dream. Everybody in group happy on this time. We eat the fruit. It fresh, not rot like other foods we having.

It go like this for long time. Some peoples die because no food. We all very thin. We always hungry. Some die because no doctor. One girl, I think not even to twenty years, she die because of the diabetic...how you say this? She get no medicine. She die alone. No family nowhere. On this day it very cold and so much rain. I remembering two solider taking her body away, and my mother cry. She not wanting the rain to falling on the girl's face. She make soldier cover with blanket. She try to asking where they will bury this poor child, but soldier don't answering. They don't tell us nothing.

Then one day, poof, Russian coming and say now war over, you go home. So we go home. It taking three day with many trains. Sometime we sleeping on floor or dirt, or the outside. We getting home in morning and my father there already. He live too! I am happy at this time, but bigger feeling is how hungry and tired I feeling.

I look up from the letter. The power-walking ladies are on the move again. They remind me of Nick and the afternoon we spent down here at the beach. Wonder how far he's power-walked away from Florida. The women rush past me, leaving behind the heavy scent of sunscreen and an eyeful of shiny bronzed skin.

I go back to the letter. The ink on the next page is blue, instead of the black on the previous pages. How many days did it take to compose this? I read a few lines quickly, then grab my phone. Words are great. Hearing my grandmother's voice is better.

"Hi Grandma. How are you?"

"Very good, sweetheart. How is this terrible weather?"

"It's not as bad as they make it on TV. We're all okay, but there's some water damage at The Point."

She murmurs an acknowledgment.

"Mom gave me the letter you sent. I've read a bunch of it."

"And you having question?"

"Uh-huh."

"Tell to me."

"Okay, well, were you ever scared? You know, while this stuff was going on?"

"Sometime yes." I hear her bracelets clink together, and I picture her shrug or roll her eyes because she gets me. Gets how I'm not built to do the thing Mom complained about this morning. *Leaving all the wells enough alone.*

"Only sometimes?" I ask.

"When the young girl die, I afraid and very sad. How terrible she die alone without families there. But not afraid all of the times. When they taking us from our home, taking our peoples, this make us wanting to live...how you say? Többet akartunk élni."

"It made you want to live more?"

"Yes. Do you understanding this? We wanting more, but not same for all. For Jew who surviving Auschwitz, Dachau, these terrible place, this not same result. They dead, even if they living."

I stare at the water as she speaks. A second seagull flies reconnaissance over my new pet crustacean. I flap my arm to shoo it away.

"Did your parents feel the same way?" I ask. "Did Eva?"

"I not knowing. We don't talking about it."

"Really?" I say. "I don't get it, and this has been bugging me for weeks. Why do so many people want to kill Jews? What did we do wrong?"

"Katika, this question nobody can answering. The religions, the moneys, the lands, the family and so much of war. You know the Jew and Arab, they coming from same place. I thinking maybe we all coming from same place. I reading book of history that saying one thing, another book saying other thing. Everyone having different idea of this. There are many of the reasons, but for me, nothing making sense. I want you to using...how you say, bibliothèque."

"Library." I translate for her.

"Yes. Go there and finding all the books. Reading all of them."

"But you just said they all say something different."

"But you reading between the linings." She giggles. "I know I saying this wrong. But read, then we talking again. Maybe you teaching to me why this happening to our peoples."

"Deal, Grandma." I say, wiggling my toes in the sand. I want to ask her a thousand more questions. I settle on one. "Why aren't you more angry about what happened?"

The line is quiet. For one, two, five, ten seconds before she answers. "For many of the years, I feel very angry. I want to giving them back what they doing to us. To taking away home, take childrens, husband, mother and father. To treating them like the bug, like they not human. To killing..." She stops and inhales sharply. "Then one day, I understand this mean we not better than they are. And we are, Katika. We better. This why I changing my mind to this thinking instead. A boldogság a legjobb bosszú."

"Happiness is the best revenge?"

"Yes. Who living the better life, the happily peoples or the angry peoples?"

"Oh my gosh," I blurt out. "That's why you always said it to me when I was little, isn't it? To be happily?"

"Yes. This is reason. If our peoples doing this, we better. We thanking the God and not pushing over our lucks. The bad peoples who did these terrible things, they full of the hate. They full of all terrible feelings. But we, Katika, we know it better to go finding the happily."

"I never knew," I say, watching a pelican skim the surface of the water. "How did it take so long for me to hear this stuff?"

"This our mistake. We should not be hiding these things from you," she grumbles, as much as a little old grandma can grumble. "I have speaking to Ee-ten's mami."

"Lena? Why? When's the last time you even spoke to each other?"

"Not for many of the years. Our family all good friends for long times in Budapest."

"I know. Ethan and I figured it out when we read those letters in the briefcase."

"The briefcase. Yes. So many secret. I calling her because I needing the informations of what she has telling her son. Does he knowing these things, or does Lena hiding this also?"

"No," I say. "She didn't hide it from him."

"Yes. Now I knowing. Also, she telling me about these terrible dreams you having."

"Oh my God." I huff and kick my left foot. Little crab is startled into action, climbing out of his cave and scampering toward the water's edge. "You know what happened to me in Denver, too?"

"I wish I never hearing about it. Milyen szörnyű volt." *How awful it was.*

"Yeah, it wasn't great. Lena told Ethan the whole story, and then he told me. Mom told me about it too. Well, she started to."

"Your mother telling you about this?"

"Kind of. She was too ston—" I stop short. "She's been pretty jet lagged. She fell asleep halfway through."

"This very surprise to me. But good that now she telling you. All the informations we don't giving you. And this terrible day."

"You said my parents told you guys to keep everything secret."

"Igen. Not good for you, Katika. So this what I wanting to say to you now."

"You don't have to say anything. It's not your fault."

"But this stupid what we doing to you. When you baby, we love you so much, we not letting nothing touch you. We are feeling this way with Nori, with all the childrens, but they here in Montreal. Close to us."

"You mean close to the family? The Hungarian spider web?"

She giggles. "This good way of saying this. But you so far away. How we keeping you safe?"

"Far away with my parents. It's not like I was alone."

"You don't understanding. You all gone."

"Oh, you were worried about Mom and Dad too. All three of us," I say, watching crab dude dart into the water. A wave crashes into his spindly legs, rushes over his shell and freaky dark eyes. Then he's gone—safe for another day, or hour, or minute.

"Yes. Of course. And when this terrible thing happen to you, our fear getting so big."

"Do you think Mom and Dad would have told me we're Jewish if Ethan's stepdad hadn't…whatever. Taken me?"

"Nem," she says *no*. "This only making it worse. Everyone here upset when this happens. We telling them to coming back to Montreal. To where we keeping safe together."

"You actually tried to get us to move up there?"

"Yes. Many of the times."

"I had no idea. Our lives would have been so different. Though staying here meant they had to double-down. Blend in, well, kind of, and erase who we were."

"Yes."

I stand up and dust the sand off my legs. "Not dragging the old life with them. Mom said that to me a few weeks ago. They had to lie to create plausible deniability."

"What this meaning?"

I stretch from side to side. "It means if I don't know about my history, I don't have to lie about it. Maybe they didn't want their kid to be a liar."

"Hm," she says quietly. "I seeing what you say. But still not good for you."

"Yet I'm still here, all in one piece."

Her bracelets clink again, "It not fair. You learning about the family in this way. Our fear costing so much to you."

"Everything costs something," I say. "Maybe this was my lesson to learn."

She laughs, "How many things you needing to learning, Katika? You have terrible day in Denver when you little girl, then trouble with bad husband, and after this you lose father? This too much already."

"I never thought about it that way, but honestly, Grandma, you survived the Holocaust. I don't get to complain about anything, and anyway, we all have our battles, right? You know, the dominoes falling over on us."

"I don't understanding this."

I squint into the sunshine. "Just something I figured out last year. It's a long story—but it means none of us get here without some baggage."

"Whose baggage?" she asks, then goes silent for a few seconds before continuing. "Who is owner of baggage you carrying?"

"That's kind of the point. If you don't take care of yours, it gets knocked down to the next generation."

"Do you think we did this?" she asks, speaking now in Hungarian. "Did we give these terrible things to you and Nori and all the grandchildren?"

I turn around and pull wisps of hair from my face. "You're not the one who pushed the lie. Mom and Dad did. They didn't like what was inside their bags, so they ignored them. Put them away."

"Into their closet," she adds quickly.

"Exactly."

She continues, still in Hungarian. "And now you carry them."

"Yeah. I guess so."

"Until now, Katika. Now you should do something different."

"I'm trying," I say, tripping, barely catching myself from doing a face-plant. I look behind me and see my torn flip-flop lying in the sand.

"Listening to me, sweetheart." She flips back into English. "You put down old baggages. You put down because they not yours. I wanting you to buy the new suitcase. The pretty suitcase, and you filling it with new thing."

I grin to myself. She sounds like she's ready to lead an army into battle. "What's the new thing, Grandma?"

She sighs, and her voice cracks as she speaks. "Sweetheart, don't you know? You fill it with the happily."

CHAPTER 57
GET RID OF IT

I hurry to the restaurant, lock the door behind me and have a good cry. My grandmother's letter feels like the missing link I've been searching for. My family, in their own misguided way, has done nothing but try to protect me. Their plan misfired, but the intention was never bad. It was love.

• • • • •

It takes a few hours to recalibrate. I spend that time alone at work, cleaning and tossing out defrosted meat from the walk-in fridge. Is it possible that I've already processed what happened to me as a child, or has the information not seeped into the part of my brain that reacts to anxiety or fear or panic? I hope for the former. Dread the latter.

By the time Jesse and Quinn arrive, I'm in the dining room waiting for a new front door to be delivered and installed. I fill Jesse in on the details of my mysterious nightmares.

"I need a drink." She heads to the old mahogany bar. "Why do people suck so much?" She finds a bottle of red wine. "I'm sorry, Katy. I'd make a joke right now, you know, say something about how it's no surprise that you're so damn weird, but, well—it seems inappropriate."

I smile at her. "Thanks for holding back."

"Anything for you." She grins. "Is it strange? Knowing what happened?"

I sit down across from her as she reads the wine label, then shrugs.

"Of course. The dude was psycho, but I don't remember any of it." I stop talking while Quinn takes a seat next to me. "I am angry, though. Can you imagine what my parents went through? That's what pisses me off the most."

"I'd have fucking killed him." Quinn says, scooting closer to me. "Straight-up ended his life."

Jesses's gaze moves between us. "You two are together now? Is this an official thing?"

"It is." He takes my hand. "She put a pink sweatshirt on me, and I was hooked."

I blush. It's been a long time, okay, it's been never, that a man was this nice to me.

Jesse fumbles with a corkscrew. "God, this is going to be annoying. I know I pushed you two together but spare me the PDA."

"Since when are you a prude?" he asks. "Need me to open that up?"

"Back off, lover boy. I got it."

I slouch in the chair and read an email from my brother. "Listen to this, you guys. I was asking Ethan why those pictures I drew were still in the little room in the basement."

Jesse pours wine into three glasses. "Right. It's been over twenty years since it happened."

"It's why I wanted him to ask his mom. Evidently, she had the room padlocked. She'd been using it for storage but got so spooked by what happened she stopped going in after a while."

Quinn picks up a glass. "Hasn't the house been rented out since then?"

I shrug. "I guess. She must not have given anyone access to that area."

"They should tear the place down," he says. "How did Ethan get in there?"

"He said the key was on top of the door frame. He didn't think anything of it. Just opened it up and went right in."

"Bet he won't do that again." Jesse slides a glass toward me.

"No thanks," I tell her. "I can barely keep food down. Wine is the last thing I need."

"More for me," she says, pulling the glass back. "I assume you're going to talk to Eudora about all of this."

"Who's Eudora?" Quinn asks.

"My therapist. She's out of town this week, but I have an appointment next Friday morning."

"Good," Jesse says, sniffing the wine. "What the hell am I supposed to be smelling?" She winks at me. "You need to tell her everything. I don't know what that dude did to you, but those memories don't deserve space in your brain. Make her do everything she can to get rid of it."

CHAPTER 58
THERAPY, SURPRISE, HIBISCUS BUSH

Dr. Jonas unlocks the front door and leads me through the darkened waiting room into her office. I won't be sleeping through this session, and we won't need to kick around the mysteries of my nightmares any longer.

"Thanks for seeing me," I say, waiting for her to switch on the lights. "And sorry…I know you don't usually work on Fridays."

She has jeans on, falling loosely on her thin legs, and an off-white button-down blouse. "No problem. We cut out early from gymnastics practice."

"You do gymnastics?" I ask. This is not a woman who is flexible. This is a woman who would snap in two if she tried to bend more than twenty-five degrees.

"No," she says. "The twins do."

Again, I'm flabbergasted. "You have kids?" I blurt out. How is this possible? How can someone with such jagged edges bear children? Last year, I could hardly get over the fact that she was married. Approachable, physically, without causing injury.

"Yes." She glances at the wall. "I don't keep pictures of them here."

I follow her gaze. "Makes sense," I say, wondering if her children are angular like her, or soft and round, the way I imagine her husband, Mr. Roly-Poly to be. Where did I even get the idea he was a roly-poly? And what the hell is a roly-poly? Is it a bug?

"Katy, you there?" She picks up a pen and swipes her finger on the iPad. "You're not blinking. Tell me what's going on."

"Sorry." I blink to convince her I'm having normal, everyday thoughts. "I found out what the dreams are about. All of it."

Her face softens. "Okay."

"It's another lie my mom's been keeping. Well, Mom and Dad. It started when I was a kid, and we went to visit Ethan's family in Denver."

She listens intently as I lay out the story. The visit, the angry husband keeping me in the basement of their old house for hours.

"I'm so sorry, Katy. May I ask how you found out?"

"It's a little complicated. Mom spilled part of it because she was stoned."

She grimaces. "Your mother smokes marijuana?"

"No," I say with a snort. "She ate some brownies."

"Pot brownies?"

"Uh-huh. She didn't know, and she had a bunch of them."

"Oh my goodness. Is she alright?"

"She was a bit groggy the next morning, and pretty moody. But she promised to tell me about all that stuff soon. You know, about Denver and her family... hiding what we are. I think she feels guilty." I shrug. "I'm not surprised she'd want to push it away."

"I can suggest another therapist for her. Do you think she'd be willing?"

"It'll be a hard sell, but I'll ask her. Anyway, I've had a week to think things over, plus I had a good conversation with my grandmother. I understand how they were trying to be protective, but some part of me wonders what else is out there. It's like my past is a Pandora's box and all sorts of crazy shit keeps spilling out."

"Absolutely understandable." She tucks her brown hair behind her ears. "Has the information sparked any of your own memories?"

"Nothing." I shake my head. "The nightmares recreated it for me. I can't imagine that I wasn't scared to death."

"Have you had any bad dreams since you found out?"

"Not the same way. Little flashes, but I wake up right away. It's been better every night. I'm angry at this point. Not afraid."

"Good," she says, typing more notes. "I want to ask something a little unpleasant."

"Okay," I say, trying to maintain eye contact. "You want to know if he did anything to me, right?"

She taps her lips with her index finger. "If you're comfortable answering."

"Ethan and Mom said I was checked out pretty thoroughly at the hospital. There was nothing." I swallow the lump in my throat. "Nothing obvious."

"That's a relief."

"I guess. Though Mom said I didn't talk for three days after it happened."

Her eyes widen. "Not at all?"

"Nope. Not one word." I slide forward on the couch. "Which would have been unusual for me. I was a chatterbox even at three. Motor-mouth, Dad used to say."

She smiles. "I'm sure you were wonderful, but suddenly becoming non-verbal happens for a reason."

"You think he did something to me?"

"He did do something to you, Katy. You were very young, obviously terrified, and in a situation you'd never been in before, with no control over your surroundings. That's trauma. It doesn't have to be sexual, if that's what you're implying."

"Is there any way for me to find out?"

"The details?" She sighs. "There's no magic wand. No guarantee you can dig into your brain and find facts. Hypnosis can be helpful, if done by a professional, perhaps EMDR to handle the aftermath."

"What's EMDR?" I ask.

"It stands for Eye Movement Desensitization and Reprocessing. It's an approach that addresses traumatic memories; the way they manifest emotionally and physically. It's complicated. Sort of like refiling the bad memories into the long-term file, so to speak. Putting them in the right place so they're not popping up and triggering you all the time." She adjusts her boxy glasses. "I'm not trained in it, so don't quote me on the technicalities. I have several colleagues who are well-versed, though."

"Should I do it?" I ask.

"I think you should consider it. But take your time. A good clinician will have a thorough intake process because it's not the kind of thing you jump into. It's been used for years to resolve trauma, but there are risks, you know—like anything. It needs to be carefully managed."

I take a mental note. "Okay."

"Again, I'm sorry this happened to you. It must have been difficult to learn the details."

"It was. Ethan told me everything over the phone. I told you I spoke to my grandmother, right?" I smile. "She said some cool things. Oh, and Quinn was there too."

"Quinn?"

"Yeah. That's the other thing."

"Tell me," she says, setting the iPad on her knees.

"Actually, can we talk about Nick?"

She grins. "Of course. Your person."

"Not so much, as it turns out. He had some of those brownies with my mom, and it was like truth serum. He said some dumbass crap about me moving to New York with him."

"Is that something you'd like to do?"

"Not after hearing how he felt about women." I tug on my hair, a thick tangle of curls. "He was so disrespectful. Like if I pass the live-with-him option, he might consider the marry-him option."

Her mouth curls into a scowl. "Oh, my."

"I know. He was going on about his pros and cons Excel sheet he made with all the other women he'd been with."

Her scowl grows. "No, he didn't."

"Yes, he did. He's been taking score, I guess. Sleeping around and deciding who would be the most appropriate. The worthiest."

Her eyes bulge. She's holding back. Trying to maintain professionalism.

"I was speechless for a minute too," I tell her. "Lucky me, right? I came out on top of the pile."

"I know I should be neutral as your therapist, but no. Just no."

"I agree, and I made him leave. He was a jerk about my dad dying, and even about my nightmares, which made it easier. If he doesn't care about something that important, then how would I ever count on him to be a good father or husband?"

Her expression becomes stoic. "This is not a question I ask often, but I'm going to do it now."

"Uh-huh." I straighten my back in preparation to receive this rare magical question.

She narrows her eyes. "How did sending him away make you feel?"

I laugh. "Oh well, I felt all sorts of things. Stupid for being naïve. Angry, because what the hell, who does he think he is? And then this weird ebbing. Is that a word?"

She drops her pen. Bends over to retrieve it. "Sorry. Yes, ebbing is a word."

"I thought so. Anyway, the whole daydream was doing that—sort of ebbing away. I'd built up this fantasy about our lives, and then, poof, off it goes. I suppose a poof is more violent than an ebb. But you know, like poking a hole in a balloon, and the air seeps out. He wasn't real. Not the way I'd created him in my head." I stop speaking, sigh, and study my chewed-up nails. "It makes me wonder what I was thinking in college."

"We all do things we hope are right," Dr. Jonas says. "It's the front end of learning."

"Front end? There's a beginning, middle, and end?"

"In a way. Learning happens through steps. You make a choice, experience a consequence, learn from it. But it can be tricky and I'm over-simplifying it. On the other hand, sometimes we don't learn, and then our growth becomes stunted."

"Makes sense. Dad talked about that last year in Bangkok." I cover my mouth to stifle a burp. I have to stop skipping meals.

"Let's return to what you were saying about college," she says.

"Oh, right. Maybe I was more gullible then. Either way, it became obvious, like a piano crashing down on my head. Nick can turn it on when he wants to, make you believe your world is his world, then the switch goes off so quickly you don't notice. Or you don't want to, so you fill in the darkness yourself, the gaps, whatever, and give him credit for it."

She juts her chin out. "Say those words one more time."

"What words?"

"The last part of your sentence."

"The credit thing?"

"Yes." She tips her head down, and I half expect my shrink to hold a doggie treat in front of my nose.

"Filling in the gaps? Giving him credit?"

"That's it. You're saying the right words, but I want you to...ingest them."

"Um." I push my fingers through my hair again. She wants me to ingest something?

"Katy?" she whispers, bringing me back.

I shake my head. "I meant he hardly ever fulfilled my expectations, or he let me down, so I filled the space in with excuses, or rationalizations, and then convinced myself that everything was great." I sink into the cushion. "Even when he sucked, I gave him a pass, and then I normalized it. Like the way you get used to something that stinks. Eventually, you stop noticing. It becomes part of the landscape. Oh my God, Nick has stunk this whole time? Oh my God, is this why I stayed with Dylan, too?"

Her lips form a happy, thin-lipped grin. "Yes, it's a big part of it. Covering up for someone else's failures. Trying to, as you said, normalize the situation lets you ignore it. But it also keeps you from moving forward, because moving forward is hard. Leaving is risky, right? The thought of being alone scares the hell out of people. They stay because it seems like the safer option."

"It's a cop-out. I was much lonelier with Dylan than I am by myself. But I didn't do it this time with Nick. I made him leave."

"Which means you're learning."

"I guess I am. It feels pretty good."

"As it should. I'm proud of you. You've been through a lot."

I squirm in my seat and thank her for the compliment. My head will surely burst from all the kindness.

"Should we talk about Quinn now?" she asks. "You mentioned he was with you?"

I rub my hands together. "He came back from his trip early because he was worried about me. I guess because of the storm and the dreams."

"He seems very thoughtful," she says.

"He is, which is kind of cool. Anyway, we got on the phone with my brother. That's when we heard the details about that day in Denver. Ethan figured out the Elevator Man was his stepdad, because that was his catch phrase. The try falling into a bucket sentence. He called his mom before he talked to me, and she spilled it. He was so sad. He was crying."

"Ethan was?"

"Uh-huh."

"It's not surprising," she says. "He may need some counseling as well."

"I told him already. But when he was telling me the rest of the story, which was horrible, Quinn was holding my hand, and it felt right." I stare at the ground. "It felt safe."

"Safe is good." She glances at the clock on the end table.

"Do you want to stop?" I ask. "I don't want to keep you on your day off."

She's caught off guard. "We have a few more minutes."

"Okay. Quinn was…um, I don't know exactly how to put it. It seemed so normal for him to be there. It's strange, I've always assumed the sour, twisty sensation I'd get in my gut meant I was in the wrong place."

She adjusts her glasses. "And how many times have you ignored it?"

I cringe. "Almost every single time."

"We spoke about this last year. Start trusting your gut, Katy. You'd be surprised about the scientific evidence showing the connection the gut has to the brain. It's real."

"I believe you," I say, then burp again, bend over and take a deep breath.

"Katy?" She scoots closer and puts her hand on my shoulder. "What's happening?"

I straighten up slowly. "I'm trying not to puke again. I haven't had any food today."

"Again? Has it happened more than once?"

"Yeah. My system is all out of whack. All this emotional crap is getting to me."

She taps her fingers together.

"I'm fine," I tell her. "It'll pass."

"Can I ask you a more personal question?" She crosses her hands on her lap. Her long, bony fingers weave, one over the other.

"More than all of this stuff?" I wipe sweat off my forehead. "Sure. I'm all ears."

"When was your last period?"

"That is more personal. You sound like my mother. But it was last week. And anyway, we were careful, if you must know."

She takes a moment before responding. "Was it a normal period?"

"Does it matter? I mean, actually, it stopped on the first day."

She rolls her eyes, slowly, with intention.

"What?" I mumble. "It was normal for a few hours."

"Katy..."

"Uh-huh?"

"What kind of birth control?"

I wiggle my nose. "The usual kind?" I stammer. "We were fully and very carefully, careful."

"Well," she says quietly. "Might it have failed?"

I imitate her low tone and calming voice, because as always, my sarcasm rises in proportion to my anxiety. "I suppose it might have."

"You know you can have a shortened period when you're pregnant. Especially during the first few months."

Sarcasm aside, I need a moment to process this information. "Are you sure? Is that a real thing?"

"It happened to me with the twins. First two months, I bled a little right when my period should have started."

"Are you serious?"

"I am. And if memory serves." She smiles. "Well, let's just say you're bringing back some memories."

Once again, time distorts, slows down. I must be dissociating, not exactly hovering above myself in the room, but no longer fully present. Her words creep in occasionally. "PTSD, prenatal vitamins, trauma, pregnancy test." Did I fall asleep on her couch again? I touch my phone to see if I'm dreaming. The screen glows with the date and time. I look past my shrink lady, who's talking about folic acid, and focus on the spider plant, the bookshelf, and a pack of printer paper on her desk. My stomach turns. I smell air freshener. Vanilla mixed with something earthy.

"Are you okay?" she asks.

"Yeah, I'm fine. Lots to think about."

She leans toward me. "You seem a little stunned. Do you need a minute?"

"A minute?" I repeat. "No. It's all good. I mean, you know, it's all good. Did I say that twice?" I stand up and gather my things. "Are we done?"

"We can be," she says. "If you're positive you're alright? We should continue talking about what happened in Denver."

"Uh-huh."

"Will you call me if anything comes up? Another panic attack?"

"Totally will," I promise, then try my hardest to smile and get outside. I don't count this time, the way I did before. Steps, seconds—that part of my anxiety has diminished. What hasn't diminished is the rolling in my stomach, which is why I race-walk to the side of the building and throw up in an immaculately pruned lavender hibiscus bush.

CHAPTER 59
JESSICA TANNER CRIES

Evidence of Tropical Storm Bethany lingers in the streets, on the lawns, and at the beach, still strewn with decimated strands of seaweed and fragmented seashells. There are a few boarded-up windows, and small mounds of debris waiting to be taken away. Dufferin Beach has once again survived the deluge.

I run into the grocery store and buy everything Jesse likes for lunch, plus two more things. A pregnancy test and a gigantic bag of cheese puffs. I've been having a craving.

Twenty minutes later I'm at her townhouse. It's moderately tidy, but filled with the usual clutter. Clothes hang off the backs of chairs in dry cleaner sleeves, a family pack of Pop-Tarts sits on the floor, and mountains of legal documents on the glass-top dining room table.

"What's the emergency?" she asks.

"Working from home today?" I put down my bags.

"The storm ripped some shingles off at the office. The roof is leaking. What's happening? Why are you here?"

"Can't tell you yet."

"Why do you have that look on your face, Kiss? Is it because you threw Nickety out on his ass and now you're all proud of yourself?"

"Not the reason. Have you heard from him since he left?"

"Not a word."

I nod. "I'm sure he'll find someone more suitable."

She puts her hands on her hips. "What are you up to? You're acting all fuckety."

"Not up to anything. I had a good appointment with Dr. Jonas this morning."

"Do tell."

"Not yet, Jess."

"God, you're so dramatic."

"I know." I fish the small cardboard box out of the grocery bag and quickly hide it behind my back. "It's about to get, um…more."

She cranes her neck to get a peek. "Why? What did you do?"

"Give me three minutes. I gotta pee."

• • • • •

I've seen Jessica Tanner cry two times since I've known her. The first was the day my dad died. The second was last New Year's Eve, during his memorial at The Point when Ethan and I recited The Mourner's Kaddish. Today is the third time, and she's ugly-crying. Tears roll down her cheeks. She snorts and blows her nose into a paper towel.

We read the test results together. Positive.

"Jesus, Katy, did you not use birth control?"

"We did. Guess it didn't work."

"Jesus, Katy."

"I know, Jessica. It'll be okay."

"You're going to have a baby. You and Quinn." She grins. "And me."

"Yeah. You and me and Quinn."

Her face screws up with concern. "Do you think he'll be cool with it?"

"I have a feeling," I begin saying. The thought has occurred to me. Will he freak out? Get angry, tell me to go to hell? Tell me it's too soon, too sudden, too much responsibility? Is he up for it? I look at Jesse and finish my sentence. "I have a feeling it's going to be okay."

She cries some more. "We're going to have a baby."

And we are.

There's a tiny human growing inside of me, and in the span of ten minutes everything shifts. I'm shocked, peaceful, nauseous, happy—all at the same time. It doesn't seem like these feelings should exist in the same space, yet they do. I'm ready to be responsible for someone else, and grateful my world has expanded beyond the borders of me, myself, and I.

All the experiences, the memories, and the details of my life bend into a protective circle. A cradle.

CHAPTER 60
ALL IN

I leave Jesse's place after devouring a healthy lunch. We're both still weepy, but happy. My baby already has a godmother who will teach him or her the fine art of misbehaving, talking back, or climbing on a counter to reach the cookie jar. I'll need nine months to prepare. To brace for whatever my best friend, and this new life, will throw my way.

Penney is waiting for me at home. I lie down on the bed and watch her latest attempt to leap, wipe-out, then resort to climbing up the blanket with her tiny sharp claws. She sniffs my eyelashes and bops my nose before prancing away. With the cover pulled up to my chin, I drift off and dream a little dream of two baby girls. The first I recognize as "peanut", the toddler who was so excited to see my phone in the hospital in Thailand last year. The second baby is swaddled in a light pink blanket. Yet to be born.

I wake up feeling better than I have in weeks. There's work to be done. The Elevator Man, what he did or didn't do, will require much discussion with Dr. Jonas and my mom. His shadow has loomed over our family's emotional function…dysfunction, for almost twenty-five years. Like Jesse said, it's time to clear him from the room.

Ten minutes later, I get a text from Quinn. He reminds me of our date tonight. My birthday dinner, and afterwards, Mom insists we come to the house for dessert, where Jesse, Russ, and some family friends will join us.

I read the rest of his message.

I'm walking dogs at the animal shelter. Come hang out with me.

He doesn't have to ask twice.

• • • • •

I find him outside in the play area with a dog who looks like he belongs on the Island of Misfit Toys. His fluffy tail wags wildly every time he returns the frisbee to Quinn.

"This guy is put together all wrong," I say, patting his huge head, which seems impossibly attached to a Beagle body.

"Beagle and Mastiff." Quinn says.

"How does he hold his head up?"

"Gotta ask him." He scratches the dog's floppy ears. "Thanks for coming down."

"Anytime," I say, wondering if the baby will have his eyes or mine. His brown hair with those impossible threads of gold, or my ridiculous out-of-control curls. The possibilities are endless, though the rules, through our DNA, already have their marching orders.

"How was your nap?" he asks.

"No bad dreams. All good." I take a deep breath. Here we go. "Can I tell you something?"

His eyebrows knit together. "Sure. Why are you smiling? What did you do?"

"Why is everyone always asking me what I've done?"

"Have you met yourself, Katy? You're always up to something."

"Fair." I nod. "But I had some help with this one."

He plays tug-of-war with the dog, then throws the frisbee again and looks at me. "You're being very mysterious."

"I'm not trying to be." I puff my cheeks out. "I got you a gift."

"It's your birthday. I'm supposed to get you something."

"It's not a big gift. I grabbed it at Target on the way over here."

"Okay," he says cautiously.

I bite my lip, reach into my backpack, and pull out a plastic bag.

He eyes it, smiling. "What's in here?"

I hand it to him. "Look inside."

Slowly, he pulls out the yellow onesie. On the front, stitched in light blue lettering, is the word *Daddy*. My heart thumps, because on the one hand I'm excited. On the other hand, though maybe only one or two fingers worth, I'm still nervous. What if he's pissed? What if he asks if he's the dad?

He looks at me. "Is this real? You're not messing with me?"

"Took two tests."

He brings the onesie to his face, covers his eyes with it, then uses it to wipe away his tears. My heartbeat slows, and for the first time in my life, I feel no anxiety about the future, and the twisty sensation in my stomach is excitement, not dread.

"Are you okay?" I ask him. "You're kind of green."

"I'm going to be a dad?"

"You are." I put my hands on my belly. "Meet your bundle of baby cells."

He puts his hands on mine. "Hi bundle of baby. We promise to give you a real name soon."

"How about Faucet?" I ask, grinning.

"Still no." He pulls me close, sweeps my hair off my face, and kisses my forehead. I hear the next words as an echo. They ring in my ears. "I love you, Katy Kiss." His hot breath on my face gives me goosebumps. "I'm all in, Mama."

CHAPTER 61
FRIDAY, APRIL 29ᵀᴴ.
THIS TIME YOU SHOULD ASK

We're late to my mother's house that evening. Russ and Jess are in the hallway arguing about college football. Mom is chatting with Mrs. Nosy-as-Fuck, and her husband, Mr. Know-it-All, in the kitchen. They're placing candles, twenty-seven of them, on the cake. Chocolate and more chocolate.

I introduce my mom to Quinn, who leaves her momentarily speechless with a hug and an enormous bouquet of off-white roses, pale green hydrangeas, and Baby's Breath.

She looks him over. Her brown eyes narrow, then soften. In Hungarian, she tells me he's very pretty. In English, she says to both of us, "Okay, this is a good start. Now is time for cake."

"It looks delicious, Mom, but I'm a little queasy."

She touches my forehead, and then my cheek. "Why are you warm? What is the matter with you? Do you have the cold?"

"Not a cold."

"Then what is wrong?" She pushes down on my chin. "Open. Put out your tongue. Are you having strep throat from Crick-ette?"

I gently push her hand away, smiling. "My throat's fine. I don't have strep."

Irritation clouds her face. "What is funny? No cold, no throat. What? Always I am feeling silly for asking if you are pregnant. Well, this time, the joke is over you. I don't even ask."

I turn to Jesse for help. She avoids eye contact by staring hard at the ceiling.

I turn to Russ, but he doesn't know I'm pregnant, so he shrugs and plays with the lid from his water bottle.

I turn to Quinn. He dips his head. Just a little. It's enough.

"So Mom, remember the thing you and Dad used to say? Even a broken clock is right twice a day."

Her face transforms again and again from confusion to shock to comprehension. I wrap my arms around her, and whisper in her ear. "This time you should ask."

Then it gets quiet.

Then it gets loud.

Because this is the end. And also the beginning.

ABOUT THE AUTHOR

G.A. Anderson is a first-generation Hungarian-Canadian, born in Montreal, Quebec. After living in Paris for a few years, her family moved to the U.S. where she has lived ever since.

She is married and has two amazing daughters and many (many) animals from the local shelters.

She began writing when friends and family on the receiving end of her emails told her she was "weird but funny." The feedback compelled her to write, entertain, and make people laugh.

Gaby has worked in the restaurant industry, commercial and group travel, private aviation, and pharmaceutical instrumentation. She currently works in behavioral health management.

Her husband calls her a renaissance woman with mad-skills. This means she can catch a softball with one hand while holding a giant turkey leg with the other.

ACKNOWLEDGEMENTS

Once again, I have many people to thank.

The Atlanta Writers Club, headed by our President, George Weinstein. If not for you…well, a bunch of us would be doing something else. Maybe rooting ferns or training our dogs to herd geese. Thank you for your endless support and occasional salty remarks. We appreciate you, probably more than you realize.

To the Roswell critique group: George Weinstein, Chuck Storla, Patrick Scullin, Phil Fasone, Deborah Mitchell, Daniel Burke, Karen Kirtland, and Ed Gruber, our senior member, who at ninety-six, continues to show us a thing or two about living well. Thank you all for the lessons in writing and friendship. My work is better because of Tuesdays.

To Reagan Rothe and the *Black Rose Writing* team. Thank you for giving my books such a welcoming home. You do an awesome job.

To my beta readers: Elyse Wheeler, Daniel Burke, Andie Zeliger, and Gail Weeden. You guys killed it. Your feedback was incredible, amazing, helpful, insightful. You found things that would have remained lost to me. For that, I am thankful.

To Amy Evans and the Atlanta Readers Club. Thank you for your support and friendship. What an amazing group of people who read to learn, laugh, broaden any horizon available, and ponder the big and sometimes strange questions.

To my Wild Women: Kathy Nichols, Kim Conrey, and Lizbeth Jones. Thank you for listening to me bitch and moan. Please don't show anyone else our texts.

To Ann Urban Herring. Thank you for being my book club partner in crime. I so appreciate your never-ending enthusiasm about the never-ending weirdness.

To my mother, Susan Reich. Thank you for listening to me go on and on and on. I hope you like this one as much as the last one. And no, you are not the mother in the book.

To Alex and Mia. All my words are for you. You have given me all the things that matter. I love you both, from the teeny, teeny tiny, to the way big.

To my husband Andy, who reads my books out loud to me before submission, and patiently waits while I screech for him to STOP, so I can make notes. I am so grateful for your support, patience, and once again, all those words. You let them loose. I catch them. It's cool how we're weird in the same ways. Thank you for still being my you-know-what. Except for the pickles in the goulash. That's not a thing. I love you.

OTHER TITLES BY G.A. ANDERSON

NOTE FROM G.A. ANDERSON

Word-of-mouth is crucial for any author to succeed. If you enjoyed *Dream a Little Dream*, please leave a review online—anywhere you are able. Even if it's just a sentence or two. It would make all the difference and would be very much appreciated.

Once your review is posted, send me a screenshot and I will email you the deleted prologue to *South of Happily*.

You can find contact information on my website, along with pronunciation podcasts, Hungarian recipes from both books, and Book Club questions.

www.Anderson-Author.com

Thanks!
G.A. Anderson

We hope you enjoyed reading this title from:

www.blackrosewriting.com

Subscribe to our mailing list – *The Rosevine* – and receive **FREE** books, daily deals, and stay current with news about upcoming releases and our hottest authors.
Scan the QR code below to sign up.

Already a subscriber? Please accept a sincere thank you for being a fan of Black Rose Writing authors.

View other Black Rose Writing titles at www.blackrosewriting.com/books and use promo code **PRINT** to receive a **20% discount** when purchasing.

www.ingramcontent.com/pod-product-compliance
Lightning Source LLC
LaVergne TN
LVHW091457090625
813395LV00035B/184